WHAT'S HAPPENING?

BOOKS BY JOHN NICHOLAS IANNUZZI

FICTION

Condemned
J.T.
Courthouse
Sicilian Defense
Part 35
What's Happening?

NON-FICTION

Handbook of Trial Strategies
Handbook of Cross Examination
Trial: Strategy and Psychology
Cross Examination: The Mosaic Art

WHAT'S HAPPENING?

A NOVEL

JOHN NICHOLAS IANNUZZI

A MADCAN BOOK

ISBN 978-1-4804-7683-7

Cover image, *New York Cityscape*, by Kurt Schumann

Cover design by Neil Alexander Heacox

Distributed Open Road Distribution
345 Hudson Street
New York, NY 10014
www.openroadmedia.com

*Lovingly, this book is dedicated to:
my Mother and Father,
without whom I could not have been;
the selfless few, particularly my wife,
without whom this book could not have been;
the folly of man,
without which this story could not have been;
and to Charles Criswell,
who, I am sure, would have agreed with me.*

WHAT'S HAPPENING?

1

IT WAS TWO A.M. Tinkling voices drifted from somewhere amidst the night-shrouded buildings and deserted, narrow streets. Though the evening's performance of *Blood Wedding* had long since ended, a clump of chattering shadows pressed the entrance of the Seventh Avenue South Theatre.

Within, the part-time cabaret-theatre, which had tables and chairs in place of rows of seats, throbbed with the clamor and din of revelers who did not want to go home or who had no home.

The room was dimly lit, almost dark. It seethed with smells: dust, beer, summer heat, perspiration. Hollow thunderclaps exploded from the stretched skin of a tall conga drum and crashed against the walls. Two spotlights in the ceiling, emitting vague green and amber beams which strained through undulating strata of cigarette smoke, tempered the darkness.

Men and women, racially interlaced like pawns on a chessboard, were crammed about tables covered with red-checked cloths. The entire room rumbled with conversation which spasmodically burst into laughter. Some people sat on isolated chairs in the aisles. Others stood in the back against the wooden bar which was illuminated from behind by a dim red bulb.

These were the Villagers. They were veiled in a face-absorbing dimness. Lenses glinted occasionally; many people wore sunglasses. Light-colored clothing and jewelry appeared through the cloaked atmosphere. White pants and shirts could be distinguished; so too tennis sneakers on feet resting on chairs. Many women wore long, silver earrings and twists of silver around their fingers. The men wore tight pants; some had beards.

The rhythmic charivari of the drum was intensified by piercing tribal shrieks from a writhing drummer standing in the shadows of the stage. His Negroid features were transformed into a grotesque African death mask by a light from inside the drum which shimmered a deathly white pallor over his chin and jaw, while his eyes stared glazedly from shadow-obscured sockets. The "yawl" of a French horn, the tinkle of a piano, the blare of two trombones further saturated the room. Pounding feet and hands resounded the beat of the drum, pulsating the very floor of the theatre. Glasses and half-empty beer bottles, their contents churning foamily, bounced and swayed on the tables.

Onstage, two couples wiggled through an Afro-Cuban mambo. Their bodies jerked and twisted, their shoulders trembled, their faces froze with bared-tooth effort, their arms stretched sideways. They danced into and out of the beams of light—from blackness to vague light and back again—living out their frenzied dance.

This was the Seventh Avenue South Theatre every night. As soon as the performance ended and the cabaret opened, droves poured in. When the place was filled, people queued outside. Everybody wanted to be on the inside living it up. The real attraction of the theatre was that one could sit at a table all night without buying a drink. Several people would chip in for a bottle of beer, used glasses were taken from other tables, and a small amount of beer poured for each person. This way everyone looked as if he were just finishing his drink.

"Man, you know, that chick Rita dances real smooth," commented a blond reveler sitting in the back of the cafe, his chair tilted against the huge air conditioner. He gazed forward, speaking from the side of his mouth to another white fellow sitting next to him. Their feet rested on the seat of a chair in front of them. The blond wore low sneakers without socks, tight white pants, and a basque shirt purposely tight to display bulging muscles. The other fellow had on ankle-high animal-skin shoes casually splattered with paint, rain, and dust. He wore tight jeans and a collarless orange shirt unbuttoned to the breastbone.

"I'm hip, man." the other answered slowly, not turning his gaze from the dancers. A pleased, almost other-worldly smile creased his face. All the while, his hands fell softly on bongo drums between his knees. "She's got beat, . . . you know, man?" His head tilted back, physically accompanying the drum beat; his eyes closed contemplatively. "Real natural beat." He opened his eyes to stare at the ceiling thoughtfully. Then he slowly lowered his gaze and both men continued to watch the dancers.

Rita's long hair flew out from her head as she twisted. Her face, contorted into a strained, wide smile by the dance, was a familiar face in the theatre. Her partner was a thin, white fellow; his face was new to the theatre. It was bony, capped with flat, dark hair. They weren't holding each other as they danced. Their bodies swayed separately and smoothly in unison as they moved through the light beams. Rita's body swayed quickly, her hips snapping, her bare feet flying. She smiled to her partner and her white teeth shone through the half dark. Her eyes glistened with the reflection of the spotlights. Both abandoned themselves to the pounding that surrounded and filled them. A final drum beat swelled from the stage, leaving the theatre vibrating with a hollow resonance. Rita and her partner swirled together, stopping in front of each other with a melodramatic flourish.

"Hey, like, that was crazy," exclaimed Rita, her smile bursting widely, revealing deep grooves of dimples in her cheeks. Her chest convulsed as she tried to catch her breath. She pushed back hair that had fallen over her face; little slicks of moisture glistened on her forehead and down the side of her neck.

"Yeah." Her thin partner panted, smiling enthusiastically. "That was really fine." He wiped his forehead with a handkerchief. His clothes were different from the clothes of the Village regulars. He wore a sport shirt, tapered, sharply creased slacks, and highly polished loafers. He looked as if he came from "Uptown" and had strayed in from Louis'. "Uptown" to the Villagers meant anywhere in the world outside their own milieu. Louis' was a tavern around the corner from the Seventh Avenue South and the mecca of the Village-goers from Uptown. They came to the Village in suits and silks to indulge their wild spirits in this legendary, off-beat world, but they went to Louis' and not the Seventh Avenue South because the revelers were too drab and unglamorous, too depressingly seedy for Uptown's sensational concept of the Village.

"I don't want to sound personal or anything," remarked the thin fellow, breathing more easily, "but what's your name? Mine's Bill."

"Rita." Between her hands, she held her flowing, long hair away from her neck.

"Okay, Rita. Why don't we sort of sit this one out?"

"Great. I couldn't make it again if I wanted to."

They smiled into each other's eyes. For an instant, the clink of glasses and ash trays and the heralds of mirth became inaudible as each of their smiles deepened in the warmth of the other's; each searched the other's face. It was warming, pleasant to see a friendly, real smile. Noise besieged them again suddenly, as they became self-conscious. They turned and made their way between chairs and people toward the the table at which Rita had been sitting. It was one of the tiny red-checked squares in the center of the room that was a table for four. A dozen people surrounded it unevenly like spokes from the hub of a shattered wheel. It instilled a feeling of belonging and confidence to sit with a group, although a glass with a single sip of beer was all that was on the table before each of them. Rita sat. Bill took a chair from the next table and sat down behind and a little to the side of her.

"I'd like to buy you a drink, but like things are kind of rough these days."

"Oh, come on," Rita protested, dismissing the need for popular concepts of social etiquette. "I've got a beer some munificent friend bought me. I'll share it with you." She smiled at him generously and sincerely, her eyes twinkling.

"Hey, that's great. I don't have a glass though," he replied, posing another problem in jest.

"Here, I'll fill my glass and you take the bottle." She smiled slyly, her eyes flitting away and then back to him as she poured the amber liquid into her glass.

"You know, baby? I dig you. Like, you're very all right. You come here all the time?" Bill talked *hip* if he didn't dress *hip*.

"When there's nothing else to do. We drop in almost every night."

"Say, Rita . . ." One of the white fellows who had been lounging against the air conditioner leaned past Bill, his hand resting on the back of Bill's chair. He glanced at Bill momentarily, and, not recogniz- ing him, looked back to Rita. "Rita, baby, like, your swaying body has moved me no end, and so I just had to get up and dance with you." He smiled, wanting to look self-assured and evil.

Rita smiled. She was pleased by the notice she had gathered.

"I'll be right back, Bill. You won't go away, will you?"

He smiled resignedly. "Are you kidding? . . . only I'm jealous."

"I'll only be a minute—and then I won't leave you for the rest of the night."

He stared into her eyes. She still smiled at him, her eyes steady and warm, then turned to make her way toward the dance floor.

"You won't?"

"Of course not," she answered playfully, her greenish eyes flicker- ing with a warm, meaningful look.

Perhaps it was the smile in her eyes, or the duration of that look, or the attitude which accompanied it, that captured Bill's attention. Whatever, it was discernible, and they both realized it and were warmed by it.

Bill concentrated on her now as she walked to the dance floor. She was not tall or slender. She was a full woman, with a body that rounded her dark, sleeveless, full-skirted dress in gentle undulations. She turned to her new dancing partner, and, without holding each other, they began to sway with the music. Her full breasts swayed beneath her bodice as she twirled to the beat. Bill watched the two people move in and out of the shadows. It didn't matter that Rita danced with someone else; she and her look were with Bill at the table. The dancers fluttered and dipped and turned. Rita glanced over her partner's shoulder, smiling faintly, momentarily at Bill. They twisted away and were again hidden behind other dancers.

"Hello," announced a small, thin voice from a small, thin girl who sat two chairs from Bill. It was a squeaky, inquisitive "hello," as if the girl who said it wasn't sure Bill would talk to her. "I'm Rita's room-mate," Laura announced meekly. She was thinner than Bill. Bill looked like a little frail rich boy whose mother always made him wear his raincoat and rubbers in the rain as she walked him to school holding an umbrella over his head. Laura was frail too, but she didn't look as if she had ever been rich. She had closely cropped hair, like the Dutch Boy in the paint ads, but hers was a lusterless brown. She was pale, her eyes lifeless and nervous. Her nose was short and upturned. Her mouth, thin lipped and liquid, twitched occasionally, as if to distract from and cover her high-voiced comments. Her clothes—pants and a man-tailored jacket—were dark and plain. She wore no make-up, and her fingernails were pale and unpainted. She seemed sad and lonely—alone and lonely in a room filled with people.

"You two girls live down here?"

"Yeah, on Christopher Street, . . . but there are three of us. Jeannie. . . . Jeannie!" Laura called across the expanse of bottles and glasses on the table.

A wide-jawed girl with short, black hair turned from a light-complexioned Negro with a shaved head to whom she had been speaking. The wide-jawed girl's face was made up very starkly, pale, in the vogue popular in the Village.

"What?"

"Nothin'. That's okay." Laura said, shrugging, an apologetic smile creasing her face. She turned back to Bill. "That's the other girl that lives with us."

Jeannie looked at Laura and Bill inquisitively for a moment, then, with a shrug, turned back to her friend.

"That's a nice little group you have."

"Yeah. They're fun most of the time."

"You mean, like sometimes it gets to be a hassle?"

"Yeah, . . . well, it's all right. Just sometimes it's not." Laura fell silent. She lowered her head, then glanced across the room. Her eyes roamed the room watching other people, glimpsing at Bill only occasionally through uplifted, frightened eyes. She scrutinized the medal Bill wore around his neck. Bill sipped at his beer. Laura still stared at his medal.

"Want to dance?" Bill asked to break the tense silence.

"No. I don't dance much. What's this?" She prodded the bright, silver medal.

"It's Saint Christopher. He protects me, like when I'm in the car."

"Are you Catholic?" She looked at him meekly from the corners of her eyes.

Bill, somewhat perplexed, nodded.

"That's good. I'm Catholic too." An embarrassed smile flickered across her mouth.

More than perplexed now, he asked, "What's so good about me being Catholic?"

"You don't meet many Catholics down here. If they are they don't say so anyway," she surrendered.

"I'm not the best Catholic in the world." He smiled a little with embarrassment.

"Oh, that's all right. It doesn't matter anyway."

"Well, I'm glad we met each other," Bill said in an attempt to turn the onrushing silence. He tried to peer beyond her face, into her eyes. Laura looked at him furtively, conscious of his stare. She stood upright in place, her eyes frantically scanning the dim room.

"Hey, Bob! . . . Bob!" she called to a fellow across the room. "Wait a minute. I'll be right back . . . in a minute . . . okay?" Laura asked Bill, her eyes searching his face. Without waiting for an answer, she turned toward the other side of the room.

"Sure, sure, . . . go ahead."

Laura scampered through a maze of people and chairs. Bill watched the little figure squeeze between the chairs and saw her start to speak to a fellow on the other side of the room. She glanced back as she spoke. Bill turned back to his beer and the group of people he didn't know. They were sitting in various attitudes of relaxation. On Bill's left, a bearded Negro wearing smoked glasses watched the dancers and listened to the music. A large, round, copper medallion hung from a thong around his neck. He beat the table in rhythm with the drummer on the stage, chanting softly, "bam, bam, ba, ba, bam, ba . . ." Occasionally he looked around the room at the other people or lifted his sip of beer and feigned drinking, perhaps to appease his own feelings.

"Say, man, you got a match?" Bill asked, an unlit cigarette between his lips.

"No, man, sorry." He didn't turn his gaze from the stage. "Bam, bam, ba . . ."

Bill looked across the table. "Say, Jeannie, you got a match?"

Jeannie turned and looked at him. "No, . . . sorry. You have a match, Josh?" she asked her Negro companion. His head was completely shaved and smooth. A small square of gold pierced the lobe of his right ear. He tapped his pants pockets under the table.

"No. I'm sorry, I don't," he said through mobile, thick lips.

"Well, I guess I go without a smoke. Thanks anyway." Bill smiled absently.

The drum beats rose to a crescendo, flying up from the background again, filling the room with their explosion. Suddenly, the air was still. Another beat; three more rapid beats and the music ended. The murmur rose again from the dark depths of the room.

"Yeah! Yeah!" the darkly bespectacled Negro on Bill's left shouted as he applauded. "Man, those cats can really wail, can't they?" he remarked to no one in particular.

"Yeah, they really move," Bill replied.

"Hello, lean one. I'm glad you waited," a female voice close behind Bill said softly.

He turned. Rita's eyes studied his face. He thought her long black hair and fair skin were a contrast in loveliness.

"Hey!" He smiled. "I almost forgot we had a big thing going. You were gone a long time."

"Don't worry, I didn't forget us." She smiled and sat down.

"You dance pretty wild. You a dancer?"

"No." She was pleased. "I go to acting class, but like all the cats that I hang around with are dancers. You know, I sort of pick it up."

"Very smooth indeed. This is a pretty nice place here, you know?" He looked around the club. "It's kind of groovy—it jumps."

"It's all right. It gets to be a little much after a while . . . the same things, the same faces all the time."

"Hey, man, dig these cats cuttin' loose on the floor," the bespectacled Negro on Bill's left called loudly. He nodded toward the dance floor. Bill and Rita looked up. A couple was writhing to the music. The male partner had long, curly blond hair that fell over his forehead as he danced. He snapped his curls back into place with a gentle flick of his head. He wore olive pants, sandals, no socks, and a boat-neck, sleeveless shirt. He danced with a dumpy, bespectacled Negro girl. She wore a pair of pedal-pusher pants and a sailor cap with the brim turned down all around so that it looked like a white football helmet. Her blouse was coming out of her pants as the two of them bounced and swayed and twirled to the brassy music. He twirled and twisted on his toes, kicking his legs, quickly and snappily, high into the air. His face was stiffened into haughty indifference, save that he glowed as the laughing crowd jeered him on. The girl bounced and twisted, a far-off look in her eye. She was just somewhere, bouncing up and down, not really knowing or caring exactly where. The blond smiled broadly as an extra high kick was greeted by extra loud applause. The crowd laughed even louder, moving the blond to almost frantic twisting and bouncing.

"Real crazy dance," howled Rita, her face shattered with laughter.

Bill laughed too. The entire theatre crackled with the noise of laughing.

The music ended and the blond jumped up, landing on the floor in a split, his arms outstretched. The revelers at the tables began to sway convulsively with increased laughter. Tears of mirth escaped Rita's eyes. One girl, doubled with laughter, fell from her chair onto the floor. The colored girl gave her blond dancing partner a helping hand and they walked back to their table in the shadows accompanied by laughter and applause.

"Is that one of your dancing friends?" asked Bill, still laughing.

"No. I don't know that couk. First time I ever saw him," Rita answered, the laughter in her voice fading. "Josh is a dancer." She nodded toward Jeannie's shaven-headed friend.

"I thought he looked like a dancer. I don't know why. You know, it's just that sometimes it comes through, you know what I mean?"

"Yeah. Lots of times people come through. You know." She spoke suddenly more slowly and seriously, reflecting on Bill, studying his face. It was a friendly, pleasant face, she thought. ". . . You don't come through though. You know, like you don't come through with any emotion in your face at all. Like it's a wall and I can't see on the other side." As she spoke, she wondered what Bill thought about her; if he thought she was nice.

"That's good," Bill said flatly. "It protects my feelings from the God damn world so nobody can step on them. Everybody else does it, don't they? Nobody shows the real picture of themselves. They put on a show of what they want to be."

She understood what he was saying, and the understanding of his bitterness made her want him to know she understood. She wanted to communicate their "sympatico."

"You're not like that, though, like other people. . . . I don't know, maybe you are, but you don't seem like that. You seem different from the rest of *people*. I don't know how to explain it but . . ." She looked at him lingeringly, her eyes warm and understanding.

"Yeah, but like when I put on a blank wall I'm not trying to fool myself, you know? I'm trying to fool other people. This way no one knows what's going on inside, you know? Like I can be myself but nobody knows about it. I can play bits without anyone knowing what's coming off. Nobody can hurt my secret feelings, laugh or mock them."

They each moved their chair closer to the other, smiling at the coincidence.

"But that's just it. When you do want to get through to a person you don't."

They stared into each other's eyes. A deeper, poignant meaning loomed behind their eyes and their words. The conversation was becoming charged with unspoken meaning.

"Look," Bill explained seriously, "when I want to get through to somebody I tell them. That's a big thing with me. I like to be frank and say exactly what I mean." He groped for a more tangible reaction on her part to the underlying excitement in their physical communication.

"Rita! Rita!" called Jeannie. "We're going to Dani's for coffee. You coming?"

"You want to go for coffee?" Rita asked Bill. Their eyes met and she was asking him with her flickering eyes too.

"Baby, I just want to be with you," he answered softly. "I'm not much on coffee anyway."

She looked at him, still studying, a slight pleased smile warming her mouth. "No. We're going to stay for a while."

"Okay. See you later."

Jeannie and Josh walked to the exit. Bill and Rita watched them. Now Rita turned back and their eyes met again, sparklingly aware of each other. The sounds of drums and people faded . . . time lingered . . . silently, . . . and now Rita smiled a little, mysteriously.

"So, you were saying you like to be frank."

"Yeah . . . ." Bill took a matchbook from Rita's hand and elaborately lit a bolstering cigarette. He shook the match, blew out a spume of smoke, and returned the matches to her hand. Her skin was warm and smooth to his touch. He grasped her hand, studied the deep lines in the palm, then looked up, peering at her intently, continuing to press her hand in his. "It's the best way to say what you mean." He scanned her face for a lead.

"I like people to be frank and come right out and say what they mean," Rita said leadingly.

Both were thinking furiously, belying an imposed outer calm. Neither wanted to make the first thrust, yet both wanted to pursue the conversation further.

"You're pretty frank," he commented.

"Why don't you be frank?"

"Okay, let's be frank. I dig you. I don't know you, and you don't know me, . . . but I like you, and I figure you might like me, . . . and why don't we get to know each other better?"

"That's a good suggestion. Anything else?" She probed further.

"What else is there? Maybe you can suggest something."

She smiled as they stared. She was not talking now. Not being able to think of what to say, Rita waited for Bill to speak.

"Well, . . ." Bill said finally, forced to take the lead boldly. He averted his eyes to stare over her head at the wall. "I don't think there's a better way of getting to know anyone than by . . . well, . . . by . . . er . . . ah . . . going to bed with them. So like why don't we sort of start getting acquainted real well tonight?" He fired this last at her quickly, watching her eyes for a reaction. She didn't bolt. She looked at him, the soft smile lingering on her mouth. She just looked, her eyes staring deeply.

"I was frank with you. Now you be frank with me. Wha' da ya say?" he persisted.

And still she didn't answer. This was—in cold, hard language—what she had rightly anticipated. And she didn't answer. She had known it was coming and she wanted to answer, but her throat was parched; she tried to swallow a sandy lump in her throat. She couldn't answer! Her thoughts were confused. She had run away from her overbearing, propriety-bridled home to be able to stand on her own feet and do what she felt she had to do. She had flown the coop to become an adult, make her own decisions, be her own master, but inside, an unsure, frightening apprehension filled her with a quivering unsureness. She wished she would awaken someplace else, away from this ordeal, someplace warm and quiet, where she wouldn't have to think, to make this decision. She looked at Bill. She took her hand from his and fingered the matchbook on the table, pensive and indecisive and afraid. She wanted to be a person, not destroy her person, and the ominous forebodings of her decision weighed heavily upon her. She still couldn't swallow.

"Come on now, . . ." Bill urged. "What are you sitting like a clam for? You're not being very frank. Let's go."

"Wait a minute." Everything inside of her sat poised in cold terror. She couldn't decide! But she had to! Here was an invitation to share in life in a big way. Thoughts of adult romance and a man danced within her. These could be hers, now. She would be a woman. *But God, . . . where does one draw the line between a woman and a whore?* She wasn't a whore. She didn't want to be a whore! She just wanted to be alive. *Oh, God, how did I get into this solitary hell inside my skull? How do I get out?* Was this not why she left home and all the molded, jaded, stagnant regimentation? Life had to be lived, and decisions had to be made, regardless of what people who were too weak to accept the necessity of the bitter with the sweet thought. She had to decide . . . either yes or no . . . decide . . . decide—child or woman . . . woman or whore—decide . . . decide . . . now . . . now. There was no easy way out. She was stuck. She had to make a decision and abide with it. She yearned to be an adult.

There was no noise of revelers now for Rita, only the sizzling pressure of silence in her ears, the sight of Bill across from her, looking intently into her face, and a millrace of thoughts. Her thoughts of home raised pictures of her family. How stupified, appalled, outraged they would be if they heard this conversation. How they would deny the reality of life . . . and seek protection behind principles and ideals, unexciting, unsatisfying, yet comforting in their universal acceptance. Familial thoughts and thoughts of blind acceptance of life without understanding angered her. *The hell with it! I've got to stand up by myself*, she screamed within herself, gritting her teeth. *I've got to . . . got to . . . got to . . . even if I'm wrong. I have to make my own mistakes.*

"Come on, let's go. You can think about it as we walk. Come on. What's the story?" Bill smiled. He stood, moving Rita's chair out so that she could stand. She looked at him, trembling unknowingly. Her stomach turned uncomfortably. He took her hand that trembled slightly. She stood, smiling, biting her lip, and they made their way out of the theatre.

2

"SO WHEN DO YOU GO TO THIS DRAMA CLASS OF YOURS?"

Bill's voice floated abstractly through the darkness of Rita's apartment. The dimness was relieved by occasional comet-like flashes across the ceiling, reflected from the traffic babbling in the street below. Rita and Bill lay on the bed engaged in naked, anti-climactic conversation, fulfilling the awkward need for verbal intercourse to affirm their humanity.

"We have class three nights a week. Phil Avery teaches us. Ever hear of him?"

She twisted onto her side to face Bill. In the shrouded room, she could distinguish only the dark outline of his head against the pillow. Her eyes strained to pierce the darkness surrounding his features but failed. Clamping her eyes shut to block out the present dim realities, Rita pondered if she had wanted—really wanted—to go to bed with Bill. It was too late, of course, but she wanted to be sure. Had she wanted him, or had she merely reacted impulsively against her fear of indecision, of immaturity? If she had assumed her present position solely out of fright, it served no purpose save to physically underscore her utter failure to stand on her own reasonable, adult feet. *Of course it was what I wanted*, she thought, furious at her doubting self. She opened her eyes suddenly, abandoning insidious thought, turning her attention to Bill and the conversation.

"No, I haven't. Should I have?"

His fingers touched her arm, slid to her hand and pressed it in his. He twisted to look at her. She too was a faceless shadow. She snuggled closer to him, resting her hand on his chest, methodically smoothing the hair there, still peering at his shadow. She wondered if she remembered what he looked like.

"Well, he was in the original cast of *Oklahoma* and *South Pacific*, and now he's in *My Fair Lady.*"

Certainly I know what he looks like, she thought angrily, forcing his image to appear before her mind's eye.

"Sounds like he knows what he's doing. But how the hell does he teach if he's in a show now?"

Another comet flashed through the slit in the curtains. It passed across Bill, for an instant illuminating his face to a cadaverous grey. Rita stopped stroking his chest; her hand rested inertly. It was a stranger's face—a face the features of which she knew only fleetingly—and yet this stranger was in bed with her, and she with him. Qualms stirred her stomach uncomfortably. *Hell*, she admonished herself, *it is only the hollow ideals about propriety my parents have crammed into me that disturb me—a lot of frightened bourgeois nonsense that means nothing, that is constantly paid lip service, and that is only adhered to by the mouthers when absolutely necessary.* Bill was fun and she was enjoying him, she concluded. She twisted away from Bill to lie flat on her back and stare thoughtfully at the ceiling.

"The class begins at five thirty and lasts until seven o'clock, that's how."

Bill folded his arms behind his head for a pillow, still peering toward her. She twisted her head toward him, gazing at his face, for which her imagination supplied the features, and smiled. It was exactly what she had wanted, she ventured to convince herself. She leaned forward and their mouths fused. They parted and she rested her head on his chest.

"How're you doing with it?"

"I've been taking lessons since I moved down here . . . . That's three months." Her jaw muscles flexed against his chest as she spoke. "I've done pretty good so far. Phil said I'd really make it if I kept at it. I will, too. I've got to," she vowed, utterly determined, her jaw muscles set firmly against his chest. "You know what I want to do—achieve? I want to be so good . . . so good that someday I'll make a whole audience . . . cry." She fell silent, inwardly choked up. "I've already won a scholarship for next term. That's good," she exclaimed proudly, thinking aloud, "I can sure use the money I'll save."

"You pay for your own lessons now?"

"Sure. You don't think my folks are supporting me, do you?" she asked sharply, a tremor of anger in her voice. She raised her head to look toward his face.

"Take it easy, baby. I don't know . . . I haven't the slightest idea." Bill didn't want an argument to jeopardize his warm position. He twisted and put an arm across her soft belly. "Come on, baby . . . take it easy. Let's not spoil it."

She relaxed again under his urging.

"Where you from originally?" he asked.

"Brooklyn. My folks still live there." Brooklyn—shady streets of black asphalt and sunlight filtering between fluttering leaves—flashed through her memory.

"So how come you live here? Brooklyn's not far. It's kind of tough having to pay for school and the rent and everything, isn't it?"

"It's better than being a brainless stooge," she fired back determinedly.

"You mean it was a hassle?"

"It wasn't that so much. It was just . . . I don't know what. They bugged me, . . . told me to wear this, hear that, say this, do that, you know? What a God damn rotten deal it was! They thought I was just a lump of clay to be smacked into any shape they wanted. I don't know why they bother to have children. They don't know a God damn thing about raising them." She snorted contempt.

"What do you think, everybody else has a picnic?"

"No, it's just that this is what I felt. I can't feel everything for everybody else, can I? I only really know the things that bother me. If somebody else has a rough time, let him stick up for himself."

"You sound harder than you are," he joshed with innuendo.

"It's not that . . ." she said, ignoring his comment. "But you've got to watch out for yourself in this world. Nobody else does it for you. Maybe that's right . . . that everybody should care for themselves. But it would be nice once in a while to relax. You know, once have somebody care for you, about you. . . ." Her voice trailed off forlornly. She reflected quietly for many moments. "Nobody can love you like your parents, you know that?" she continued.

"I never thought about it much."

"Well, everybody is out for something. You know, they treat people nice if they can get something for themselves out of it. Your parents, they love you all the time—they should anyway—not because you do anything, can do anything, but like you're theirs . . . you're you, part of them."

"I guess you're right. Like I said, I never think about it."

"It's a bitch when they don't even give a shit about you! Take my parents, . . . please?" They laughed momentarily. "I don't know why they had me," she continued, serious again. "I guess for the same reason they do everything else—it's the *thing*! They didn't want to be out of the race, you know?" One thought led, through painful association, to another, and Rita's anger spilled over. It was a sort of relief, however, to give these thoughts their freedom, to be able to vent her true emotions and feelings to someone without polite suppression or fear of retaliation. It felt like being alive and real inside herself for a change.

"They think the only thing they have to do is go to bed and make babies. They don't know they have to care for children, that everything they do influences their children. They think a kid is a dumb clod. But it isn't. A kid is a little person! They think they're kidding you when they lie to you—you know, white lies—to get you to do things, to go to the store for them, to act nice—stories, nonsense—as if, well, someday the kid'll understand. But you don't. You resent the lie. When you can't rely on your father, where is there to go?" She fell silent for many moments.

"I wasn't treated like a person. I was a nothing . . . a dummy they pulled strings on," she continued. "They want animals, little nothings, not children. It's just like some people have dogs, you know? They want the dog to be cute and to do tricks, see? But when it comes to the dog being a dog, you know, he wants to do his business, or he wants to play when his master isn't in the mood—Wham!" Rita grimaced, cutting the air viciously with her hand. ". . . right across the head with a strap. People like that ought to buy paper dolls and paper dogs; they never move unless you want them to."

Bill still held her across the waist, listening quietly, breathing slowly. He thought her story a bit trite and tedious; it was her problem. He restrained his feelings, however, being in no position to be annoyed.

Bill's quiet, firm support, his understanding, calmed Rita's doubts about being with him.

"You know, they even held my God damn acting lessons over my head. I was planning to take acting lessons and they agreed to pay for them. But when anything went wrong, the first thing they said was they wouldn't pay for my lessons. They thought I was nuts, you know? The jerky kid wants to be an actress. They humored me so they'd get me to behave. They humored me like I was a fff . . . a dummy. Stupid bastards!" she hissed between clenched teeth. "Who needs it?" she yelled angrily, sitting up in bed.

"Hey, take it easy." Bill sat up too. "Don't think about it." He put his hands on her shoulders and tried to ease her back to a prone position.

"Oh, leave me alone," she said coldly, shrugging him off.

"Listen, baby, I'm trying to help. If you don't want help, like we'll sort of forget the whole thing."

His angered threat of sudden desertion, aloneness, cooled her raging. She turned to him, forced a smile, and slowly relented, lying down again. Bill slid his arm over her waist again.

"I live here with the girls and nobody tells me what to do," she continued, slowly, sullenly. "Sure it's tougher than living at home in a couple of ways, but then, man," she smiled a little now, "if I were home I wouldn't have this pad and you wouldn't be here with me." She slid her hand across his chest, wanting to forget the unpleasant past. It was the warm and pleasant present that was important, and she wanted it to be real, tangible.

"That's right too." Bill smiled. "I'm glad you don't live home."

He twisted on his side to face Rita, becoming conscious of his presence and surroundings once again. He moved closer and kissed her. They embraced. Their bodies touched, and slowly began to pulsate.

It was warm and tender and nice here, she thought. She was a woman here. She was no longer a child here.

Bill's hand slid along her flank. He jerked her closer to himself, lifted himself, then enclosed her in his arms. They were engulfed in a writhing, blind passion. The room and the bed no longer existed. All that could be seen was the other's face—twisting mouth, biting lips, gnashing teeth.

Slowly, the room returned into focus. Bill lay on his back. Both breathed heavily, saying nothing, studying the ceiling.

"What do you do, Bill?"

"I'm a photographer."

"Really? Who do you work for?"

"Myself. I'm my own boss."

"Gee, that's great. Maybe you'll take my pictures for my composite?"

"Sure, why not?"

They were silent again. A slick of perspiration covered their bodies. She thought of being in bed with Bill, and then she thought of her bed in Brooklyn. How foreign this scene was to that other bed. How appalled her parents would be if they saw her with Bill.

Presently, a scratching sound was heard as a key slid into the lock in the front door. Rita bolted to a sitting position, thinking momentarily that it was her father entering her bedroom. After the initial shock, she realized she was in her own apartment, and that no one had more authority than she. Though she still waited cautiously to see who it was, fear relaxed its grip. Bill, too, had lurched to a sitting position instinctively. Rita put her hand on his chest to assure him with a confidence born of her feelings of adulthood, just now confirmed by her realization of independence and by Bill's nervousness. She felt very adult about her entire position now.

"It's all right," she whispered, "only one of the girls. Shh . . ."

They both watched the slit in the drapes that separated the bedroom from the middle room.

The apartment was three rooms. Rita and Bill were in the bedroom. The middle room, into which the door from the hall opened, was a kitchen-dining room. In it was an old refrigerator with the large exposed coil on top, a tub supported on claw feet and covered with a porcelain top, and a low, wooden-inlaid Chinese table which was used, while people sat around it on large colored pillows, as a dining table. The front room had two windows that faced Christopher Street four stories below. One wall of the front room was covered with frosted mirroring. The room contained a couch, heavy stuffed chairs, and paintings on the walls.

Suddenly, the light from the outside hall flitted through the open door. It shed a ray of light into the middle room. Bill saw Jeannie walk into the apartment. She stood just outside the curtained doorway of the room in which he and Rita were, talking to someone in the hall. She told whoever was out there to wait until she lit a lamp.

"She'll be coming in here?" Bill whispered.

Rita was still sitting up, also gazing through the split in the drapes. She held the sheets up to her neck.

"No," she whispered, "Jeannie sleeps outside in the living room. Laura and I sleep here. Don't worry about Laura, she won't be back for a while."

Jeannie turned the light on in the middle room. Its rays passed between the curtains that separated the rooms. The voice of the person to whom Jeannie spoke was familiar, but Bill couldn't place it. Suddenly, the curtains parted and the shadowy outline of a head appeared in the slit. A stream of light from the outside room fell across the bed. Bill and Rita cringed self-consciously.

"Anybody home?" Jeannie whispered with anticipation into the darkened room.

"Yes, it's me. Scram!" Rita commanded, trying to retain her composure and firm control of the situation. She looked furtively at Bill, then back to Jeannie, staring at her imperiously, wanting her to leave.

"Oh . . . okay. Sorry." Jeannie slipped her head out of the slit and returned to her guest.

"Who's there?" Josh asked loudly enough for Rita and Bill to hear.

"Rita."

"Say Rita . . ." Josh called.

"What?"

"Are you going to make it to the studio tomorrow? We're having that party, you know?"

"Oh, sure, I'll be there," she acquiesed, not wishing to converse.

The light was snapped on in the front room. They could hear Jeannie and Josh moving further away. The phonograph was started and music began to filter through the apartment. Rita and Bill lay back in the bed.

"Josh goes to dancing class tomorrow. They have a party about every two weeks. Josh invited me to go with him! It's something to do," she explained whisperingly to Bill.

Silently they listened to the music. The apartment began to vibrate as the two in the front room danced. Rita's hand entwined Bill's. They were still somewhat nervous, but they pressed each other's hand to assure confidence. The ceiling was now turned steel-grey from the light stealing through the curtains. Two long, pencil-thin lines of brightness were etched across the ceiling. The music ended. Jeannie and Josh returned to the middle room. There was the clatter of pots being taken off the door of a closet. Rita and Bill breathed lightly to minimize their presence. They felt the slight moving of each other's body as they twisted occasionally, heard the squeak of the faucet as it turned, the rush of water through the pipes, and the water falling into a coffee pot. All reality seemed to be magnified in the darkness, and they could hear all the sounds in the world, as if they were right in the midst of society—a society that was aware of their being in bed and was waiting for the right—the most embarrassing—moment to expose them.

"Anybody want any coffee?" asked Jeannie, directing her question to the bedroom.

"I'll take a cup," called Rita. "Do you want any?" she asked Bill softly.

"Sure, I'll take a cup . . . black," he whispered.

"Two cups of black, please."

"Okay, just as soon as it boils."

"Somebody in there?" Josh asked curiously.

"Sure there is, . . . Rita."

"No, . . . besides her?"

"What makes you ask that?"

"The two cups of coffee. Is there anybody in there?"

"For a bright boy you talk too much. Take some cups out of the closet and stop asking so many questions."

China clinked as it was taken from the closet.

"Say Rita," Jeannie called," Josh thinks he should get married and settle down. I told him he was crazy. What do you say?"

"Are you nuts?" Rita sat up in bed. The covers fell to her waist, revealing her breasts. Her hands lay outside the covers in the hollow between the two bulges of blanket that were her legs. "I think you just need a woman."

"That's true too," agreed Josh, "but I was thinking it might be nice to live with a chick that I really dig. I don't mean get married and all that crap—you know, a ceremony and all that corny jazz—I mean, like living with some chick who is really great, compatible. I think that'd be kind of groovy."

"Well, that's not a bad idea. Heaven is supposed to be great too. But you're on earth, man, and you won't find any customers for that jazz around here. We like our freedom. When you live with a cat, besides a whole bunch of garbage and dull crap and fights and things, when you fall out, man, there's a big hassle over the apartment, and who belongs to what, and this is mine. No sir, man, who needs it?"

"Sure," agreed Jeannie, picking up the conversation. "This way, man, you pick up your hat and coat and split any time. Oh, oh, the water's boiling." She rushed to the stove. The tinkle of china again drifted through the curtains. Rita turned to Bill and continued the conversation privately.

"I figure this way I can meet all the people I want and do whatever I want and not have anyone tell me I should go out with only him or do this or say that. You know? I don't think I want to settle down with one man right now. I'm not set for it. I have to live a bit first. I want to look around the world, have a little fun first. What could be more of a ball? We live here and no one bothers anyone. We all have our own friends and ideas and it works out fine."

"Here's your coffee," said Jeannie as she backed through the curtains. She held two steaming cups in her hands. As she entered, the curtains parted, and Bill saw Josh sitting cross-legged on a pillow in the middle room. Josh held his coffee cup in his hand as he tried to peer into the bedroom. The curtains fluttered closed and Jeannie handed Bill a cup.

"Hi," she said, looking at him with interest, a vague smile coloring her mouth. "Weren't you the one who wanted a match at the Seventh Avenue before?"

"Yep. Thanks," he said curtly, a bit annoyed at his disadvantageous position. He took the cup from her hand. "Oww . . . God damn it, this is hot," he exclaimed to distract from his discomfort.

"Well, what did you expect, cold coffee, silly?" asked Rita. "I keep a good maid who knows how to make coffee for my friends." She looked at Jeannie and laughed, partly to cover her own discomfort.

"Maid?" Jeannie feigned annoyance. She pulled the pillow from behind Rita and dropped it across Rita's head.

"Watch out! Oh, for shit's sake." Rita jumped up. "Now you got coffee over the whole God damn bed."

Jeannie burst into hysterical laughter. She fell back and slumped against the dresser for support.

"Jesus, what an ass you are sometimes, Jeannie." Rita stood on the bed, her cup in her hand, oblivious, in her excitement, to her nakedness. She jumped off the bed and held the sheet off the wet spots. Bill remained in bed on the partially dry side. His laugh was deep-voiced. He and Jeannie filled the room with a counterpoint of mirth. Josh, hearing the howls of laughter, gladly stuck his head through the split in the curtains. He wore a big smile in preparation to laugh at something funny. He added his deep-throated laugh to the melee, his eyes eagerly studying Rita's nakedness. Rita let the soaking sheet flop down on the mattress hopelessly, aware of and now turning her attention to disposing of the embarrassing intruders.

"You should have seen yourself jump out of that bed," gasped Jeannie laughingly. "It was the funniest thing . . ."

"Oh, it was funny, was it?" Rita took the pillow and slammed Jeannie with it, knocking her toward the door. "You'll see how funny it is if you don't get the hell out of here, you bitch."

Everyone resumed the laughter that had started to ebb. Jeannie became so hysterical she stumbled to the door. Rita again batted her fiercely with the pillow. Josh stood at the door, smiling, still ogling Rita. Jeannie bumped against him, pushing him back through the doorway as she made her way away from the flying pillow.

"Daughter-of-a-bitch," shouted Rita half laughing, half serious and annoyed. She stood at the doorway staring at the drawn curtains. In the other room, Jeannie and Josh were still laughing. Jeannie had the ability to laugh, once started, for many minutes on end, and she was now laughing uncontrollably. Her laughter kept everyone else laughing.

"Hey," Bill called softly to Rita, amusement coloring his voice, "come over here . . . . It's getting cold here without you." He studied her body as she walked toward him.

Rita smiled with resigned politeness. She reached for the covers. She was embarrassed and wanted to hide herself from Bill's eyes. This scene left her disenchanted, feeling cold and slutty. She wanted to let Bill play out his part and be rid of him, be alone; she felt hot tears in her eyes.

"I'll have to sleep on your side of the bed . . ." she forced herself to say playfully. "This side is wet."

"That's okay, we only need one side of the bed anyway." He grinned.

Rita's face streaked with a smile as she slipped under the covers.

"Hey, Rita," Josh called from the other room, ". . . man, you're looking great . . . . No kidding."

"Hey, you bald-headed bastard," scolded Jeannie. "You stop flirting with the other girls in this apartment or I'll give you a bust in the mouth."

"Wild, baby, wild," Josh exclaimed enthusiastically. Jeannie laughed. There was the sound of movement in the other room.

"Stop it, you crazy bastard . . . Stop it!" Jeannie protested playfully. "Ohhh, . . . ohhh, Josh." There was a shrill scream, followed by wanton laughter. "Ohh, Josh, . . . you're driving me crazy." There was a bumping shuffle of movement, and a hurried rustling of clothes, mingled with gasps. Neither Bill nor Rita paid any attention to it.

3

THE DOOR LEADING INTO THE APARTMENT was eased open by the pressure of Laura's hand. Light from the outside hall pierced the opening, slicing a slim V out of the dark interior. Portions of the rug and furniture were illumed. A white blanket covering the convertible sofa bulged with sleeping figures. Laura caught a glimpse of the double bulge and instantly jerked the opening door to a stop. Dumbstruck, her mouth fell open, her eyes widened. She angled her head to better see through the small opening between the door and its frame. The blanket, not completely covering Jeannie, revealed her naked arm stretched across Josh's shoulders. Laura stared blankly at this apparition for many minutes, all her muscles still, tense. Then she shrugged forlornly. Pressing the door, she swung it further open slowly and quietly.

The entire apartment was cast with the dim light from the hall. Laura's vague figure was projected hugely on the far wall. Jeannie and Josh slept on undisturbed. Laura removed her shoes, tiptoed into the apartment, and eased the door shut. Groping, she felt her way through the dark toward the bedroom. Finding the door frame, she glanced back at Jeannie's bed. The form of the sleepers was now silhouetted against the deep blue-black of the windows in the front room. Laura turned, and, in the naked quiet, she could hear the bones in her neck pivoting.

Nothing stirred in the bedroom, Rita's presence being discerable only by her breathing. The breathing, however, was peculiarly heavy, uneven. Laura froze, her eyes straining against the dark void, peering toward the bed, toward the source of the breathing. Gradually, two reclining, purplish bulges seemed to rise from the murky depths, so close together as to appear to be one gigantic, slumbering monster. The irregular breathing had caused Laura to suspect the presence of a second person, yet she stood gaping at the bed flabbergasted.

Laura's astonishment at the scene before her was intensified by the thought of having her bed—her own, one and only, bed—usurped, . . . and by Rita! Rita was sleeping, sharing the bed with someone else, without even asking Laura. This, her refuge, the only place wherein she was safe and warm, was now not safe, or warm, or even always hers. *Oh well*, she shrugged helplessly, resignedly, her lips pursing to stave off tears. *Rita didn't do it to be mean. She's just trying to have some fun. She just forgot to tell me.* Laura tried to smile, but her face twisted into an agonized grimace. With the hand not holding her shoes, she slid open the top drawer of her dresser. The drawer ground with a wood-on-wood friction sound, punctuated by the sharp metal clink of the drawer pull falling back into place. Laura listened, hoping she had not disturbed anyone. The breathing did not falter. She reached inside the drawer, her hand fumbling toward the left side. She felt beneath handkerchiefs for the crispness of folded bills. Finding them, she sifted them through her fingers, selected one, and put it in her pocket. Her hand replaced the remaining notes under the handkerchiefs and slid the drawer closed. The drawer jammed, the friction sound replaced by a loud squeal.

"Who's that?" inquired Rita's sleep-muffled voice.

"It's me," whispered Laura in a voice slighter than usual. There was a hint of whine in her tone.

"I'm sorry, honey. We fell asleep. Here, I'll give you my pillow . . . . Please don't mind sleeping on the couch."

"No, that's okay," Laura assured her vaguely, not wanting to disturb anyone, "I think I'll go out for a while anyway."

"Don't be silly," Rita whispered imperatively. "There's a couch inside. Don't go out."

Laura didn't want to disappoint Rita, but she just had to get out—out into the fresh air—and breathe. "No, I feel like going out. I'm going to meet someone. I'll see you later."

"Come here, will you, for crying-out-Christ," called Rita more loudly.

Bill stirred, cleared his throat, then twisted toward the outside of the bed. Both girls silently watched him.

"I'll be okay," Laura assured Rita in a whisper, backing toward the curtains. She parted them, quickly stepped across the room, opened the door, and exited into the hallway. Rita sat up, guiltily listening to Laura's fading footfalls on the steps.

The metal guard on the edge of each step clattered under Laura's feet as she descended through the dismal, yellow-walled halls. The yellowness was intensified by the single, extremely dim, almost tan, bare bulb burning at the top of each flight of steps. Dark brown doors were set in pairs at each end of the landings. Two additional doors were cut into the side wall of the narrow landing passages. These were the common toilets the tenants shared—two end door apartments to a toilet. Laura became conscious of the loudness of her descent, and apprehensively tiptoed down the remaining steps.

The last flight of stairs led through a short hall out to the front door. Metal mailboxes, green with time, were set in the wall on the right. Lidded garbage cans, like squat sentinels, formed ranks on the left. Laura drummed her fingers across the lids as she walked to the front door. She stood on the one-step stoop, her head craning to view first one end of the street, then the other. The door, shutting behind her, nudged her out into the street a bit further.

The street was silent, deserted, filled with harsh shadows. The dismal pattern was relieved by the inverted V of light falling from the eye of a street lamp on the corner. The lamp was bent over, as if wilted from long years of suffering noise-filled days and friendless, lingering nights. Drizzle, floating on a slight breeze, passed in diagonal patterns through the beam of light. The street was coated with a slick that reflected the street light in a wavy line that reached toward Laura.

Befuddled, Laura sat dejectedly on the stoop next to a covered garbage can. The can was coated with a film of mist, but Laura ignored the wetness as she rested her weary head on it. She bit her lip hard, feeling a scream rushing up her throat.

A car passed and stopped on the corner for a red light. Through the steamy back window Laura watched the shadowy forms of the driver and his passenger; diffused red images kissed. The light changed, the wet tires rolled with a sucking, hissing noise, and the car turned the corner and disappeared. The street was again deserted. Feeling deserted like the street, Laura looked toward Sheridan Square to the left. The bright lights of Jim Atkin's Food Shop and the other shops on Sheridan Square which were still open, flared through the mist, hazily belying the time.

"Hey, pal, could you have a heart on an old veteran," begged a disheveled figure who emerged out of the shadows across the street, tottering toward Laura. "I need a dime . . . that's all, only a dime."

The drunk slurred his words as he stood in front of her, his hand stretched out imploringly. Laura smelled cheap, sweet wine floating on the air about him. He swayed, staggered, then caught his balance again. Laura was now further confused. She felt sorry for him, but she hadn't enough money to buy drinks for him.

"No, I'm sorry. I don't . . ."

"Ohhh . . . ," he wailed with drunken discovery, "excuse me, sweetheart." He smiled, his beaten, bearded face wrinkling like a prune. His head lolled to the side involuntarily. "I didn't know what you were." His hand groped into his back pocket; he lost his balance momentarily. "Wanna drink some good wine?" His torso swayed forward and back as his feet remained planted on the same spot.

"C'mon, go away. I don't want any crap," Laura snapped nervously, her mouth twitching. "Come on, leave me alone."

"What's a matter, . . . you don't like my company?" he asked with a vicious snicker. "Whatta ya think, you're too good, hanh, baby? . . . too sophisticated?" He leaned forward, a sneer on his face.

Laura felt trapped. She leaned back, but there was no room, the door being closed behind her.

"Ahhh . . . get the fuck out of here, you God damn wino," she yelped frightenedly, jumping up. She bolted toward Sheridan Square where she knew there should be people and safety. After the first few steps, she slowed her pace to a shuffle, trying to appear calm, her eyes straining to the sides to see if the drunk was following as she made her way toward the lights.

"Hey, come back here you little trollop," yelled the tramp in a hoarse, wine-destroyed voice, as he remained in the same spot.

"You son-of-a-bitch." Laura dug an empty food tin out of a garbage can, wheeled and hurled it with all her hurt power. "I'll give you trollop, you bum."

The can caromed off the sidewalk in a series of bounces, its clatter hollowly resounding between the buildings. It rolled to a stop against the curb. Laura turned and continued walking, looking back only once to see the tramp zigzagging toward the far corner, muttering unquietly. He leaned against the street lamp as Laura turned into the Square.

Most of the streets leading to the Square were sepulchral, disturbed only occasionally by passing cars or hollow footsteps. It was Tuesday night, and over New York somber silence prevailed. Yet Sheridan Square was ablaze with neon lights from food shops that stayed open until very late. There was always someone who couldn't sleep in the quiet night wandering around the Village until the early morning.

Laura crossed the Square, meandered past the myriad of now darkened shops lining West Fourth Street and halted at the Avenue of the Americas. Despite the passage of time since its name-change, most New Yorkers still called this Sixth Avenue. She stood at the curb gazing up and down the empty avenue. The Waverly Cinema marquee was dark. Large, illuminated numerals depicting the time on the side of a building near Eighth Street read "3:15." A cab filled with noisy men pulled out of Third Street. The striptease joints were still open.

Laura stepped determinedly toward the Club Lisa. A covey of young men from Uptown walked ahead of her, talking loudly. They argued whether to go home or go into one more club first. They cupped their eyes against the large picturewindow in front of one of the strip joints, peered in for a few minutes, then passed on. Laura, out of curiosity, stopped to peer through the window. A bleach-blonde woman was shuffling around the stage in an Arabian-type dancing outfit, complete with concealed zippers.

"Ey . . . you, . . . up da dock, . . . beat it," threatened the doorman. He looked sneaky and cruel and was festooned with a garrish maroon-and-gold uniform hat and coat over shabby grey trousers and scuffed shoes.

Laura moved on. Ahead, another doorman automatically opened the door of his club for the passing men.

"Step right in," he called, "no cover, no minimum. New show just started."

A brassy singing voice filtered through the opened doorway. The Uptowners continued walking and the doorman at a third club held his door open.

"Come on in . . . beautiful girls . . . all-girl review . . . ya get some hot stuff here." The doorman fluttered his eyebrows evilly.

Laura turned at the corner of MacDougal Street and climbed the steps of the Club Lisa.

The Club Lisa had the stale look and smell of any cheap beer-joint. Despite the time, it was fairly crowded. People lined the bar. Big squares of mirror covered the wall over the half-oval bar, reflecting yellow fluorescent border lights. Bottles of cheap whiskey on shelves behind the bar were lit from behind with white bulbs. Lining the wall opposite the bar was a small checkbooth for coats, a few tables at which some people were sitting, and a cigarette machine. Over the door of the checkroom was a sign: "Not Responsible Unless Checked." A partition separated the bar and the tables from a back room which contained wooden booths, a jukebox blaring brassy music, and a dance floor. Several couples were dancing. At the very back, the entrance-ways to the rest rooms were cloaked from the view of the patrons by partitions fabricated from dark, thick, floor-to-ceiling drapes. The matron, required by law in ladies rest rooms, sat outside the entrance to the rest room near the jukebox.

"Hi, Laura, . . . what's happening?" asked a little figure with a D.A. hair wave standing at the bar. D.A. stood for Duck's Ass. It was so called because the short hair at the back of the head swept together in the fashion of a duck's tail-feathers. The person addressing Laura wore pegged pants, a black shirt open at the neck, and tasselled loafers. This was apparently a man, but underneath the rough, black shirt were the breasts of a woman, neglected yet immutable.

"Hi, Phil," Laura answered eagerly, glad for the opportunity to speak with someone. "Nothing much happening with me . . . How about you?"

"Nothing to shout about," replied Phil, her high voice intoned hard and tough. "I'm waiting here for Billie. You know Billie, don't you?"

"Yeah, sure. Give me a beer, Sonny," Laura called to the bartender.

Laura sat on the stool next to Phil, took a cigarette from Phil's pack on the bar, lit up, and blew the smoke from puffed, uninhaling cheeks. She twisted on the revolving stool and faced the back room.

One couple was now dancing, swaying with the music, rotating their kissing pelvises synchronously in a steady rhythm. The dancers both wore men's pants. One had dark kinky hair and a shirt and tie. The other had straight, slickeddown black hair and wore a red sweater with the sleeves rolled to the elbows. They twirled and faced Laura—the male role of the couple was played by a kinky-haired "butch" Lesbian; the female, a saccharin-faced "faggot" in a red sweater. Challenging and oblivious contentment comingled on their cheek-to-cheek faces.

The countenances surrounding the tables in the booths around the dance floor were strange, petite, feminine featured, completely pale for lack of make-up, unnaturally twisted into callous sneers. The Lesbians were gathered, as if assembling their forces for a fight to the finish, at any moment, with the men and the world that had somehow disappointed and betrayed them. Most of the Lesbians wore their hair cut short, almost to a man's length. They wore men's clothing, intending to make themselves look like tough punks. Their naturally wider hips, however, gave them a pear-shaped appearance. Some Lesbians, however, wore feminine-styled hair, and looked normal to all outward appearances. They were different, though; they only dated male-like females.

"Today's my birthday, Laura," Phil commented, re-capturing Laura's attention. Phil was a small woman, tiny in proportion.

"Hey, that's great. How old are you?"

"Twenty-seven." She looked like a fourteen-year-old boy.

A waitress dressed in skirt and blouse walked up to the bar to fill an order.

"Hi, Jo, what's happening?" Phil asked the waitress. "You want to meet me here tomorrow and get drunk for my birthday?"

"Sure." The waitress's mouth revealed overly jutting, crooked teeth. She lifted the tray of drinks and turned toward the back room. Two fellows standing by the doorway of the partition grinned and softly remarked to her as she walked to the back. They were two guys from Uptown getting a big charge from the Lesbians. They were so convinced of the reality of their own world, they failed to realize some things are not funny to some people.

"C'mon sweet, smile," taunted one of the two Uptowners as the waitress returned to the bar. Her eyes flew to the side of their sockets, riveting on him angrily. Her face set hard, hatred flaring from her nostrils.

"Hey, man, dig this chick that just walked in," Phil remarked to Laura, twisting to look at an attractive girl who had just entered the club with a male date.

The girl was draped in a clinging, tight, light-blue dress. She and her date were well-groomed Uptowners. Their faces were unusual in this club. They hesitated at the door, looking around, and then, spying the back room, walked to the back and slid into a booth. Lesbians twisted around to look at them as they passed, many admiring the girl.

Unlike the conventional rites in which male approaches female, or vice versa, all formality is disregarded by the sexually abnormal. Perhaps it is the almost maddening need to be loved and appreciated which drives the emotionally upset person toward others with such frenzy, and allows imbalanced people to fuse together on contact. Besides a groping, grasping, impulsive reaching toward each other, they hold each other with frenzied passion and flare up at each other with equally uncontrolable impulse.

"Aw, fuck her," remarked Billie, who had just arrived at the Club to meet Phil. Billie stood glaring from the girl to Phil and back again, while Phil continued gazing at the new girl. Billie was a "fem" Lesbian, in women's slacks and a sweater, her hair worn long. Her face, though made up, was hard-featured.

"That's what I'd like to do," Phil replied smilingly.

"Oh, you would, hanh? I'll tear every bone out of your head," Billie threatened menacingly.

"You will like shit."

They glared at each other angrily.

"Hey, come on. She was only kidding," Laura interposed in defense of Phil.

Billie glanced to Laura momentarily, then back to Phil. A smirk twitched her face. She shrugged off her anger. Billie had entered with and was standing next to a tall, dark, somewhat heavy-set, pimply-skinned man.

"Hi Frank. How're you doing?" Phil asked the man.

"Hello, dears, . . . and what are you up to tonight?" he asked in a purposefully sing-song fashion. He rolled his shoulders inside a heavily padded, tough-guy jacket.

"I'm going to rip this little bastard in two." Billie pointed to Phil. "She's eyeing that chick in the back room."

"Why not? She's a nice-looking chick. But I'd rather have you, baby," he said grasping Billie's wrist and pulling her toward himself. He put his arms around her waist and lifted her into the air. "I don't care what the hell you broads think you are, you're broads to me and I'd go to bed with every one of you. Say, . . . that's not a bad idea." He fluttered his eyebrows in licentious reflection. Billie was grimacing in his bear hug. Frank let her loose and she dropped onto her feet.

"You couldn't take it, Frank," remarked Phil.

"It'd be a hell of a lot of fun trying." He burst out in laughter, watching for the girls to appreciate his remark. All the girls laughed with him.

"You're going to get your fucking false teeth knocked back into your throat if you don't shut up," boomed the waitress's voice as she passed the two Uptowners standing at the partition door.

The entire club silenced ominously. All heads turned menacingly toward the two men—the intruders—whose presence was known and barely tolerated by the Lesbians. The men began nervously chatting with each other, wishing to be inconspicuous. The waitress looked at them with contempt, then turned to the bar. The Lesbians' interest lingered a moment longer then returned to their friends and drinks.

A wide-hipped girl in men's clothing entered the bar. Had she been dressed in women's clothing, she would have appeared heavy. In men's clothing she resembled a penguin, earth bound. Some horrible madness drives vain woman to this ludicrous appearance. Two ferns with long hair and women's clothing, and make-up entered with the earth bound one. One of the two fems was a tan Negro. The butch Lesbian removed her windbreaker and threw it brusquely on the counter of the checking booth.

"You didn't take a check," called the girl behind the counter. "Hey . . ."

The butch ignored her and walked toward the back room.

"You didn't take your coat check," the checkroom girl yelled again.

The butch sat at a booth with her fems. The coat-check girl's eyes widened with anger at the public affront. She threw open the door of the coat room and swooped into the back room, butch's coat in her hand.

"Here . . . ," she yelled throwing the coat high into the air.

The coat floated upward, downward, landing on the floor at the feet of its owner, who jumped with surprise. The butch glared at the checkroom girl, then bent forward and picked up the coat, putting it on a chair next to her. She continued to glare at the coat-check girl, who in turn stared boldly back. It was a standoff. The checkroom girl pivoted and walked back to the checkroom.

"Hey, Omar . . . ," a tall Negro yelled as he stood next to one of the tables on the bar side of the partition.

Omar was another Negro, sitting dead drunk at the table, his head resting on the table top. Omar's arms hung limply from his shoulders, his hands touching the sawdusted floor. He wore a western-type hat, the wide brim bent beneath his inert head. Long strands of hair stuck out from under the sweat band. He wore boots, and his pants were tucked inside them.

"Hey Omar," his friend yelled again, pounding the drunk on the back to wake him. "Come on, man, . . . you can't pull a sick in here, . . . come on."

Omar picked up his head from the table. It moved slowly through the air to an upright position, continued backward and bounced against the partition with a dull thud. A long whisp of hair hung down the center of his face and touched his nose. He forced his eyelids open half way but they struggled to close again. Two little circles of blue peered out dully, unfocused. Omar glimpsed at his friend, tried a feeble smile, then the eyelids clamped down again.

"Hey, come on . . ." Omar's friend started to pound Omar's chest. It sounded as if he were pounding a side of dead beef. "Come on, man . . . come on." He became annoyed and hit Omar harder. Omar's body started to ease forward; the weight of his head came into force again. His head crashed solidly and bounced on the table top. "Come on now, man." He put his hands under Omar's armpits, lifting him on to his feet. Omar stood erect, his friend balancing his swaying body, then pushing Omar toward the door.

The coat-check girl was talking to a woman about thirty-five years old, dressed in men's clothing, with a streak of silver dyed into the front of her man-styled hair. They watched unconcerned as the two men stumbled out. The friend dragged Omar down the steps and pushed him toward Eighth Street and coffee. The Lesbians at the checkroom turned and continued their conversation.

Laura was now dancing in the back room with another girl. Her dancing partner, Lucille, who was called Lou, danced Laura toward the jukebox. Suddenly, Laura was pulled behind the jukebox on the opposite side of the drapes shielding the women's rest room. Lou encircled her arms around Laura's waist, pulled Laura close, and leaned forward to kiss her. Laura jerked her head back. Lucille was persistent, following Laura's head with her own, trying to find Laura's lips. Finally, she grasped Laura's head between her two hands and pressed her lips against the small mouth. Laura stared perplexedly, terrified, over Lucille's shoulder. She suffered Lucille's arms, not knowing what to do, not sure if she should rebuff her. After all, someone cared for, desired her. Even this was better than the hollow emptiness.

"Hey, man, that Laura really swings after all. See her swapping spit with Lucille back there," Billie remarked, watching Laura and Lucille from the bar. "She's a pretty fair chick, you know what I mean, . . . a little mousy, but nice."

"You son-of-a-bitch," said Phil half joking. "I'll cut you into little pieces if you start that kind of crap." Phil, Billie and Frank laughed together. The music ended and Laura and Lucille walked back toward the bar.

"Hey you . . . You little bitch," Tony the bouncer yelled loudly at Laura as she returned to the bar. "You know you shouldn't be making out in here, don't you?" he said loudly, menacing her by thrusting his head close to hers and staring into her face.

"So . . .?" she asked nervously.

"So?" he asked imperiously. He enjoyed picking on her because she became so frightened and nervous. A butch would have punched him in the mouth if Tony had done that to her . . . but Laura shrank away. "Well, if you wanna stay here now you gotta give me a blow job. You're a blower, ain't you?" Tony said, smiling viciously, looking around for popular approval.

"You rotten bastard. Fuck you," yelped Laura defensively, edging away from him.

"Come on, you little blower." He grabbed her hand. "Here . . ." He put her hand on his manliness.

She stood frozen with terror and surprise, then squeezed him hard where it hurt.

"Aughhhh," he bellowed with intense pain. "You little bastard whore." He lashed his fist against the left side of her head above the ear.

Laura fell back against the wall. She stood still, her eyes bulging with terror, her hands feeling for the wall behind her. She was like a trapped cat, studying her attacker, thinking furiously of escape. As he approached her, she slid cautiously along the wall to the door, bolting down the steps just as he kicked at her. Whimpering, she ran down the street, and rounded the corner into Minetta Lane.

"Rotten son-of-a-bitch," she murmured through tears as she strode quickly through the unlit lane toward the light of the Avenue of the Americas. She passed under the canopy of Raoul Johnson's bar. Someone tapped a coin on the window from inside. She stopped and peered through the window. A friend waved to her to enter. Frightened and alone, unable to go home, she entered the bar.

"Hi, Laura," said the blond fellow who had tapped on the window. He was dressed in jeans and a white T-shirt. "What's happening?"

"I don't know, . . . nothing," said Laura with a weak, resigned shrug. She sat on a stool, looking blandly over his shoulder at the wall.

"I thought we were going to get together one of these days . . . What's the matter? We'll go to the movies or something."

"Okay, . . . one of these days." She wasn't really paying attention to what he said. She looked at her friend with the pathetic look of a lost puppy, holding the side of her head, tears still streaking her face.

"What happened?"

"Oh, I got kicked out of the Lisa."

"How? What happened?"

"The bouncer called me something and wanted me to do something . . . and I told him to F himself . . . and he punched me."

"Oh, that's real nice. You hang out in all the best spots, don't you?"

She looked at him guiltily. His admonition only presaged the annoyance that Rita and Jeannie would display when Laura told them.

"Hey Laura," a tall curly-haired fellow in the back called. Laura looked to the back, then at her disapproving friend.

"I'll be right back," she said, escaping toward the back. She sat on a stool next to the fellow who had called. He was a tall, thin fellow named George.

"Whatta ya been doin', baby?" he asked with affected, one-uplifted-brow casualness.

"Nothin' . . ."

"Listen, I got some smokes that'll make you fly. Whatta ya say you and me go to my pad and have a ball?"

Laura made a face of disapproval. George chuckled and began to explain what kicks it would be. He bought her a beer. After many minutes she stood, turned, and shook her head all the while walking back to the front of the bar. George stared after her, shrugging disappointedly.

"What do you call right back?" asked the blond fellow. "Like you were gone for days."

Laura smiled weakly out of the side of her mouth and half shrugged. Sammy the bartender put down a beer for her.

"Hey . . . don't you even say hello?"

She looked up at Sammy. "Oh, I'm sorry, Sammy . . ." She wrinkled an excuse for a smile. "I didn't see you. What's the beer for?"

"Your buddy bought it for you." He jerked his thumb at the blond.

Laura looked to the blond and flickered a smile. She appreciated his thoughtfulness. She didn't even know his name. They had met at a party, but she had never found out his name, and now she felt badly about asking him what it was. He stood taller than she, watching her. She became flustered and sipped her beer, looking around, still pressing a hand to the side of her head.

Josh Minot, Jeannie's shaven-headed friend pushed the door open and walked into Johnson's.

"Josh!" Laura called to him, half lifting her arm to wave.

"Hi, Laura," he said walking over to her, "where'd you go? Like everybody was worried about you." He looked over her head at the people seated around the room. She noticed his lack of interest.

"Just for a walk," she said unimportantly. "Is that other fellow still at the apartment?"

"No, everybody split for their own pad. I'll see you later," he said, seeing a friend in the back of the bar.

Laura turned quickly to her blond friend.

"I'll be right back." She put down her drink.

"Hey, don't go, baby, the night's just beginning."

Laura dashed out of the cafe and started to run. She ran across the Avenue of the Americas, up Fourth Street, and across Sheridan Square to Christopher Street. Out of breath, she walked very fast the rest of the way to the house and dashed up the stairs two by two. Cautiously, she opened the door of the apartment. The V of light cutting through the darkness revealed only one figure on Jeannie's bed. Laura walked in slowly and quietly and shut the door. She peered through the slits in the curtain until her eyes made out the lone figure in bed. Rita was asleep, her arm stretched out across Laura's side of the bed. Laura walked into the room, undressed quickly and slid into bed, curling up to keep warm. Laura lay her head across Rita's arm, cuddled close to her warmth, and fell asleep.

4

The warmth within her family's house could not penetrate the cold fear trembling within Rita. She was nervous; a queasy feeling rushed from her gnawing stomach into her dry throat. It was as if she were in some unknown, horrible place wherein ominous dread dwelt and from which she wished to fly. In the rose-print-papered room that had been hers, she sat before the plush scallop-shaped mirror of the dressing table brushing her hair with a silver-handled brush. This room, still reserved for her, brought back many memories. She looked at the reflection of the room in the mirror—at the bed, at the chair upon which the small dolls her father had once bought for her sat silently, at the white window curtains she had helped Mother sew, although Rita had really contributed merely occasional distraction. This nostalgia should have made Rita feel as if she belonged here. These surroundings were luxurious and nice, and yet they stirred up memories of intense adolescent violence, of seething tension and disagreements. Rita returned her attention to brushing her hair.

The aroma of the meal being prepared rose to greet her. It was a thick, warm, inviting aroma, . . . yet it added to the chill of fear within

Rita. Her fear was increased by the apprehension of the scene she was sure would start at dinner. One always did.

Why had she come? she pondered. Why did she bother, when each visit only set off additional misunderstanding and hostility? She had returned because she wanted to be part of them; she wanted to belong to her family, she admitted to herself reluctantly. Not that she wanted to be a part of their socially dictated society, but that she wanted to be part of a warm, loving unit where the stress of the world would be forgotten in velvety, warm love. She insisted on being a whole part though, an individual part, not an undistinguished lump contributing only passive existence to the mass.

Rita conjured up the scene during the course of the meal when Father or Mother would begin preaching of the evils of the Village and of the disapproval that all good, honest, respected persons had for such a place and those who lived there. Rita's parents couldn't understand why a nice girl like she lived there. Hadn't they given her everything she could have desired—clothes, toys, vacations—things comparable to that which children of only the *best* families received? *"She'll come around,"* she continued, conjuring up their thoughts and words. *"She'll come around to our way of thinking when she realizes all the good things that our existence has in comparison to the degradation of the Village." They want to assure themselves, perhaps to fill their lives with other vague dreams instead of stark reality*, she interjected to herself. Something shall go wrong, something has to happen to upset the entire evening, Rita assured herself. She wished that just this once things could be different.

"Rita!" Mother called from the kitchen downstairs. It was that familiar, prolonged call that grated against Rita's mind. It wasn't just a call, it was a yell—and yet it was more than a yell. It was a demand, an order. It manifested a complete disregard of Rita's integrity and privacy. But more than this, the reason it chilled Rita to the bone, Mother's yell was prompted by laziness. Mother strained her throat to obviate the necessity of walking. Rita had learned to despise people who yelled—lazy, slovenly people who would rather tear out their lungs with screams than walk ten feet and talk quietly like human beings. Rita avoided these sorts of people because they were actually dead, although frighteningly alive-looking. It was the foolish, unwilling-to-accept-difficulties approach to reality which this yelling manifested that most angered Rita.

Mother yelled Rita's name again.

Rita brushed her hair more furiously, concentrating on each stroke, on the hand movement, on the quality of the hair. She wanted her mother to scream her lungs out . . . *Scream, scream, scream, you dumb witch*, Rita prayed inside herself, her head pounding with rage, *scream till your throat is sore and aching . . . till you can no longer talk or even whisper . . . till you die . . . then perhaps you'll realize what it's all about. . . .* She gritted her teeth.

"RITA" Mother yelled again, a hint of desperate, annoyed frustration prolonging each sylable until the name became a chant, filling every passageway in the house.

You rotten lazy bastard. Rita's head shook with rage. Rita knew Mother was now disgusted, afflicted and tortured because her screams were not answered. If only she were sensible enough not to yell, not to demand, order, . . . once, . . . just once. Rita held her hands to her head to block out the haunting screams.

Someone knocked on the door. Rita looked up quickly. Before she had a chance to bid the person enter, the door opened and Father peered at her inquisitively, suspiciously, frowningly.

"Well? What's the matter with you? Can't you hear your Mother calling you? You need a special invitation?"

"I'm sorry," she apologized automatically. "I'll be right down."

She turned back to the mirror to check if she had adjusted and changed her make-up and hair sufficiently to look the way she knew her parents would think presentable. "Presentable" meant whatever was accepted and worn by Mother's and Father's friends, other people, the world in general. Mother's and Father's friends also only wore things that were "presentable."

Father was standing in the doorway, Rita noticed, still studying her reflection in the mirror. Father was short—short and stocky, tending toward the paunchy. He hunched over a little with age, though he was only fifty-five, and waddled slightly duck-footed. His face, once seemingly bold and fearless, was putty-like, haggard, without conviction, forceless. He had been brave and tough, had fought to keep for his family that small glory he had achieved by his labor. He had been able, by incessant toil and adherence to a principle of conformity to social dictates, to lift them above the wretched life he had spent in a cold-water flat as an immigrant laborer's son, to give them a comfortable existence in one of Brooklyn's most luxurious sections, to make them respected in their Temple and neighborhood. And now he wanted only to be quiet, sleep and rest; his family was comfortable.

"Well, come on. Dinner's ready." He continued watching and waiting. He searched for some physical defect or weakness, for the joint in her Village-wrought armor, against which he could loose the tirade of the respectable on living in the Village.

Rita stayed in the chair purposely, annoyed at his insistence in treating her like a child, like a mindless lump of clay.

"Well?"

"All right!"

Rita couldn't remember when this now-open conflict had started. When she was young everything had been fine. As she matured, feeling her own will and weight a bit, enjoying the social equality and freedom Father struggled to provide, the conflict began to rise. Perhaps it was because Rita didn't seem to fit exactly into the stereotyped position her parents felt they, and, therefore Rita, had to reflect. At first, this stereotyped position demanded that Rita supress only minor feelings or thoughts. As she grew older, however, the position became more arbitrary, demanding, oppressive. It was vexing to hear, This is what *they're* doing. This is what *they're* wearing this year. Why don't you be like *everybody?* Wasn't she a person too? Couldn't she decide for her own being? She, like Thoreau, wondered *"by what degree of consanguinity they are related to me, and what authority they may have in an affair which affects me so nearly . . ."* Who the hell are THEY anyway? This outside direction began to back up in Rita's mind like a log jam, until she felt *they* were prescribing her entire life.

She remembered how she began, just for spite, for kicks, to do things that this unwritten, unnameable code wouldn't have approved: how she stole cigarettes from Father's package, how the smoke tasted awful, and how she beat the smoke out of the bathroom window with a towel. It was an exciting feeling to have done something unusual, something daring, something she had thought of by herself.

After a while, this socially-dictated position which Rita was supposed to reflect became so ludicrous in her mind that she was able to follow the precepts which her parents and *they*dictated only with the same precaution required in taking vile medicine: swallow hard and grimace. This made her more sick and more restless, however. She couldn't stand the stifling rules imposed on her without reason; she couldn't stand being a lump of clay. She wanted either to enjoy life or to end it. Thus, she fled from her family's house to find the freedom and tolerance and independence for her own opinion in the Village. Then, whole areas of darkness fell away from her eyes. Like a newborn child, she began to discover hidden aspects of herself. Suddenly, she disagreed with her parents about more things than ever before. Somehow, they seemed even more stagnant, static, molded, the way *everybody* was.

Rita followed Father down the stairs toward the kitchen, wishing there might be a way through which they could understand each other more.

Their house was large and spacious. It was a private, three-story wood-frame house with turrets and ramparts and terraces reaching into the sky like a medieval castle. The architecture of all the houses on this street was similar. Each new house followed and matched the time-worn, approved pattern of the one before it. Father had had it built for Mother ten years before, and what a wonderful present it would seem, except that it was a demanded present, dedicated only to the neighbors, and erected not by love, or for the comfort of those who lived within, but by a need to have an external monument to the prowess of its owner.

Rita thought the house foolish, like everything else in it—wasteful, tasteless. It was foolish to build a house using modern materials to falsely recreate ancient expediencies—supporting beams which did not support but hung, just as the people within did not support changing life but clung frightenedly to prescribed traditions. "*If it was good enough for others, it's good enough for us,*"

The interior was decorated gaudily. Her parents and their friends were influenced in their tastes and followed those modes that were expensive, massive, and patently luxurious—regardless of the needs of the room. Velvet drapes hung in huge folds from a cornice across an entire wall in the living room. Ornate scallops topped these cornices, and flimsy curtains underscored them. Plush overstuffed chairs and couches were spotted about the room. A thick rug with a design of flowers and vases covered the floor. A piano that no one played and candelabra and knicknacks, all bedecked with designs and gilt, completed the ostentation of the room.

Her parents' entire life was, like this house, equally without reason. All undertakings bore witness to the fact that they could be afforded; money was spent for the sake of spending it, regardless of the tasteless, choking effect.

"You sit over here, dear." Mother pointed to Rita's seat at the kitchen table. The kitchen was the family room, where the family spent its time. The gaudy, rich trappings in the other rooms were preserved and enshrined to the honor of *Pecunia Rex*. The family remained in the kitchen, content with the warmth effulging from the other rooms, not deeming themselves worthy enough to enjoy a luxurious life. Those rooms were reserved for friends and other worthy people.

The way Mother said "dear" annoyed Rita. It was hollow, and Rita wasn't deceived by this false show of sweetness. Had Mother called her a Village tramp, Rita might believe her. This sweetness was contrived and phony. Mother was too busy with the house and bridge games ever to have many real emotions.

"Randy," Mother called to her young son. "RANDY." The yell sent a shiver up Rita's back.

"Randy. Will you come to dinner . . ."

Randy was a hulking boy of thirteen, with glasses, a bent nose, thick fleshy lips, and crooked teeth. Mother loved her poor little Randy more because of his imperfections. He was Mother's favorite plaything and lover. Often, Rita had been revolted while sitting watching television at home, Mother in a shabby house dress and curlers in her hair, Randy lying on the floor like a bloated oxen in pajamas, when suddenly, about bed time, the boy would begin to hug and kiss his Mother. Randy knew that Mother liked to be told he loved her, and he would play his cards to the full to stay up late to watch another T.V. program. Rita felt sorry for Mother; Father was usually out and Mother alone. But these scenes with Randy were repulsive. Father, when he was out, was usually with another woman. *Why shouldn't he be?* Rita asked herself, considering the benefits of staying at home with his wife, her mother—the benefits of staying at home with a cretinous woman of forty, who felt firm only with the love of a child; a woman beyond whom adult love lay as a barren island; a woman who didn't know enough to get out of bed in the morning to get her husband's breakfast; a woman who wasn't woman enough to keep herself attractive for him; a woman who still enjoyed the childish gossip that she had enjoyed when she was eighteen; who got a kick out of smutty little tawdry jokes; and who coyly flirted when she was out with the "girls" on the town. Randy was the only human with whom Mother could feel at ease emotionally, and even this would change when Randy was old enough to go out with friends at night. Rita thought that Mother would soon have to realize that one had to be capable of love to be capable of being loved and that love wasn't something stocked up in a magazine, toy, or candy store. Love had to be understood and nourished for itself; in this house, Rita thought, they were lucky their bodies were nourished, much less their souls.

"Come on, Randy, sit down," Mother urged lovingly, looking at him intently, admiration rippling her mouth. "Your soup is getting cold."

Randy sat and Mother sat.

"Oooszp . . . oooszp," Father sounded, drawing in his broth.

God, how Rita had learned to love quiet! She writhed inside with each spoonful Father sucked in. She hated everything about this place,—she loathed it, she despised it. So as not to hear Father's sucking, Rita concentrated on hating and loathing. Hate, she thought as she looked at the other people at the table bent over their soup, was a rather beautiful, meaningful emotion, reserved for things once loved. A lover hates with passion his lover who has spurned his love. Things can be disliked, loathed, resented, sickening, despised; without love there is either indifference or dislike. But hate gives rise to love, and love to hate, and each can become the other by a hairline change. Lovers should always be encouraged if their partners hate them in anger, for then they are truly loved.

The "ooszp . . . ooszp . . ." tore through Rita's concentration. She stared hopelessly into the lines etched on the surface of her soup. With her mouth set firmly after each opening, and a hand squeezing the napkin in her lap, she forced herself to eat with her family.

"So how's your apartment?" Mother shot at her in an offhand manner, smiling to instill confidence.

"Fine, . . . fine." Rita looked up perfunctorily so that no one could start a discussion about her not raising her head and speaking with respect.

"And your roommates?"

"Fine, . . . they're fine . . ."

"Oooszp . . . oooszp." Father tilted his plate to pull in the last few dregs of his soup. He was completely unconcerned with the other people around the table.

"Why don't you bring one around so I can take her out," Randy suggested giddily, a childish sneer on his mouth. His eyes darted to Mother. She indicated a slight smile, then looked quickly at Father from the side of her eyes.

Father glanced at Randy sternly, annoyed, then down to his soup again. Father did not approve of talk about the interrelationship of boys and girls in the presence of his family. Consideration of these subjects was reserved for the bodies of Father and his girl friend, and the ribald, evil humor of his friends as they regaled themselves, ostensibly in secret, with crude stories.

"I don't think they'd be interested," Rita replied with restraint.

"Why not? If they like you, they can't be too hot."

Rita winced. This was a parent-approved way for Randy to speak because he was only a boy, a little child, . . . a child that did not know better, who could learn about life by chance as he got older, and besides, Rita . . . well, Rita lived in the Village.

Rita drew in an extra breath to squelch her rising anger. Her mouth chomped on the inside of her cheek as she stared at Randy. She looked down and tried to concentrate on her soup.

"What else do we have?" asked Father.

"Liver . . . mashed potatoes." Mother stood to bring out the rest of the food.

"Mmmmm . . . a meal fit for a king." Father rubbed his hands together with delight. "What else are you doing?" Father asked Rita as he waited.

"Working, you mean?"

"Anything. What are you doing at all?" He continued the general inquisition.

"Nothing much, . . . still a waitress, . . . still going to class three times a week."

Disgust flickered on Father's mouth. His head began to nod with the weighty problems of the patriarch. He enjoyed even this grief of leadership.

"Well, I can't explain you anything, can I?" he asked. "You're gonna do what you want no matter . . ."

"Pop, let's not start another argument. I came home to see how everybody was, not to discuss what I'm doing. Can't we leave it at that?"

"Wait a minute! You don't mind if I tell you something?" He aimed a finger at her face, his eyes narrowing. "If you're so worried about us, you would be home more . . . so don't hand me that crap. I don't know yet what you want, but you're not gettin' nothin'. You live in that, "Green-witch" Village and then you come home and expect whatever you expect from your poor mother and me," he snorted. "I let you get away with too much. I should give you a good slap in the mouth and make you come home, that's what I should do. I'm too good to you. Other fathers would let their daughters go and live in the Village by themselves, . . . hhmph. They'd cut their kids' legs off first."

Rita absorbed this tirade silently. Father was quiet for many minutes, contemplating.

". . . but I want you to find out for yourself, and do what you think is best," he began again mildly, solicitously. "Do you think daddy yells at you because I like it? I know what you're going through, and I want to help you. I was young once. But if you don't listen to me . . ." Anger flared for an instant. "I'm doing these things for your own good. If you don't listen though, you're gonna be sorry. To tell you the truth I don't wish you any hard luck, . . . but you'll be sorry. Wait! You'll see I was right," he concluded with infallible finality, raising a finger into the air, then opening his hand in a sign to stop all conversation, as Mother put the steaming serving plates on the table.

"Ahh . . . this is good," Father said enthusiastically as he dished out the liver.

Rita sat quietly, wondering if Father really thought these little pieces of liver, thrown into an oven and, still in their cooking platters, onto a bare table without napkins, really was a meal fit for a king. He had eaten this sort of plain, uninspired, poorly served food all his life, and he wanted to think it was good, the best. *Everyone molds a kingdom with his own hand out of his own possessions.*

The others at the table were still moved by Father's indignity and they reflected embarrassment for Father and themselves. They resented the whore from the Village that was a member of their family.

The word Village was a curse in itself. It signified the filthiest of the filth, the lowest of the low, the cesspool of humanity to which drained all the waste matter of the world, the refuse of society. And to think that a relative of theirs had elected to live there, with all the degenerates and queers and nuts—Father's own daughter, flesh of his flesh. It was an affront to the family dignity.

Father was resigned, though, as any good man should be, and he accepted the burden that the Lord had given him. He graciously dropped the subject and chomped a large hunk of liver.

"You know . . ." Father began again, his mouth full, "you've been there long enough. Maybe its time to come home. Maybe you come home and talk to Rabbi Mayer. Daddy'll go with you. Let him decide— talk to you anyway. What could be fairer? He's a smart man—a good man."

Pulverized particles of white mashed potatoes and brown liver stuck on the end of Father's tongue and caked in the crevices between his teeth. Rita turned away disgusted.

"Maybe . . . Let me think about it," she said, wanting to avoid discussion. She attempted to force down her liver.

"C'mon, eat the liver. It's good for you," Mother urged Randy. "Don't waste any; it'd be a sin. Sixty-eight cents a pound it cost." She shook her head, accompanying her gesture with a *tch tch* sound of sadness.

That's all she worries about, thought Rita, *whether or not she wastes her money and effort . . . not if her family eats or feels well.* Rita's thoughts were filled with sadness.

"Eat, . . . c'mon eat," Father demanded of Rita. "You look terrible. You need a good meal instead of all the sh——"Father almost forgot not to be himself for the moment. ". . . The crap they have in those creep joints down the Village. You look run down. What are you doing to yourself?" Father was still sure he would flush out some hidden sordid secret; she would admit the filthy error of her Village ways.

"Probably staying up all night at parties," Randy injected, mixing his words with thoughts he had heard expressed before, thoughts with which he knew the family would agree.

"That's enough, Randy," Mother said protectively. "Eat the liver . . . it's good."

"It's the truth, ain't it? I don't want any liver." Randy made a face.

"Well, eat some of it anyway. I cooked it just the way you like." She smiled encouragingly. "It's good for you. It gives you brains."

Father was still contemplating Randy's words silently. They ate into his brain. Rita felt the rack she was on begin to pull her head from her body. She began to feel trapped. She wanted to leap from the table and leave. Yet she couldn't bear the scene that would inevitably ensue. Why had she come? Why had she come? Why? . . . Why? . . . Why? She had had to—that was why—she just had to. They had her mailing address, and if she hadn't come, one day she would answer a knock on the door and there he would be, Father, resplendent in his most austere, his most self-righteous, dominating, searching, disapproving look. It was far less an ordeal to return home first. And yet, beside this imposed need to return, Rita often truly felt she wanted to come home, she wanted to be part of her family. Time has a way of indulging memory. The mind turns from the unpleasant, the difficult, until one day, the qualm is no longer extant, and seeming pleasantness alone remains. This morning, Rita had awakened and felt the warmth and want of family love. The same warm blood that ran through the veins of Father and Mother and Randy surged through her, warming her thoughts until she had decided to return. She allowed their disagreement might be her fault, and perhaps they could try once again. Time's indulgence of memory may be barbed, however. Rita had been allowed to forget, but her parents had not forgotten to be. Rita contemplated how she might tactfully leave early and return to the peaceful, unenforced happiness of her own apartment.

"Is that what you're doing?" asked Father, thoughts of Randy's words having gnawed at him sufficiently, ". . . out fooling around all night, wasting your time?" He paused. "I don't want to be hard on you." He groped gracelessly for warmth and sincerity.

Rita had experienced his attempts at warmth before. She knew they were always emitted to sway her to his will.

"I just want you to settle down, . . . to get set in life, . . . get a husband." He shook his head, completely crushed by his daughter's imprudence. He was disgusted, sorrowful, and he didn't know how to convince her she was all wrong.

"There's that nice Marty Rosenstein," Mother added. "His mother was telling me he has a nice job in television. They're nice people. His father just bought a new store. You should come home and meet nice boys."

"Sonny Cashman still asks for you," added Randy.

"Another nice boy. Come home, meet these boys. You'll change your mind about those terrible people in the Village. Ughh, . . . they give me the creeps." Mother shivered with distaste.

"Look," Rita pleaded, ". . . I didn't come home to get fixed up. Please let's forget about it, . . . be happy and enjoy."

"That's all, Rosie, . . . forget it," Father ordered, his anger and annoyance mounting. "Bbbbbrrrucccck." He belched blatantly, raucously.

Rita absorbed the sound and cringed. Her stomach turned.

"I'm gettin' a nervous stomach on account of you," Father threatened, leaning toward Rita. "You know that?"

"You're probably getting a nervous stomach on account of yourself. Maybe your girl friend is giving you a hard time." She had to lash out for protection. She was immediately sorry she said it. She didn't want to hurt Mother.

"Maybe that's so," replied Father, his headlong attack grinding to a halt. He did not flinch, however. Often he purposely spoke of a girl friend as a topic of family conversation. He had found that the most daring, obvious way was the easiest way to confound a weak person like his wife. He purposely provoked the ultimate question he knew she would not ask. Of course, supposedly, he was joking when he spoke this way. Yet he did have a girl friend. He kidded about her and kept her, and whenever a thought of her real existence was brought to the fore, he substituted the old joke for the real and his wife couldn't tell one from the other without creating an embarrassing scene. It frightened Mother to face the world alone. Father smiled at the age-old joke, but Rita knew it was an embarrassed smile.

"But I'll tell you this," Father started ahead again, "I want you to stop this nonsense, and stop it soon, otherwise you're going to be sorry. That's all. I don't want to hear any more. Just remember, you're all mixed up now. You don't know what you want. I know it's tough. All this stuff you think now—this acting, and dressing up in those creepy clothes and the rest of the junk—it's just a passing fad. You'll forget it. But I want you to forget it soon. How'd'ya think I feel when people ask me where my daughter is? I'm ashamed to tell them. Me, . . . I'm ashamed of my own daughter." He gritted his teeth in a contorted grimace of anger and mortification.

"Take it easy, dear. Don't get yourself upset," Mother urged consolingly. "What do you want for dessert?"

"I don't care . . . anything . . . I'm so disgusted." He turned angrily from Rita.

Rita absorbed all he had said silently. Her mind exploded with disgust and loathing and hate. She hated them all, all of them. They were ashamed of her—ashamed!—because she wanted to be herself as they had made her herself. They couldn't cope with the strength they had unknowingly infused into their monster. They refused to admit there was anything on the other side of the Brooklyn Bridge, anything past the corner of this very block. Ashamed! They didn't care about anything but themselves. . . . They weren't worrying about Rita, they were worried for themselves—only themselves—and not even themselves, only what other people would think about them. Angered thoughts flashed and re-flashed through Rita's brain.

Mother served the dessert, a small pound cake on which she had turned back the cellophane so that it hung on the cake like a woman's drooping stockings. Rita hated the slovenly, lazy way Mother served food, the laziness of her entire existence. Rotten pound cake from the delicatessen! Night after night she served the same things, and if a disparaging remark was made, Mother was as offended as if a sumptuous banquet she had created had been criticized; and for Mother, perhaps, the pound cake was the farthest outpost of her creative ability.

Father began to chomp his cake and suck his coffee with the same "oooszp" he had used on his soup.

Rita braced herself and shuddered at each repulsive sound. She was hardly able to contain her disgust.

Father lifted his cup, and poured some coffee into the saucer. He lifted the saucer and began sucking from it. Rita stared dumbfounded. Realizing she was staring, Father lowered the saucer from his mouth and turned to her inquisitively.

"You're kidding, aren't you?" Rita asked.

Father chuckled, cognizant of his indelicacy. He was a bit embarrassed. "That's the way I like to drink my coffee. Isn't that the way they do it in the Village?" He chuckled more defensively.

"Jesus Christ! If you aren't the most unmannerly person I have ever had the misfortune of eating with. That goes for the whole bunch of you," Rita lashed out, sweeping the others with her eyes. "Noises . . . belches . . . drinking from saucers . . ."

"Un, hahh, . . . Miss Prim," said Randy with a mocking lilt.

"Randy, go inside," Mother implored, wanting to shield him from the imminent violence. Mother looked dumbly to Father. Father stared at Rita, his anger mounting. Randy walked to the door, turned and stood watching, enjoying the spectacle.

"This is my house," Father thundered. He pounded the table with his palm. The cups and dishes jumped. ". . . and I can do what I want in my house."

"Well, if you want to be a God damn pig, go ahead," Rita exploded, ". . . but don't tell me what to do if you don't know what you're doing yourself."

Father chuckled again—an embarrassed chuckle. "If I didn't think you were kidding I'd slap your teeth out." He watched her eyes. He didn't want to have to cope with this scene either.

"I'm not kidding," Rita said flatly, challenging him. "My friends in the Village might not have as much money or put on as big a show as you and your friends, . . . although you wouldn't know that because you've never even been in the God damn Village in your life, . . . but they're a lot more mannerly and less hypocritical if you're any ruler to measure them by."

"Why, you ungrateful little bitch. I've given you everything you got . . . everything you wanted . . . . What am I supposed to do now? Am I supposed to sit here and listen to you tell me that the creeps and whores you hang around with in the Village are as good as my friends?" He stared at her with angered eyes that had not yet decided on a course of action.

Rita stared back boldly, defiantly. "I don't know what you're supposed to do," she answered. "Why don't you make up your own mind for a change?"

His hand whipped, smacking Rita's face. Tears began to flow between fingers of the hand she raised to her face. Father gaped at her, perplexed, angry yet sorry that he had hurt her.

"Go ahead, . . . go ahead, . . . you God damn animal, . . . hit me again. I expect as much from you, . . . you big, strong, . . . pig." She pushed away from the table, her chair falling to the floor. "That's all you know . . . ." She stood away from the table catching all of them in her view. Father glared at her. Mother didn't know what to do. "A smack in the mouth, . . . just like the animal you are, . . . that's all you know. Too lazy to think about life . . . beat it to death . . . but that won't eliminate the things you're afraid are true, the inner voice . . . and you know it. One of these days somebody ought to smack your teeth out. Maybe you'd like that, hanh? You ill-mannered . . ." Rita was so angry she couldn't speak. She tried thinking of something to say, but her mind overflowed with rage. She turned and bolted into the hall, picked up her coat from a chair, and ran to the front door.

"I hope she suffers, that tramp. I hope she suffers like she's making me suffer. I'm so humiliated I can't even face my friends," Father screamed.

Rita's teeth ground with anger. She twirled and ran back to the kitchen. "So long, . . . you unmannered animal." Her hurt strength flowed into her farewell through sobbing gasps. "I hope you and your friends are very happy together . . . I hate you . . . I hate you . . . I hate you," she screamed as loudly as she could, venting her rage, wanting to repay the hurt.

Fortunately, she had not turned from Father. She ducked from the doorway as a plate hurtled through the air and splattered on the wall behind her. A spray of chips sprinkled on her as she ran blindly for the front door.

"Stay outta here," thundered Father, standing in the kitchen door-way. "I don't ever want to see you again. I have no daughter."

Rita heard Mother console Father, their voices fading to the background as Rita reached the bottom of the stairs and dashed out into the noisy, peaceful, lonely street.

5

THE STREETS IN THE VILLAGE are laid out as if the mold of the city had softened over the fires of the kiln and the portion that was to be the Village had melted and twisted out of shape; Tenth and Eleventh Streets cross Fourth Street, Third and Eighth Streets reach a dead end at the Avenue of the Americas, Bleeker Street straddles the Village in a big arc that bisects the Avenue of the Americas then feeds into Eighth Avenue, and there's Little West Twelfth Street, Commerce Street, Cornelia Street, and Jones Street, each one block long, and Gay Street is the shortest block in the city, and a maze of crooked, short lanes and alleys crisscross between and behind the larger streets.

Patchwork streets and artist-supply shops, schools and theatres, a variety of handmade jewelry, shoe, and clothing shops, burger shops, studio skylights, and quiet tree-lined residential streets set the Village apart from the rest of the city. The mercantile hustle is not here; it is Uptown. Here, even the streets are separate and apart from Uptown, and people live differently, quietly, friendly, indulging themselves, both mind and body.

Small shops line the main streets. The variety of objects sold is profuse: rings and jewelry, leather goods, shoes, clothes, pottery, china, housewares, records, books, paintings, Mexican serapes, leotards, and thousands of other commodities. Many of the objects are actually made in the little Village shops by hands which stamp a veritable trade mark of style into them. The Village approach to style most often strives for newness, creativity. Many things are presumptuous and contrived, but with so many new ventures in style, many fine, interesting combinations of old formulae are arrived at by the miscreants in the Village, and are afterward acknowledged and accepted by the socially proper, avant-garde Uptowners.

In the evenings, during warm weather, the crooked streets of the Village tremble with the footsteps of roaming hordes. The sidewalks become so crowded, people walk in the streets. Tall, thin men with narrow pants emphasizing a gaunt stylistic elongation, casual shirts, and dark glasses veer between crowds of slower walkers, heading toward an espresso shop or a cafe. They falter momentarily to remark to girls strolling casually, lugging large Village-made handbags, wearing tight slacks or formless full dresses and sneakers, leather-thong sandals or dancing slippers, their faces chalky with pale make-up, their eyes heavily mascared, contrasting darkly. Often, the men who falter to chat with the strolling girls continue to the cafes, but occasionally they forego that activity for the night.

In the midst of this nocturnal rambling are the inevitable, curious, insatiable tourists. The tourists amble along, gaping into store windows, peering into the apartments at street level, nudging each other, suppressing amused smirks when a Villager strikes an odd or curious note for them. They rifle through the little shops, stare at the paintings, leaf through books, finger the hand-crafted leather, follow the strokes of painters painting in stores used as studios, buy mementos of their excursion, stop off at an espresso shop for coffee—they call it *expresso*—and return home entertained, with exotic tales to fill the halls of their uneventful lives.

Many girls from Uptown come to the Village to get picked up and be taken to a wild party, to meet the "weirdo" guys, to have some different, exciting kicks. Men from Uptown come to the Village to meet some wild, way-out women. Often, however, the Uptown men end up with some stray women from Uptown, but all of them are happier for it in their vivid minds. Uptowners are an intrusion, an invasion upon the privacy of the Villagers, yet their presence betokens an unspoken admiration for the existence, the vitality, the freedom of the Villagers.

While the weather permits, crowds of Villagers form outside coffee shops. Everyone waits for some friends to arrive, or for something interesting to happen. They wait outside because they can't afford to buy Rose Water and Lime at forty-cents a glass; they prefer dryness to support by their families. Usually, the roaming groups stop at all the popular spots, walk in, look around, stop outside for a while, and if nothing exciting happens, continue to the next spot.

But now, winter enveloped the city rapidly. The weather grew colder, and the Villagers retreated into hibernation. The myriad of Village espresso shops which had witnessed the gaiety and color of summer and early fall with outdoor tables on the sidewalk, with people chattering casually on warm breezeless evenings, were all encased with shutters. Only rust marks remained outside the shops where the tables had been. Now the migration had decreased. Only by short, valiant treks, by braving the frigid blasts of wind which felt even colder because of the memories of the recent warm weather, did people migrate from one espresso shop to another. Yet the Village and its people continued their boiling, off-beat activity. The faces of the Villagers now decorated the insides of shops, and they sipped cafe espresso, cappuccino, or hot cider with cinnamon sticks. They sat and talked and read, sitting and waiting for something to happen.

The scenes of the Fall Outdoor Art Exhibition and thousands of brightly colored paintings hanging from the wire fences bordering parking lots on the Avenue of the Americas and on fences and walls of houses lining Washington Square Park were only memories rekindled about glowing belly stoves. This was the time for the preparation of collections which would be hung at the spring exhibition. The jewelry makers, the sculptors, the leather crafters, the painters, had all taken down their wares, stacked them in their homes and shops to await occasional, intrepid winter customers and the next outdoor exhibit.

Twice each year, in the spring and fall, there was an outdoor art exhibition for people to come to and admire and buy paintings and handicrafts, and spend enough money, it was always hoped, to keep the artist fed until the next show. People from all over Uptown flocked to the Village during the art exhibition to see the paintings and to have an excuse to see the picturesque people who, by legend, lived in the Village. Usually they were not disappointed.

Some artists came out for the show calculatingly resplendent in casual, dirty, paint-spattered attire, sat on the sidewalk or in little wicker chairs, occasionally barefooted, and sold their work for more than it was worth. Other artists were actually retired folks who had never made it and who would have looked more at home in quiet country scenes, rocking in chairs, but they were exhibiting paint- ings—still in there kicking. Some of the work was fine, but mainly it was the dabbling of people who wanted to be part of the great artistic confraternity and whose main achievement was keeping the art-supply stores and the Greenwich Village Outdoor Art Exhibition functioning.

At night, during the exhibitions, individual oil lanterns were lit, and crowds milled on the sidewalks around temporary jewelry coun- ters and trinket booths, and in the streets, eating ice cream off the stick, gaping, nudging each other, and sometimes laughing at the painters. It didn't matter that most of the painting was wretched, since the taste of most of the spectators was worse. It was a side show for an invading horde of preying hypocrites, but the milling crowd warmed the hearts of the would-be artists.

While at the exhibition, many Uptowners had their caricatures sketched by artists who set up easels near the main flow of human- ity. Some of the caricaturists were capable and did renderings which resembled their subjects. Some others were either just fooling them- selves or were fakes who owned paper and pencil; they made everyone look the same. But the crowds wanted to pay $1.50 or $2.00 to see themselves drawn. It made them feel important, as if someone wanted their likeness to keep as a treasured memory. Crowds jammed around the caricaturists, and friends dared each other to have a rendering done, no one agreeing until all agreed to be drawn. Then each sat gladly. The others would stand around and watch their friend being drawn, and joked and poked fun. When each in turn was seated, he just grinned, embarrassed, as his standing friends laughed. The one caricatured laughed when he saw the rendering of himself, trying to show he thought it was a big joke.

The concerts in Washington Square Park were also only memories. There were no longer weekly concerts attended by people sitting on the benches, or reclining on the grass, listening to harmonious strains of music floating over the park on warm, rustling breezes. The loud-speakers and wires that had been strung through the trees to bring music to the far ends of the park had been taken down. The bust of Alexander Holley standing on a pedestal near the center of the park, around whose neck wire had been irreverently and chokingly wound, was also glad the wires were down.

During the summer, even on nights when there was no music, the park was filled. Talking groups would sit on the grass, and men sat under the lamp post playing chess on the cement chess tables. Crowds of young people gathered and talked and sang as they sat inside the empty circular fountain in the center of the park. A multitude of dogs was brought to the park and let loose to run and mate promiscuously, each adding its sound to the din. Many dogs were used as a conversation starter between fags looking for a pick-up. Dogless faggots sat on the railing, sometimes known as the meat rail, along the outside of the West end of the park and waited for other kindred souls to appear. But now, the dogs that had romped and played scurried hurriedly, steam puffing from their mouths, on the end of leather leads.

The police too were happy now that winter had come to the park, for they didn't have to scamper after singers and musicians congregating on the benches and in the fountain. In the summer, the colored cop had often chased groups of folk singers with guitars and an inverted wash tub from the fountain, as four mandolin players singing Italian songs started drawing a crowd on the other end of the park. The cop would rush there to stop them while yet another group's harmony might waver on the air from someplace else. Life had a will of its own.

But now it was winter. It was cold. The wanderers were inactive, quiet. But within the dark shops and cafes, the Villagers maintained their vigil.

6

DANI'S COFFEE SHOP WAS WARM INSIDE—the belly-stove kind of artificial, thick, pleasing warmth. The winter sun, partially secreted behind the buildings, blazed a blinding, almost white, warm patch of brightness through the front of the coffee shop; the front consisted of two large windows separated by a double set of glass-paneled doors. Symphonic music filtered softly from loudspeakers located near the ceiling at the corners of the room. Only a few of the square, marble-topped tables were in use; the customers were sipping coffee, quietly reading or gazing at the people outside drifting past the shop. Occasionally, a page of a newspaper being turned fluttered the silence.

Ronnie sat at a table by one of the windows. He was an unhandsome white fellow. He constantly wore the same striped sweater and soiled chino pants; the clothes looked as if he constantly wore them. He had battered tennis sneakers on his feet. The table at which he sat was half bathed in the clear winter sun. He leaned back in his chair, a cigarette dangling from his lips, reading the latest issue of a theatrical newspaper.

Rita, carrying an armful of books, entered the shop. She was bundled in a heavy coat; a scarf was bound about her head, its long trailing ends hanging down over her shoulders. She looked around the coffee shop; no one she knew was there except Ronnie. He looked up and saw her. She approached his table.

"Hiya, baby. How ya doin'?"

"Hi, Ronnie. Have you seen Jeannie or Laura?" She put her books on a chair.

"No, not yet. What's happening?"

"Nothing much. Just cut out from school. We had an extra class today." Ronnie furrowed his brow. "You know, that drama group on Sheridan Square," she explained.

"Oh yeah. You go there?"

"Sure. Been going for months now." Rita removed her long scarf, then her coat. Under it she wore a full, black, wool skirt, a heavy red sweater, and long black stockings.

"You're looking kind of nice," Ronnie remarked, admiring her legs and bottom as she bent from the waist to put her coat on a chair.

"Thanks." Rita sat and blew warm air on her hands. "Give me a cup of cappuccino will you," she said to the waitress who had walked to the table.

The waitress noted the order on her pad and turned toward the back of the shop. Ronnie's eyes followed her the entire distance to the espresso machine.

"What's happening with you, Ronnie?" His attention was still at the espresso machine.

"Hmm, . . . oh, nothin' much." He turned back to Rita. "School and studying by myself and like that. Nothing much else."

"Have you been working lately? I mean, have any shows turned up?"

"Nah. Like things are slow all around. There's a show opening up next week at the Albee. A friend of mine is working in the chorus. He said there might be a spot for another chorus guy, but I don't know, . . . you know how it is."

"It'll be real cool if you get it."

"You're not just kidding—if I get it."

He lifted his feet onto the chair in front of him, tilting his chair back against the wall, his thumbs thrust into his pants pockets.

They were silent for many minutes, gazing out the window.

The waitress brought Rita's coffee to the table.

"Want anything else?" she asked, her pencil poised to write a check.

"No. That's all Juanita. How're you today?"

"Working. What else is there?"

"You still in that play at the Orchard Players Theatre?" Rita asked.

"Mmph, . . . that lousy show split the scene after two performances."

"No kidding?" Ronnie chuckled.

"Anything else coming up?"

"Not that I heard of." Juanita looked up and studied something outside the shop. Ronnie and Rita twisted to see what she was looking at.

Josh Minot was outside, pressing his face against the front glass, a spume of steam marking the window just beneath his nose. His hand against the window shaded his eyes from the bright sun as he scanned the shop.

Rita tapped on the window. Josh looked down and saw the two of them at the table. A smile spread across his face. He turned and walked through the first set of doors into a glass vestibule. He wore a yellow, rough-textured Tyrolean hat with the brim down all around and a vari-colored feather stuck in its band, tight black pants, and a soft natural-colored suede jacket with a belt. A tiny gold major clef pierced Josh's ear lobe.

"Hey, baby, how you doin? Hiya Ronnie. What's happening that's exciting, babies?"

"Usual—nothing. Sit down, man." Ronnie removed his feet from the chair.

Josh hesitated, looking inquisitively at Ronnie. He took out a handkerchief and wiped the chair.

"You kidding me, man?"

"Sorry, man. Like I didn't know you were wearing your spun-gold pants."

"They're not spun gold, man, but I like *my* pants clean."

"What's that supposed to mean, Dad?"

"Oh, come on," Rita injected with a slight chuckle to break the tension. Josh glared at Ronnie. He turned to Rita and his face softened.

"You go to class today?"

"Yeah, I just got finished. How did you know? Hey, did you see Jeannie?"

"No, man. Like I haven't seen her in weeks. Where she been hibernating?"

"Oh, she's kind of tied up lately. Going Uptown with some guys from her office."

"Wow, I mean, like really gone these days, hanh?" Josh exclaimed with mock enthusiasm. "Stepping out with that very swinging Madison Avenue bunch, hanh? I hear a girl's gotta watch herself with them, like they sweep you right off your feet with Guy Lombardo music and that kind of jazz."

"Yeah, man," Ronnie added, "that's really going. I hear those cats with their three-button uniforms really know the know, you know? Like they swing the end—mad cats."

"You're right, that's the way I heard it," Rita chimed in. "I hear they're real hip."

Josh grimaced, dismissing the ludicrous subject. "What's happening tonight—anything?"

"Nothing much," Ronnie shrugged, "unless there's a party going. You know of anything?"

"No, I haven't seen anyone all day. I guess I'll drop in at Pandora's Box."

"What's to do there but drink coffee?"

"Something'll turn up."

"You want anything, Josh?" the waitress asked.

"Nothing you sell here, baby."

Her face tightened into a stern stare.

"No," he corrected himself awkwardly, "I'll just be squatting a minute, and like I really don't want to spring for the price of a coffee."

Juanita smirked and returned to the back of the shop.

The three sat silently at the table. The entire shop was silent save for the soft music. The espresso machine hissed impatiently.

"I hear you got yourself a job, Josh?"

"Yeah Ron, me and Anna, my partner, we're dancing at this little cafe up on the West Side in the twenties.

"Hey, that's great. I didn't know that."

"Yeah, we've been there two weeks."

"Does it include waiting tables?"

Josh glared at Ronnie, then glanced to Rita who was watching him.

"Once in a while we help out—when they're really busy."

Josh studied the other two for their reaction.

Ronnie frowned.

"What the hell man, . . . at least *I'm* working."

Neither Ronnie nor Rita spoke.

Josh looked up and saw a girl he knew outside the shop. He stood, grabbed his coat, and ran to the door.

"See you, gang," he called over his shoulder as he pushed open the first door. "Hey, Dolores," he called, running out to meet the girl, putting his jacket on in the street.

Ronnie and Rita watched them through the window.

"Who the hell needs that kind of a job? I'm an actor, man, not a waiter," Ronnie remarked, not turning his gaze from Josh outside.

"I'm hip, but at least he's getting experience. He has a chance to be what he wants—even if he's waiting tables."

"Who needs it?"

"Most of us—me."

"Not me, baby, not that bad. I've got my pride."

Puffs of smoke escaped Josh's mouth as he spoke to the girl outside. Frankie, a young Mexican, approached the shop. He stopped and motioned a greeting to Josh. He then turned and walked through the doors, hesitated, then walked toward Ronnie and Rita. He was short and wiry, with a springy-fast look to his frame. This was accented by a bouncing skip in his walk. He seemed to be hopping on the tips of his toes for people to see him better. Under his chin a small triangular patch of shadow followed the shape of his muscular jaw.

"Hi, boys and girls," he waved, "what's up? What's happening?"

He put books down, removed his jacket, put it over the back of the chair Josh had just vacated, and walked to the back.

There was a large vertical supporting beam in the middle of the room. A bulletin board was nailed to it. Frankie read the posters announcing the local events and the signs indicating the available actors and actresses and their phone numbers, the models and their numbers, and clothes or books or furniture for sale. As he read he started into a shuffling tap dance. When he stopped reading and dancing, he made his way back toward the table. Juanita, the waitress, walking toward the back, passed him in the aisle.

"Get me a cup of espresso when you get a chance, will you, baby?"

"Okay."

"Say, Ronnie," Frankie called, walking to the front again, "do you want to make it to a flick tonight?"

"Which flick is that, man?"

"You know, the one at the Plaza Theatre. The new Italian flick with Vittorio de Sica."

"No, man. No bread. I haven't been working lately. Besides, like I'm not worthy to mingle with the great people outside the wall. I'll catch it when it comes down here, . . . and save some loot besides."

Frankie chuckled patronizingly. "Don't hold your breath while you're waiting."

"Don't worry, baby. I parcel out my gasps very sparingly to say the least. Never know when I may need an extra one."

They studied each other.

"What's with the shadow under the chin, Frankie?" Rita asked, interrupting the incipient dispute.

"My womb broom, baby," he said smilingly, glad she had noticed. "You know, one of these chicks at school asked me what it was. I told her it was a womb broom, . . . and, man, . . . she flipped. I mean, she thought I was off my rocker to speak, like, so nasty, you know?" He chuckled. "You know, some of these chicks that just got down here are the squarest you've ever seen. Like they're nowhere. I'm trying to give them a few pointers though." He smiled slyly.

"Say listen," said Rita standing. "I'm going to split out of here. I want to get a little chow for supper and I have to find Laura. Like she's got the bread with which we buy the bread which we will break this eventide." She put on her scarf and coat. "Here's a quarter. Pay for my coffee, will you."

"How about paying for me?" Ronnie suggested.

She laughed. "See you guys later."

"Yeah, we'll be around. We'll find something." Frankie assured her.

"You gonna be at Pandora's tonight?"

"Yeah, we'll be there."

"Crazy. See you later." She smiled and went through the doorway.

Ronnie and Frankie followed her with their eyes through the glass side of the compartment between the two doors and out into the street.

"You been making it with her?" Frankie asked, both of them watching until she disappeared down the street.

"Not yet, man, . . . but I'm working on it." Ronnie nodded approvingly. "She'd be kind of nice, you know."

"Yeah, man, . . . like I'm hip. What's the story with her?"

"It's there, man, it's there. You just can't rush these things, you know."

"I know it's there, man," Frankie acknowledged, "and I'm not in a hurry. I've got plenty of time and nothing better to do. I'll fit her into my schedule one of these days."

"Yeah, . . . like I'm hip you're so busy you need a schedule to keep track of them."

"Don't be too sure, man. I do all right."

"Okay, baby, okay."

"I'm going to split." Frankie was a bit annoyed with Ronnie.

"Yeah, me too. These places depress the hell out of me in the afternoon. They're all like a vacuum, . . . devoid, nothing . . . you know? Juanita!"

Juanita was in the back. She stood on her toes, peering over the coffee machine.

"I'll leave the money for you here," Ronnie called, putting some change on the table. "Take it slow, hanh."

"What else?"

7

THE VILLAGE WAS WIND-RIPPED and very cold. The wind withdrew from the canyons of the streets to lurk cunningly at the edge of every corner. Thence, it slashed forcefully, whistlingly, unexpectedly at exposed faces and ears and hands. Its chilling fingers reached through the heaviest clothing, freezing the defenseless wearers. The few people on the street walked quickly, leaning down into the wind, holding their coats close about themselves, their faces turned from the wind.

Rita, Jeannie, and Laura quickly descended the steps leading from Pandora's Box, "the coffee shop with an aroma." Tom and Stan, fellows the girls had just met over coffee, followed just behind them. Tom was of average height, wiry. His hair was parted and combed slick. Stan was tall and broad with curly, black hair. The five of them, caught up in the Village's nocturnal wandering, turned toward Johnson's. The frigid wind felt its way into their coats. It froze Rita's face into excruciating numbness. Her forehead ached as if many little wires were stretched across, agonizingly cutting into the skin. She began to stride faster.

"Come on, girls, let's move a little faster. Come on," Rita urged Stan and Tom, "you're buying!" All the girls laughed. So did Stan and Tom.

"These chicks are all right," Tom commented to Stan as they moved to catch up to the girls. "Hands off that Rita."

"Cool, man," Stan agreed readily. "I dig that Jeannie, you know? She swings all right. But listen, let's not spring for too much in Johnson's. You know, Dad, like this pocket hasn't much in it, and like the rent is due soon."

"A couple of beers, what the hell?" He smiled as they now caught up to the girls.

"C'mon, woman," Stan snapped with sham imperiousness, gripping Jeannie's arm to physically urge her to speed her steps. "It's rather chilly out here tonight."

The five reached Johnson's. A bare bulb over the door cast a denuding white glare into the darkness of Minetta Lane. Stan ducked his head under the canopy, pushed open the door, and they entered.

Johnson's was a narrow cafe. The people at the bar and at the tables were immersed in a dim, yellow, murkiness. The jaundiced haze emanated from dim, yellow bulbs burning in an occasional socket of the octopus-armed chandeliers hanging from the ceiling. The bulbs and chandeliers were coated with a thick fuzz of dust. (Many Village bars, noted for quaint dustiness, retain their aged atmosphere with a flit gun and a mixture of oil and vacuum-cleaner dust.) Calypso music filtered through the thick air.

The wooden bar was parallel to the wall on the right side. Small, round tables lined the left side. The floor was coated with sawdust. The bar extended only half the length of the cafe; beyond were more tables, rest rooms, and a jukebox. From the jukebox, dim red, blue, and yellow alternately beamed up the walls and across the ceiling. The rest rooms were marked *hombres* and *muchachas*. From a hamburger grill against the back wall, greasy smoke swirled up to an exhaust fan in the wall. A door next to the grill led to a garden in the rear which was used as an outdoor cafe during the summer.

The atmosphere in the cafe was splashed with all varieties of color from a confusion of decoration. A huge snake skin stretched across the wall behind the entire length of the bar; a picture of a middle-aged man with glasses, inscribed "to Bill from Dad" was tacked to the men's room door; all sizes and colors of bottles hung from strings tied to pipes near the ceiling; travel posters from all over the world, torn for a casual effect, were pasted to the walls and ceiling—so were bullfight posters, photographs, composites of actors who frequented the place, caricatures of others, weird paintings by customers, old hats, stuffed fish, African masks, a bullfighter's cape, banderillas, rifles, foils, fake hands, maracas, brassieres, a torn jacket, a bullwhip, a baseball bat, and a kiddies car in the shape of an aerial bomb marked "Sputnik." These decorations were always being altered. If one had not been to Johnson's for a time, one would find many new *objets d'art* casually increasing the confusion.

It was hard to know if Johnson's was an authentically casual cafe with weird decor, or a place contrivedly casual and weird. Once the decorations were hung, it was difficult to say. Only time distinguishes the genuine from the phony. The genuine is the flexible, self-determining, self-complementing predecessor, while imitation only follows dogmatically, without understanding or reason, save that this is the way the original was fashioned. It is far easier to know if a person is a phony than if a place is. A place must be taken at face value, but a phony person, once he speaks, can hardly sustain the false impression he attempts to convey. A picture is said to be worth a thousand words, but a person, with a few words, can expose his hidden background so disastrously that the picture that had existed disappears into nothingness. With people, a few spoken words are worth a thousand pictures. Places, however, do reflect their owners, . . . and Johnson was a phony.

Not only were the decorations on the walls of Johnson's always changing, so too were the waiters, cooks, and bartenders. When things got rough, regular customers, or other Villagers they recommended, changed their status and became employees, working their way through school, earning enough to take some lessons, or keeping from falling back into society's maze. Johnson's was in the Village, was part of the Village, and was the Village.

Just as the waiters and bartenders and cooks were replaced constantly, so were the people living in the Village. The values and ideals remained, the principles, the rules, the code of the revolutionaries, but the people believing in them varied. The people living there last week had gone away, perhaps to surrender and live home again, or to go to

California to get away from the grind of the Village, or to paint closer to nature, or to tour with summer stock, or to live with someone who lives in another part of town, or to do any number of things in further search of peace. Their places were eagerly filled by others. Male and female flee to the Village attracted by the lure of excitement, of freedom, of tolerance, of peace and security, to escape from the harsh, unthinking world—but many leave very soon, most leave after a while, with more tolerance for the world, but some never go away and never find it.

"Hi, Rita," said Sammy, aproned, standing behind the bar. Sammy was a rare Villager. He was the most constant feature of Johnson's beside Johnson himself, who was present seven days a week. Johnson was always there to keep his eyes open and the people drinking. He had to;half his profits were absorbed by other interests; those politicians who had to be payed off because they secured Johnson's liquor license; the hoods who had a death grip on all the clubs in the Village. The only thing sacred to Uptowners is money; that's why they're Uptowners; that's why there are Villagers. Sammy was always bartending at Johnson's, and the bar somehow never looked the same without him.

"Hey, Sammy, how're you?" Rita answered, smiling.

"Fine." He nodded slightly, drawing his thin lips back over his teeth. He had a way of holding his mouth so that even when he wasn't smiling he looked as if he were. He was Negro, with a soft voice and smile. Sinewy biceps bulged at the edge of his short-sleeved shirt. Contrasting against the dark skin of one hand, the overhead yellow lights reflecting on it, was a large, silver ring, hand wrought in the Village. It looked like silver worms entwining Sammy's finger, holding up a green stone.

"Hi, Tom, Stan, Jeannie, Laura." Sammy nodded to the rest of the group.

"Say, Sam. How about five beers? You want glasses?" Stan asked the group.

"No," said Jeannie. Rita shook her head negatively. So did Laura.

"I'll take a glass," said Tom.

"See that! Anything to be different, hanh, man?" Stan shook his head woefully.

"Will you come off it, man? Do you mind if I drink out of a glass?"

"Yes, yes, I do mind," Stan taunted playfully. "You think you're better than anybody here, don't you? Well, you're not, man, . . . you're not. You're just like everybody else. What was good enough for my father is good enough for you" . . . Stan began to laugh; he fought down the laugh ". . . and you're going to drink out of a bottle like a respectable person. Got that, man?"

"Yeah, Pa." Tom shook his head sadly. "This is too much. This boy is really sick. Sam," he said deliberately, smiling, peering at Stan from the side of his eyes, "five beers, one with, please, . . . even if my father objects."

"Right you are. Come on, Daddy, . . . get hip," Sammy admonished Stan. He slid the cooler door open and lifted out five bottles.

"You guys always come on like this?" Rita asked amused.

"Yeah, man, like you guys are bugged, you know," Jeannie added. "Like you're flying."

"Are you turned on, or what?" asked Rita.

"You fly, man?" Tom whispered, feigning mysteriousness.

"Once in a while," Rita replied.

"Talking about flying—we went to a party the other night, oh wait, listen to this." Stan recalled a story. He put his hand up to ward off other conversation or interruption. "I got a date with this chick, and I go to pick her up at her old lady's pad, you know? She's a model, you know, a real nice-looking chick. Her old lady's one of these real watchful-type old ladies, you know? She always wanted to be an actress or somebody and she never was—but she's gonna make sure this chick is, whether the chick wants to or not. So, the old lady makes sure the chick gets home early, and if she does this, and takes care of her career, and takes care of her clothes, and if she goes to the bathroom regularly and all that kind of crap."

Sammy put the beers on the bar. One of the bottles had a glass inverted over its neck. Tom grasped the five bottles and carried them to a table opposite the bar.

"Let's sit over here," Tom suggested.

They all walked over and sat around the table, the girls on a bench built into the wall, Tom and Stan on chairs.

"Well, anyway, to continue . . . ," Stan said after taking a draught from his bottle. "So I go to the door and I say, 'Is Sally home?' And the old lady tells me, Sally's not here. 'Wait a minute,' I say," he recounted with a chuckle of surprise as he re-enacted the scene. "'This is Sally's house, isn't it? She lives here doesn't she?' The old lady says, 'yes.' 'I don't think you understand,' I tell her. 'I have a date with Sally. She told me to pick her up here at eight-thirty . . . That's what time it is now. She's got to be here.' The old lady smiles a little, you know, a little whimper of a smile, and tells me she's not. So you know, like what can you say? Anyway, it turns out . . ." He bent forward, emphasizing each word ". . . the chick meets me a few days later and tells me she was hiding in the bathroom because her old lady wouldn't let her go, on account of some modeling job the next day, and she was so embarrassed, like she couldn't face me. I mean, is that wild?" Stan concluded with a laugh. "How much can an old lady want a career?"

Everyone laughed.

"Anyway, I go to this party myself," he continued. "Well, Tom was with me, but like that's as good as coming on by yourself." He snickered. "Anyway, I meet another chick there . . . with an English accent." Stan now assumed a haughty British inflection. "And she says, 'You have a mini docka?' 'Got a mini docka,' she says. 'I like to fly a bit you know.' Man, she was out of her head, this chick. You know, a real couk. Anyway, she got high and started cursing out this guy she was with like mad because he didn't come through or something. And I mean, real swinging talk, I tell you. And this guy she was with was a little guy . . . embarrassed . . . he had to hide in the bathroom until they threw this chick out. She had a knife in her hand and all . . . Talking about flying reminded me of the party . . . and like that."

Tom looked at him perplexed. "That's a nice story, Stan. Remind me to take you to my next party so you can entertain the guests with your great stories."

"I'll be there."

"What's a mini docka?" asked Rita.

"A little pot, man, you know, pot?" Stan suggested.

Rita nodded.

The juke box started to push a calypso chant and beating drums into the room. This music wasn't popular anywhere else, but the management put its own selections on the juke box to please the unorthodox tastes of the customers. Their appreciation was wide, restricted only by imagination and a loathing for popular demand.

Raoul Johnson, the owner, had been standing in the back, talking to a tall, thin, specter-faced girl whose blond hair cascaded to her shoulders. Now Johnson started to chant loudly with the jukebox. He was a tall, light-complexioned, blue-eyed, handsome Negro. His clothes were form fitting. He wore them as much to be noticed for their difference as to be clothed in a style that he liked. Precious few act merely for an enjoyment of the thing done. Fads and fears trammel discretion, replacing it with stock solutions to the desires of life. Individuality only adds confusion and responsibility to the mass that progresses intellectually only far enough to realize that everything must be convertible to material reality to be worthwhile.

Johnson, in tight white pants and light green shirt, danced forward from the rear of the cafe. He called for a pair of maracas. Sammy pulled two pairs off the wall behind the bar, handed a pair to Johnson, and took a pair for himself. Both rattled them loudly as they sang with the jukebox. All the people around the bar joined in at the chorus. The place overflowed with mixed singing voices. Johnson danced solo in the center of the space between the bar and the tables. He had a supercilious smirk on his face; his eyes narrowed to slits. He knew everyone was watching him. This was the same look he effected when there was a girl he wanted to impress with the fact that he was Raoul Johnson, man, *Raoul Johnson*. When he approached a girl, he'd shrug his shoulders, and say softly, with a sly smile on his face, a flutter of eyebrow, 'hello, baby . . . what's happening?' Or, if she was with a guy, he'd start singing loudly to attract her attention, and then he'd give her a sneering once-over and perhaps pucker a kiss for her when her boy friend wasn't looking. The girls from the Village had become hardened to his passes; they ignored him for the most part. Girls from Uptown got a big, exotic charge out of it.

The chant from the jukebox ended in drumfire. Johnson ended his dance next to the table where Rita and her friends sat. Looking down, he contrived surprise at seeing Rita.

"Hello, baby," slid from the side of his mouth. His eyes fluttered as he gave her the once-over, or as much of a once-over as possible, considering she was seated. He wagged his head slightly, his eyebrows raised, a leer in his eyes. This was to convey that he was appraising her sexually. "Baby, let me tell you I dig you." He took her hand in his and kissed it very slowly, raising his eyes to peer into hers in the manner of the European. He had a penchant for trying to make white women. "Let's get together sometime when you're not busy." He stood straight, his eyes still narrowed, and fluttered his eyebrows again.

"You're so full of shit, Raoul, it isn't even funny," Jeannie remarked laughing. Everyone at the table laughed.

"That's right," he snapped. His face suddenly hardened. "You ought to know better than to say Raoul Johnson is full of shit, baby. I spit on better white meat than you."

"Well, why don't you just keep doing that then, man," said Rita. "You certainly don't need us."

"Listen, baby, forget it, you know?" he said with disgust. "You don't have nothin' special, you know. Hahaaaiii . . ." he cried out lustily in accompaniment to the new selection on the jukebox. He began to dance away. "C'mon, man, . . . let's swing tonight," he called to the bar in general. "Hey'a, . . . c'mon." He danced toward the back and the specter-faced blonde.

"That God damn clown gets on your nerves sometimes," Rita commented, watching him dance away.

"He's a big man with the women, though, baby," Stan added.

"So would you be if you made a pass at every and any bitch you saw in this bar. Big shit," Jeannie discounted.

The front door opened and a girl that Rita knew walked in. Her name was Moira. She was one of the girls that went to acting class with Rita. She was dark haired, with a fleshy, aquiline nose. Her mouth was wide, her lips thin at the edges, so that the middle of her lips fell together in a mass, giving her mouth a pouting aspect. Her eyes were lined in heavy black pencil and deepened with greenish eyeshadow.

"Hi, Moira," Rita called.

She turned, saw Rita, and smiled. She walked toward the table.

"I didn't know you came in this place," Rita added.

"Hi, Rita. I don't usually, but I felt like it tonight. Every place else is dead." Moira looked at the people at the table, smiling the slight smile of the unacquainted. Rita introduced her to the others. Moira smiled to them and stood by the table talking.

Johnson was now behind the bar, still smarting from the rejection. He saw the new arrival, whom he had met once before to his dissatisfaction.

"What are you drinking there, baby?" he called out.

"I don't want anything right now."

"You can't come in here if you don't want to drink anything, baby," Johnson called loudly. "What the hell do you think this is? I throw my own kind out; you think I'm going to leave you stay here standing around, sucking up the heat for nothin'?"

Tom twisted toward Johnson, his brow wrinkled. "She'll have a drink in a minute," he said softly, determinedly. "Right now she hasn't made up her mind. Don't be such a bug, man. She'll drink when she feels like it. Don't worry about it."

People at the bar watched silently.

"Listen, man, when somebody comes in here they gotta spend. If not, forget it."

"We're spending," Tom continued, staring at Johnson. "Sit down, Moira."

Johnson looked at Tom viciously. Angrily, he turned to serve other people at the bar.

"You want a drink Moira?" Tom asked.

"No, I'm going to take off," she replied, smiling thankfully. "I can't take that bastard too much."

"Yeah, let's all cut out," suggested Jeannie irritatedly. "Let's take off."

"Let's go," agreed Stan unconcernedly.

"I'm going to stay here a while," said Laura as the others stood. She felt like a fifth wheel.

"Oh, come on. You're not going to start that?" said Rita, looking at Laura impatiently.

Laura appealed to her with her eyes. "Let me stay here. You cats go ahead. I'll meet you later."

"Come on. There's no coupling here or anything," said Tom.

"No, . . . I'd really rather stay here for awhile. Frankie, Frankie . . ." she called to the short Mexican who was standing at the rear of the bar. She wanted to assure them she wouldn't be alone. "I'll stay here, . . . and I'll see you later."

"Okay, if you want to," Rita relented.

Tom payed the bill, and they walked out. Rita said good night to Moira in front of Johnson's. Moira walked toward MacDougal Street. Rita and the others started toward the Avenue of the Americas. They all fell silent as the cold began to bite them again. Tom walked with Rita; Stan and Jeannie followed behind.

"You know, I've never seen you around before tonight," Tom said to Rita to start conversation. They crossed the avenue, walking toward West Fourth Street.

"I've been around awhile, about six months."

"Funny, I've never seen you. Where do you keep yourself?"

"I keep busy around, doing the usual things, you know?"

"Me too, but I've never seen you anyway."

They fell silent again, leaning into the wind. They passed under the marquee of the Waverly Cinema.

"Hey, dig what's playing," Stan called from behind, "*To Have and Have Not.* That's one of Hemingway's, isn't it?"

"Yeah," Tom answered, not turning.

"You see it?" Rita asked.

"Yeah," Tom answered. He hunched deeper into his coat to counter the wind. "You see it?"

"Yeah. It was pretty good. That Bogart was really . . . well, he was really terrific, you know? Really believable. He put such a depth of feeling, such facial gestures, such . . . well, everything he did was so great that you could believe him, identify with him. He really felt his role."

"You sound like you studied the picture."

"I did. I study all the pictures I see. If you want to act you have to learn from people who know how."

"You study acting?"

"Sure over on Sheridan Square—with Phil Avery."

"Hey!" exclaimed Tom, stopping with surprise to look at her. "I know a couple of chicks that go over there." He started to walk again. "What the hell . . ." He tried to remember a name. ". . . Sybil . . . Sybil Owens. You know her?"

"Sure. Sybil and I are partners in a one-act play." Rita smiled. "We were rehearsing together last night."

"No kidding? That's crazy. She's a great chick. Sybil and I used to hang around together, you know, like we were kind of very chummy for a while."

"Yeah, I'm hip," Rita smiled knowingly.

Tom smiled and shrugged his shoulders to indicate that that's the way life is.

Stan and Jeannie fell further back and began to talk about something else. Each had his head down into the wind, their hands in their pockets as they continued forward briskly.

"You from New York originally?" Tom asked.

They reached the corner of Fourth Street and turned West toward Pandora's and Sheridan Square.

"Yeah, if you want to say Brooklyn is part of New York."

"Brooklyn? No kidding?" Tom exclaimed more surprised than before. "How great is this? You know Sybil and now you're from Brooklyn. I'm from Brooklyn too. This must be a portent of something great."

"It could only be a harbinger of calamity. I didn't think anybody else ever found his way out of Brooklyn."

"There are a few other people still awake in this little old world."

"You don't still live there, do you?" she asked.

"Yeah, I still stay over a lot with my folks."

"Man, you've got what it takes. I couldn't do that for all the money in the world."

"Yeah, well, you know, like I work in Brooklyn, and like it's easier to get to work from my father's place. I have a pad down here I stay at on weekends though."

"Man, I left Brooklyn and my mother and father six months ago, and all of a sudden I realize there are lots of things on the other side of the Brooklyn Bridge . . . things they never even dreamed of, still don't."

"They gave you a hard time, hanh?"

"That's being charitable. I couldn't take those people any more. So I figured it would be less frustrating for me to move out on my own, . . . even if I can't give myself *all the things I ever wanted,*" she mimicked savagely. "You know?"

"Yeah, like I know the scene. Same bit, different players." Tom chuckled sadly. It was a laugh brought up to overcome embarrassment or sorrow. "I've been through that scene so many times I can play it blindfolded. I guess everyone has."

"So why are you sticking at home?"

"Like I said, it's easier for me to get to work this way. I don't stay there much. I get my food and a pallet to sleep on and I have a pad down here for my friends. You know, . . . and like that?"

"Yeah, I'm hip, and like that. What sort of work do you do?"

"I work in a shoe store. I sell shoes to old bitches that cram their big, fat feet into ugly little shoes."

"Shoes? You like selling shoes?"

"I make a couple of bucks at it. It's not a hobby or pastime or anything. What the hell, a job is a job. Nobody bothers me; the boss let's me dress the way I want, as long as I look neat and all, but he doesn't insist that I wear grey flannel, or be his religion, or agree with his politics, or any of that crap. He just wants me to work for him. You know? It's a nice switch. Of course, it's not one of the up-and-coming professions. *They* don't consider it chic . . ."

They looked at each other, smiling simultaneously. They passed in front of Pandora's. Tom turned to Stan and Jeannie.

"Hey, you wanna see who's inside?" he called. "You want to go inside?" he asked Rita.

"No." She shook her head, her face wincing with the cold. She huddled her face down farther into her coat collar. "I'm cold and tired. I think I'll pack myself into bed."

"Okay, . . . I'll walk you home."

"Crazy. I'm afraid of the dark." She smiled, pleased.

"I want to go inside for a cup of coffee. I'm freezing," said Jeannie.

"I'm going to the pad." Rita shivered through the shoulders. Her lips were a bit blue.

"I'll be along in a minute," said Jeannie. She and Stan started up the stoop to Pandora's.

"Okay. So long," Tom said. He and Rita started walking hurriedly toward the Square.

"So how're you paying the rent in this place, and going to school, and all that?" he asked as they walked. "You working?"

"I'm a waitress. Besides, I have two roommates. We sublet this apartment from two guys real cheap—furnished and all and a telephone for twenty-six a month, and like that."

"What? Twenty-six a month? You're kidding? Man, they just don't make apartments like that, do they? Where is your place, under the river?"

"Right here," Rita nodded toward Sheridan Square. "Right around the corner on Christopher Street."

"I gotta see this pad. It sounds too much. It's wild. Twenty-six a month. Wow! How great is that, hanh? We pay seventy a month for ours, me and Stan. How many rooms do you have?"

"Three."

"Three? Me too, and the seventy doesn't even include the phone."

They reached Sheridan Square and stood at the curb waiting for traffic to cease. Streams of cars swarmed from Uptown on the wide, cobblestoned street, their sealed-beam eyes glaring whitely into the black shadow of night.

The Square was a broad, flat, open space into which six streets emptied. Twelve corners surrounded the Square. Most of the corners blazed with lights and signs in front of shops and cafes. Directly across from Rita and Tom was a cigar store. Next to that was a Riker's food shop, and next to that a delicatessen. On the other corner of Christopher Street, across from the cigar store, was Jim Atkins eat shop. On another corner was the Riviera Bar. On another corner was a small park. On the corner where Rita and Tom stood, there was Mother Hubbard's Food Shoppe, Simple Simon's Eat Shop, then the Seventh Avenue South Theatre, and next to that, the Limelight, an espresso shop, then a book store, then two dark, closed shops, and a gas station.

After the cafes close and the tourists leave, the Villagers converge to this square. It is difficult to note exactly who the Villagers are. The term and reference is applied to far more people than those who live within the actual, physical boundaries of the Village and excludes many who do. Physically, the Village is small. Yet, its reputation for bearded poets and painters and writers and starving actors and uninhibited licentiousness and queers and Lesbians and all sorts of sensational, dreamy, romantic, exotic, erotic stories is far more extensive than its crooked streets could possibly harbor.

The Village that has spawned this sensational reputation is only a small part of the actual Greenwich Village. There are thousands of people living on the quiet, residential, crooked, forsaken streets in and around all of the mad excitement which, as legend has it, is continually broiling up in the Village, who rarely seem to notice it, and never partake of it. People who live away from the main stems of weirdness and life—Eighth Street between the Avenue of the Americas and Broadway, Fourth Street from Sheridan Square to Broadway, MacDougal Street from Eighth Street to Bleeker Street, West Third Street from the Avenue of the Americas to Broadway, Sheridan Square, and Washington Square Park—live quietly, peacefully in little houses, on age-old streets, go to work Uptown each morning, appear to be tourists to the tourists, but only want quiet living, and are Villagers nonetheless.

There is also a large Italian settlement in the Village. This is another of the worlds of Greenwich Village, right within this framework of weird life. Pushcarts, Italian-provisions stores, dark kids, and old men who chomp black cigars, can't even speak English, much less hip English, and think Americans are a little *pazzo*, are part of the Village too.

At the same time, all the legendary Villagers, who populate the joints till all hours of the night, who exist according to a sensational, social code, purposely and diametrically opposed to the social code of the outside world that has rejected them, live not only here, but all around Uptown—in the Gas House District, the Murray Hill District, the Chelsea District, the Bronx, Harlem, Brooklyn—and come to the Village to meet and find a little life.

The Village is really only an idea. That which people from Uptown consider the Village is something not outlined by streets or avenues, but by minds and ideals and souls struggling within themselves, by heart and sinew needing their own personal *raison d'etre*, not some union-made, impersonal spirit. The Village is reputed to be the capital of these rebellious idealists, but more often they flourish forsakenly miles away, and only come to the Village for companionship.

The Village is a place of exile for rebels condemned to remain there by misunderstanding people too lazy-minded to think of a true answer for those things which they do not understand. It is far easier to condemn than to understand, to reject than to befriend newness or strangeness. And the excuse offered is that these strange rejected creatures do not want people, do not love people. But it is rather that these unhappy creatures do love people which sends them from society's mindless non-people.

To those who flee to the Village, it is not a sewer but a place of refuge. Those who have no place else to live, who are rejected because they do not fit into a mold, who advocate individuality, who are fast enough to bolt, come to the Village with the anticipatory hope that they will find tolerance, acceptance, relief from the outside molding pressure. To those outside, the Village is a place of repulsion—those who live here, have been repelled from the outside; it is a place of insanity—those who live here are adjudged insane by the people outside; it is a place of degradation beyond compare, beyond description, for so the people here have been accused. Yet this is a place where many people learn to grow up, for outside they have been accepted only as young and childlike. This is a place where thinking is attempted, for outside, thinking is repressed. This is a sanitorium, a place of rest, a place for thought, a place where the afflicted, seeking fellows afflicted in like, and in worse, manner, take courage and stand up to the masses outside who find it easier to discharge than to recharge the sinking lives of these hungerers for life.

Here, early in the morning, one finds only Villagers. The people from Uptown who make fun of the Village, yet feed their dull minds and lives by coming for a look at the mad, crazy Village and the things that Villagers do; the drunken sailors on leave who want to live it up; the gangs of men from Jersey or Brooklyn, wearing their windbreakers, who laugh violently at their own remarks passed to the guys they think are queer; the smart guys looking for a "quick piece of ass" from the wild Village chicks, have all gone home to their own, warm, safe apartments. Left only are the people who stumble to the Village, who stagnate here, who live here, who more than just abide here.

"The light changed. Come on, let's go across," Rita said to Tom, tugging impatiently on his arm.

"This place is furnished too?" Tom jogged across the street, his hands in his pockets. Rita pulled him by the sleeve of his right arm.

"Contain your curiosity, sir," she affected gravely. "You shall see in a minute."

They turned and walked along Christopher Street and entered the dim hallway. It smelled stale, but it was warm. Tom followed her up the stairs to the apartment. She unlocked the door and entered first.

"Come on in," she called as a light from inside flashed through the slot between the door and the frame.

Tom walked in and looked around. He was taken short by the front room with its plush furniture and the smoked mirror covering one wall.

"Oh! oh!" he cried out painfully, falling on the couch. "I'm sick. I'll never be able to leave this place." He feigned pain. "I think I'm paralyzed. You might have to move out and leave me here."

"I'm not moving out," Rita laughed. "I guess you'll have to stay here with me and the girls."

"Hey, that's a better idea." He was suddenly without pain. "I think I'll stay paralyzed for a while. Man, this place is a palace. I thought it was just one of the ordinary beat-up pads the cats usually rent, but this place . . ."

"It doesn't have any heat though."

"With a place like this, man, I'd generate my own heat."

Rita looked at him slyly out of the side of her eyes. He smiled a bit.

"How about a drink? I have some Vodka. That's about the only thing we have in the place."

"Anything you got'll be fine . . ."

Rita reached up into the cupboard suspended from the wall above the covered tub. Tom sat on the sofa just inside the doorway of the front room. He watched her, and slowly, as if a vague screen had fallen from his eyes, he saw she was a woman. Oddly enough, he had not thought about it until this moment. Rita was a soft woman . . . he and she, boy and girl, here they were and he hadn't even thought about it before. He stood and walked into the middle room where Rita was mixing the drinks. He put his hands on her shoulders. Rita shuddered with surprise, then twirled to face him. He put his hands on her waist.

"Baby, I've been with you all night, and suddenly I realize that you're a woman, a lovely woman."

"You mean, suddenly, like, we're alone, and like what the hell, hanh?" she asked indignantly. "Here's your drink." She thrust the cold glass into his hand and walked into the front room, sitting on a chair between the front windows.

Tom sat across the room on the couch facing her. He was embarrassed. Rita stood and walked to the phonograph and started a record on its way around the spindle. Anita O'Day's singing rose into the room.

"I dig that Anita O'Day," Tom said to start conversation again. "She really swings, doesn't she?"

"Yeah."

"Did you ever hear her Honeysuckle Rose?"

"Yeah."

"Oh, come on, . . . come off it. I mean, what's the big bit? I'm sorry," he said seriously, appealingly. "I thought we were grown-up people and all."

"I thought you were too . . ."

"What's the bit?"

"Somebody ought to tell you that maybe a girl likes to . . . well, . . . she doesn't like to be . . . fucked," Rita blurted out angrily.

Tom winced. "Wait a minute. I dig you." His eyes were serious and he pleaded for her to believe him. There was an urgency in his appeal because he felt badly that he had hurt her. "You know, like, I think you're the greatest, and like that. I really do. Bricks don't fall on me to clue me in to people. I don't feel like jumping off the roof just right now, but man, like, I think you're really nice, and I like the way you talk, and walk . . ." A slight smile flickered on his mouth, ". . . and everything. Don't go getting all shook up or anything, baby. I mean, I didn't mean to shock you. I just put my hand on your waist. Besides, we're from the same town. We've got to stick together." He smiled, trying to induce her to smile. "It's not that you're just any girl. I like being with you, you know, I think you're the greatest chick I've met in a long time. I mean that. Just because I thought about wanting you doesn't mean I don't dig you. I think it means I do; I do dig you . . . and what else is there?" He stared at her, trying to see if she understood and forgave.

Rita's hard, staring visage slowly wrinkled into a smile tinged with sadness.

"Yeah, we're from the same town." She shook her head with a sudden reminiscent sadness as she stared into space above Tom's head.

Anita O'Day began singing Honeysuckle Rose, only it sounded like "honey suck a rose."

"Boy, . . . I can't take that Brooklyn, man. What a hell hole," she reflected, still looking over his head. Tom sat back and just looked across the room at her, relaxing a bit, feeling that she had understood. They commiserated silently.

"Where you from?" Tom asked.

"Who cares? Shit! Want another drink?"

"Sure. Sure thing. They must have given you a real rough time."

She took his glass and walked to the kitchen.

"They did. They do." Ice cubes clinked into the glasses. "Here's your drink." She sat on the couch a bit away from him, staring across the room at the windows. "I want to be me, that's all. I want to go to acting class and show them I really know what I'm talking about, you know, that I'm really somebody . . . those dopey bastards," she howled in an angry burst of hurt.

"Take it easy. They're not here now."

He reached out and touched her hand and pressed it in his assuringly. She looked at his hand on hers, then to his eyes. She smiled slightly, thankful for his desire to help. She looked forward again. Tom leaned back, resting his drink on his stomach.

"Sometimes people don't understand how they twist their kids' insides, . . . even by just ignoring them," he said, trying to show her he too understood, wanting her to feel better. "Parents can be so parental."

"I don't know," she said bewilderedly. "They still bug me. My old man tells me I'm a disgrace and he doesn't want his friends to see me looking the way I do, dressed the way I dress. Not that those sons-of-bitches don't look at me like they'd like to make it with me every time I see them. But he wouldn't tear into them for their lecherous gaping, . . . no, he'd be too embarrassed to embarrass his friends. Let them look. 'Why do you have to be different?'" she mimicked viciously. "And they can't understand when I insist I am different. You know, not like I'm great, . . . but only that I'm me! I tell them, 'nobody else is named Rita Fisch.' That's my real name, but I use Rita Farren now. 'Nobody else is named Rita Fisch and has you for a father and you for a mother and went to P.S. 116 and all the other things I've done in my few years. I am different, . . . not big deal, . . . but I am me . . . and that me is human, with a mind.' *They* are only human too, so why shouldn't I do the things I want instead of the things *they* want. When I talk to them like that, they look at me like I'm from Mars. Then they say, 'pass the butter.' Man, . . . I can't stand those people . . . those dopey bastards . . ." Her eyes filled with tears that teetered on the brink of her eye sockets. "They just want to be numbers, . . . just numbers." A clear droplet slid slowly down her cheek, leaving a path bathed through her make-up.

"Take it easy, baby. Calm down. Christ, . . . I won't bug you." He twisted toward her. "Hold it." He squeezed both her hands tightly, trying to calm her with understanding. He looked into her face, his eyes conveying sincerity. She gazed steadily back to him, her tears stopping.

The room was quiet, save for the sound of the phonograph needle recoursing over the end track of the record. Rita looked into Tom's eyes. They were steady and searching, deep, penetrating. They revealed that he knew what she was talking about, that he wanted her to know that he understood. *He knows, he understands,* she felt inside herself as she continued to look into his face. *He really understands.* Her hand wiped across her eyes. She felt wetness on the back of her hand. She smiled slightly. Her smile became more firm, more sure, as Tom smiled back softly. They continued to look at each other and smile. Finally, he freed her hands and stood to turn the record over. He turned one of the lamps off, so that only the light in the far corner picked out the objects in the room. From the other corner, the little red light of the record player stared out at Tom and Rita as they sat silently on the couch. Tom held his drink in his hand. Rita had a lit cigarette between her fingers.

"Want another drink?" Tom asked.

"No thanks." She smiled gratefully.

Tom slipped an arm around Rita's shoulders; she leaned her head against him. They stared forward, not speaking for many minutes.

"I know how it is, baby," Tom said softly. "I mean, I get that too, . . . only I've got a job, so like what can they say. That's the big thing with them. As long as I'm working, everything is great. I could be emptying sewers, or carrying the honey bucket, . . . they couldn't care less. As long as it's a job. They don't understand anything except everybody should have a job. Sure, maybe they had it rough when they were kids, or maybe that's the way things were then. They had to toe the line pretty much and work pretty hard to be accepted or something. But what the hell does that make me. That's all over . . . it's different now. I'm accepted! But they don't understand that. I'm only a kid compared to them, and I should understand them? That's like these jerks say, 'when are you gonna find yourself?' Did you ever see a guy's lost watch find the guy? Anyway, I throw in a few bucks a week, and they think I'm a great son. Can you imagine? It doesn't matter if I'm there or not, just as long as someone has my name on a work sheet. This way they can face their friends."

"Yeah. Well, I wanted to go to class, and, ahhh . . . ," she wailed hurt and hate.

Tom's arm around her shoulder hugged her tightly to hold her closer, more firmly to his understanding.

"They said they'd buy me a car and new clothes if I stayed," she continued, ". . . not in so many words, you know, . . . but I had to stay and shape up to what they thought was proper, . . . proper! They were blackmailing me! They were trying to buy my respect. They didn't deserve it," she rasped angrily. "I had to get away from there. It wasn't doing me any good."

"You're right about that." Tom's arm still held her tightly. She snuggled closer to him, pulling her legs up under herself. "You've got to be yourself," he said, "and do the things you've got to do. If you're not yourself with your own things, . . . who are you? Why bother, you know? If you want to act, that's what you've got to do, but you have to work at it. A lot of these jerks that come down here slopping around the Village like slobs think it's just going to fall into their laps. I'm not putting anybody down or anything, that's their business. But they're just not going to make it. They're rebelling so much against the world they're not even willing to work for what they want. They're too busy being angry. Actually, they haven't the guts to face it. Sure, it's tough and cold, but you've got to stand on your own feet and fight for what you want. Nothing just happens."

"You're not kidding. I work harder at acting than I ever did at anything in my life. It's a lot more work than talking about acting like some of the kids in school. And I'll make it too, I know I'll make it."

"If you want it and you work for it, it's gotta come. If it's inside of you to make it, no matter what people do to try and stop it, it'll come out. The only thing in the world that can stop you is yourself."

"I just know I'll be great. I just feel it."

They were silent again. Tom leaned toward Rita, his lips touching her mouth. She twisted toward him, her arms grasping him. They embraced tightly. They parted and looked at each other. There was a softness, a gratefulness passing between their eyes. He kissed her again. It was pleasureful to kiss like this, Rita thought. It made one forget the coldness of other things. Suddenly, she broke away from him.

"Don't, Tom, let's not," she said calmly, feeling the beginnings of a mutually understood warmth buiding up within her.

"Don't what, Rita? I just want to kiss you."

"I know, I want to kiss you too. But there's more to it than that, you know that too."

"I know, but why fight it, baby. I can't."

"This isn't good for us. You know what I mean. You understand. We just met. Can't we leave it at that?"

He took his arms from around her and sat back on the couch. One hand fumbled with an ear. His jaw set hard.

"I know, . . . I know, . . . shit!" he burst angrily. "Why is the whole world like this. Every time you want something nice, meaningful, something else messes it up? You never get anything in this world but a lot of heartache and coldness. I don't mean you, you know," he explained.

"I know."

Tom stared across the room at the wall. Rita looked at him compassionately, now able to return his understanding. She suffered for herself as well as for him; for within her, there was the desire for warmth. However, there was also a feeling that revolted at the idea of promiscuity. *What a lousy mess of a life*, she thought to herself.

"I think maybe I'd better leave then." He stood up.

Now he is leaving. Rita was sitting on the couch alone. *Soon I will be completely alone*, she thought, *alone, alone, always alone.* She didn't know what to do now. Again the quandary—child or woman, woman or whore? *The world is but a series of decisions and life merely the outcome.* Confused, she reached out impulsively and touched his hand. He looked down. Her eyes were warm, sorrowful, confused, understanding. They gazed silently into each other's eyes for many moments. Tom sat. Rita lowered her eyes, remaining silent.

"Kiss me again," she asked softly, not lifting her eyes.

Tom kissed her again. His mouth caressed her eyes, her cheeks, her neck.

"Oh, Tom, we shouldn't. You know, you're doing things to me."

"You're doing many wonderful things to me too."

"We can't, . . . not here. Stop," she pleaded, now sorry she had not been strong enough to have let him walk out.

"Don't try to stop it, baby. It'll hurt even if we stop. It's good for us. It is . . ." His mouth caressed her neck.

She turned her head away from his kiss. "I know it's good, . . . and I want it to happen, but we can't . . ." She was breathing heavily now.

"Why not, baby? I want you so much. I'll be careful."

Rita wedged her arms between Tom and herself, holding herself away from him.

"The other girls will be back soon, and I don't feel like putting on a show."

Their eyes spoke love. She relented and his arms enfolded her again. She began to weep softly, half out of desperation, half out of desire. Tom felt her shaking with tears. He lifted her face and kissed her tears.

"Baby, we've just got to. We've got to. You've driven me out of my mind," he pleaded.

"I'm going out of mine too. But we can't here . . ."

"Let's get out of here then. Come on, let's go to my place. Come on . . ." He stood and took Rita's hand to help her stand.

She looked up, still retaining her seat. His eyes pleaded with hers, longing shining through grief and need. *Why can't I decide these things before they happen,* she asked herself, *instead of being thrown into a quagmire of confusion each time.* Impulsively, she stood and picked up her coat.

The metal strips on the edge of the steps resounded the descent of the two sets of feet to the remotest depths of the hallway. Suddenly the footfalls quieted. The lock in the front door clicked back into place.

8

KEYS JINGLED IN THE SILENT HALLWAY. A key turned in the lock of the front door of the apartment. The door swung open revealing one lamp in the front room still lit. The only sound from within was the monotonous circling of the phonograph needle on a spent record.

"Wonder where the hell Rita went in such a hurry? She didn't even turn the record off," Jeannie exclaimed.

Stan entered the apartment behind her. "I don't know. Maybe they decided to go out and get some coffee."

"Yeah, but like she could have shut off the machine or something."

Jeannie selected another record and placed it on the turntable.

"We got this new record the other day. Josh Minot, . . . you know, the colored guy, light complexion, shaved head? He's a dancer? Somebody made a record of African drums and chants—and it's the end. Josh's picture is on the cover." She handed the album cover to Stan. "You know Josh?"

Stan, now sitting on the couch, looked at the cover. On it, a dancing native was leaping before ritual fires, "I've seen this cat around. I don't know him though."

"Oh, he's really a great dancer. I was up at one of those belly-dance places—in the West Twenties?" She looked at him inquisitively, patronizingly, wondering if Stan knew what she was talking about.

Stan nodded to indicate his awareness. "You think I'm square or something, baby?"

"Well anyway, of all people to run into, I saw Josh. He was dancing there—terrific."

Jeannie placed a cigarette between her lips and handed Stan a matchbook. He looked wonderingly at the matches for a moment, then up at Jeannie. She watched him impatiently.

"Oh, . . . you want a light, hanh?" He struck a match.

"I wouldn't mind. I know it lasts longer this way, but the flavor isn't the same." Jeannie studied Stan for a reaction to her remark. He only watched the flame lick the end of the cigarette. Her face smirked with displeasure at his unawareness.

"I think I'll take a cigarette, too." Stan looked around for the package.

"There're some in my purse."

Jeannie sat in a chair near the phonograph. She increased the volume and now the entire room vibrated with the sound of thundering drums and wailing people.

"Where the hell are they?" Stan inquired as he rummaged in her large leather handbag.

"I don't know. There's some Camels in that little jar on the table behind you. You probably don't like Parliament anyway."

"Sure I do, man. I like the filters the end." He smiled at his own pun. Jeannie remained straight-faced. "I have very expensive appetites too, you know," he said, effecting a German accent.

"That's what I thought. Most people do when they're not paying for it."

Stan's face froze into a question.

"If you're going to be broke cause I took one of your nails, like forget it. You know, like this isn't the last place in the world that has cigarettes, and like you're not the only chick in the world that has Parliament. Don't be so impressed with your little self." His eyes were riveted upon her fiercely.

"Oh, come off it, will you? I'm kidding."

"No, you come off it, off that jazz about Parliament and the rest of that crap. You know, like you're not doing me any favors at all, baby."

"All right, for Christ's sake. You want to argue all night, or what? I mean, like forget it will you? I lost my other head for a minute . . . so?" She attempted a smile, waving her hand to indicate that what's been said has been said.

"I just get annoyed with people who give me bullshit. I don't like to listen to it anymore."

"So forget about it. Let's stop talking about it." She crossed the room and sat next to him on the couch.

"God damn it! I hate bullshit!" He sprang to his feet.

Jeannie stood up next to him, slipping her arm through his. "Come on, sit down. Can't you forget it . . . please?"

Stan sat down again. Jeannie sat next to him. She started to speak, but in mid-word, her head jerked forward, her eyes and mouth opened wide, her head quickly nodded again, and she sneezed.

"God bless you."

She looked at him inquisitively. "You talk about God an awful lot. What are you, a priest or something?"

"What do you mean, am I a priest? 'Cause I say 'God bless you,' I'm a priest?"

"Yeah. Only a frig-ass priest would ask some god to bless me. You don't really think somebody marked down a little blessing in a book for me, do you? One blessing for Jeannie Sorrent . . . from Stan. What's your last name? But what's the difference, God knows you. God knows everything, doesn't he?"

"Look, baby, all I said was 'God bless you.' What are you trying to do, bug me tonight? I mean, like come off it, off the kick, will you? Yeah, I believe in God. I don't flip on the bit, I live it up, but I still believe in God, and like that, and like do you really mind? And will you stop bugging me? I mean, will ya?"

"Okay, Father, I'll stop bugging you; I don't want you to get excited. You might start doing penance in here for my soul. Do you whip your-self, or do you just wear a hair shirt? Let me see, do you wear a hair shirt?" She thrust an inquisitive hand between the buttons of Stan's shirt front. "No hair shirt, Father, but nice hair on your chest." She smiled coyly, playfully rubbing his chest. "Even if you do say your prayers every night you have a nice chest."

"I thought you were going to come off this bit, for Christ's sake." His jaw muscles set firmly. "What the hell is with you?"

"I'm coming off it. I'm just teasing."

She stood and walked to the kitchen. "You want a drink?"

Stan nodded stiffly.

"I can't reach the glasses; could you get them down for me, Stan?"

"Yeah, I'll get them."

He walked into the kitchen and reached into the closet. He lifted one glass out. He stretched himself up on his tiptoes, his hand groping blindly for another glass on the top shelf. He found one and let himself down from his stretched position.

"What happened, no more 'Father' anymore?" Annoyance was still etched on his face.

"You know I was only kidding you, don't you, Stan?" She moved close to him, pressed herself against him, her hands sliding up and down his back.

"What do I know if you were kidding or not?" He looked down into her face.

"Well, I was." Jeannie moved her body in an almost imperceptible circular motion against him. "I just get annoyed at preachers. You know, like I don't dig God, and preachers are always trying to convert you, you know what I mean?"

"Yeah, I know what you mean, baby. I mean, like I'm not the most holy guy in the world, you know?"

"Come on, let's sit down and talk for a while."

She pushed herself away from him and began mixing drinks. The music of the jungle flew up from the background, hollowly vibrating through the apartment again. Jeannie handed Stan a drink and took his free hand in hers, leading him to the couch in the front room. The screaming natives and pounding drums shuddered through the room. Jeannie lowered the volume. She turned.

"Do people come up to you and tell you that God exists, and that you should heed His word, and be righteous, and do all sorts of things or He'll be unhappy and hail fire and brimstone or sticky marshmallows on you? Do they?" she inquired, waving her drink in the air.

"Sometimes," Stan nodded affirmatively.

"I hear that all the time, you know? It used to be worse. My father's a minister, you know? We're from West Virginia. So, he's got this little parish down there. I mean, that's all right; some people want something to believe in; they've got to have something they think is all-powerful, that can give them their wishes and prayers. This way, they can figure life's not so tough. Good things can happen just like that, out of the blue; it's just that you have to pray hard enough. And when nothing happens, they say God isn't pleased with them and they have to pray harder. Some people need a crutch, some vague hope of something good, something besides themselves to blame for their failures, you know?

"Sure," Stan answered, "if they believe there is some god, they don't have to face the reality that one day there's the sleep of death, and then nothing. That's frightening, . . . death."

"So's life. That's why they pray to God. God can give them the easy life, grant their wishes—all they've got to do is pray. That's easier than working hard, laboring, thinking—just pray. That's life made easy all over again. Just repeat the magic words. And my father, . . . he used to stuff that pray bit into me as if I was a sausage. He was always telling me I was the community's example, and I should be good and do this and that. I got tired of being an example! I just wanted to be me. That really shocked my old man. You're not supposed to just want to be yourself. As a matter of fact, you're supposed to beat into your breast that you're worthless, that you shouldn't enjoy anything—any pleasure is sinful. The lousier time you have in this rotten life, the better person you should feel."

"Yeah, like I know how you feel."

"Well, when I started acting up a bit—you know, I just wanted them to know I was there—the old man really got annoyed. When he got really annoyed, he punished me. Then I started to get angry. I was only a kid playing pranks; I didn't mean anything by it at first."

She walked to the couch and sat down next to Stan.

"First they treat you like children," she continued, "don't tell you anything, protect you from the truth and harshness of life. And then, all of a sudden, they don't treat you like kids any more. Overnight you're an adult. And then you're supposed to know everything, in one night—all the things they protected you from—suddenly, you're supposed to understand them, with no help from your parents . . . as if knowledge came in an apple on a tree. They don't feel any obligations, . . . all a kid has to do is eat the right apple.

"My old man didn't want to face the responsibility of raising children either. So he blamed it on me. Said it was me that wasn't pious or something. He was sure *he* was okay. He was saying all the right prayers. He couldn't figure it, but he knew it was me. And, by God, his righteous indignation was hailing fire and brimstone on this dumb little hick kid."

"How long have you been here?"

"About two years. I mean I left there about two years ago. I went to college first. He thought that was the answer. It's amazing, you know, how many ready-made answers people can manufacture to take the sting out of life—the easy way out. They don't want to stop to think that you've gotta figure your way out of this life all by yourself."

"That thinking stuff is no good," Stan injected. "It ruins the country. Just do what you're told and everything'll be fine. When people start to think they bring up too many problems. Just open your vacuum-packed jar of life and you got all the answers. Don't think though."

"That's it, that's it exactly. My father's vacuum-packed jar was called God, and he tried to stuff it down my throat. I kept asking him why. What a word—why? Terrific. All you have to do is ask *why* and you could stop the earth from turning."

"You're not supposed to ask why. Just do it. Who are you to ask why, when everybody else does it without asking questions?"

"But I always asked why. And I never got the answer, just fire and brimstone. And after a while, I was sick of God and a stuffed throat, . . . and I told him. I said to my father, I don't believe in God. Not that I really didn't. I didn't know God, that's all. I wanted to understand the why about Him—not parrot. My father almost hemorrhaged. He couldn't believe that his sweet little daughter didn't believe in God. He was a failure, a disgrace. Not that he worried too much about me; he worried about how I'd affect his place in the community. He kept me hidden in a closet after that, at least until I left. But people still won't leave me alone. Even today, somebody will be saying something and then you mention that you don't believe in God—that's the way I am, . . . I have to say exactly what I think. But that's all you have to do, mention that you don't believe in God, and wow, like they won't leave you alone. They've got to convince you that there's a God. I say to them, I'll allow if you want to believe, but leave me be. But they insist that you believe in their ready-made answers, because if you can live without their answers, then maybe their answers are wrong, and it'd be too confusing for them to have to find other ready-made answers. They want to be right, even if they shut their eyes in order to believe it, even if they have to kill you to shut you up."

She sipped her drink and sat quietly.

"God never did anything for me," she blurted suddenly with annoyance. "I never saw Him. He never sent me a letter asking me to join His troop. I never even saw His picture. I've seen a lot of crap paintings. You know, the real nice ones, the ones with halos, and all the creeps looking to heaven and the birds and all that jazz. Like they're not even good paintings. Anyway, I don't know Him, and He don't know me. I really don't believe he exists.

They sipped their drinks and gazed at each other silently. The beating music rose freely from the phonograph.

"How could He?" she pressed. "If a God existed, then the world wouldn't be the rotten filthy hole it is, and life would be a hell of a lot easier. I mean, what are we doing on this rotten piece of dust, . . . what?"

"I don't know, . . . to have a ball, no?"

"Well, who the hell is having a ball? It's all a bunch of shit, just like God is. You have a ball for ten minutes, and the rest of the time you're miserable, paying for it. What are we suffering for—to prove how good we are, so we can go to heaven and be with God; or how bad we are, so He'll know we don't deserve heaven and we go to hell? That doesn't even figure, you know? If God wanted us to be with Him, we'd be there now, not here, trying to prove something that doesn't even mean anything."

Stan looked at her with silent, absorbed interest.

"I mean what does it prove," she continued. "Everybody is morally neutral when they're born, not good or bad, but morally neutral. And God put us here so we can prove ourselves? What kind of crazy shit is that? He shouldn't have to test anything. He'd know what the outcome was going to be. Not that he'd direct it, but we're born in a certain environment—sometimes a good clean, healthy one, sometimes a filthy hole of an environment—and all of us are influenced by that environment. We can only expand within the limit of our experience. When its squalid and seamy, when kids go hungry to bed, there'll be a lot of people stealing—money, love—people with below-par morals. They have to be that way to eat regularly. And when there's an environment where it's easy to be good—perhaps money, or comfort, or just plain love and peace—the child is influenced by that. And when you grow older you do things according to the influences you've had. If somebody's been in a poor environment, he may do rotten things and not even consider them rotten. They're just everyday occurences in his way of life. He doesn't do it to be evil, just to be good really. Even a murderer murders because he thinks good for him will come out of it. So here you're supposed to have God putting the neutral humans on the earth, in an environment that influences either to be bad or good. And when you die, God is going to condemn you because you were bad, because you did something you didn't know enough not to do—something you probably weren't even aware of? What bullshit that is! If He does exist He's almost forcing you to hell or heaven. God wouldn't do that, God would be so much bigger than that, so much more kind, merciful—if he existed! But there's no one who is kind existing. You've got to shift for yourself and make the best of this life. It doesn't prove a God damn thing, except it's a pain in the ass, and it's miserable. This earth could be a great place except for the rotten people that treat you like shit. God is a bunch of shit that somebody cooked up, because we're here and we can't do anything about it anyway. Half the people don't even become intelligent enough to know God, . . . so what'll He do? Save them anyway because they're simple?

Both of them leaned back on the couch, thinking of the masses of adoring people. Neither spoke. The music from the phonograph heedlessly rose and beat and swayed, and the Africans wailed.

Stan brooded pensively. Now he looked at Jeannie, just staring at her. He nodded his head slowly, continuing to look at her. She turned. They gazed intently into each other's eyes. Stan put down his drink.

"Come over here and stop all the talking."

She moved toward him. He reached out and pulled her even closer.

"Hey, . . . don't you know God doesn't like things like little boys and little girls doing this sort of thing." She laughed.

"Come on, will you, knock it off." He held her tightly in his arms and kissed her. Her arms swung around his shoulders. She held herself against him tightly.

"But God won't like it," she said breaking away, gasping slightly.

"But if there isn't any God like you say, then He don't know about it." Stan bit her neck lightly.

They kissed again. They leaned over and lay next to each other on the couch. Stan tangled one of his legs between Jeannie's legs.

"But if there is?" she injected breaking away.

"We don't know for sure, . . . and like let's not waste the night finding out."

They kissed more firmly and actively. Their bodies began to pulsate. Stan picked her up in his arms and walked toward the room in the back.

"This the bedroom in here?"

"Yes, . . . but I sleep on the couch." She was cradled in his arms. "We'd better stay out here. Laura and Rita will be home soon." She kissed his ear, caressing it with her tongue as he carried her to the front room.

Stan stood over the couch. He kissed Jeannie, still holding her in his arms. They kissed long, passionately, and as they kissed, Stan sank to his knees on the couch. He lowered Jeannie onto the couch and lay next to her.

The whirling monotonous "zzchh" of the completely played record soon filled the room. Two people breathed deeply in the darkness, moving actively, ignoring the record.

9

THE SHADOWS IN JOHNSON'S were not as dense as they had been earlier in the evening. Laura was alone as she returned from a walk to Dani's. She stood in the doorway, closing the door behind her by leaning against it. She blew on her cold hands as she studied the wilting shadows, hoping she knew one of them, wanting to talk to someone. She was feeling abandoned and alone again. Silently, she wished that she didn't mind being alone. She wished she could become accustomed to it.

"Hi, Sammy."

"Hi, Laura." Sammy was behind the bar drying glasses. "How're you doin'?"

"All right." Her words were snappy, monosyllabic. She feared saying anything too long, involved, or loud, afraid someone might hit her, or make fun of her, or in some way make her feel foolish. "Rita or Jeannie come back?"

"Naw. They were here with two cats before—you know, you were with them. But I haven't seen them since they split about an hour ago."

"Ohh, . . . Thanks."

She sank even further into her feeling of being abandoned. Now she couldn't even return to the apartment for fear of again intruding awkwardly on Jeannie or Rita. None of her friends were standing at the bar. She spied Gene leaning against the jukebox in the rear. Except for the whites of his eyes and a white scar across his left cheek, his opaque, ebony complexion blended into the dimness of the cafe. The scar gave him a savage, brutal appearance. No friend he, Gene reminded Laura of a Nazi, or some other such barbarian. Gene was cruel—vicious mouthed and sarcastic. He was always mocking and deprecating everything around him.

Laura walked toward the back; even Gene's contempt was more acceptable than aloneness. Around Gene's neck, from a leather thong, hung an uneven-shaped medallion of intertwined silver fingers.

The Villagers, throwing off the robes of Uptown's oppressors, taking up those of the Village, inundate themselves in a stream or mores and tastes as muddy and beclouded as the one abandoned. The garb, the mannerisms, the ways of speaking, the ideals, the pictures to see, the books that are a must, the beards, the women's long, flowing, styleless hair fall into conventional Village patterns. The world of the outside is replaced by a world banded by other frenzied conventions. The Villagers have only run a short way, and now stand waving their fist at the cold oppressor, resenting and rejecting every aspect of the outside world. But they have not run fast enough, nor straight enough, nor long enough to get away from themselves. They are the same inside; they are only garbed differently.

Laura walked to the back and sat on a stool by the end of the bar. She twisted on the swivel seat until she faced the jukebox and Gene. He stared at her coldly, not speaking a word. His arms were folded on his chest. Laura too was wordless, she from apprehension. She became self-conscious.

"Hi, Gene. How're you?" she said finally.

"I'm okay, baby." Only his lips moved, and they slightly. "How's yourself?"

"Okay. Where've you been lately? I haven't seen you in a while."

"I been workin' my way through the A.A." Still he did not move or smile.

"You're a real card tonight, Gene." She tried to chuckle.

His face remained stone. Laura stopped chuckling. Nervousness began to mount within her.

"Always, baby, . . . you know that."

Gene enjoyed being cruel to Laura. It bolstered his feelings of power to viciously taunt a weak, helpless person. It made up for his own inadequacy.

"Yeah, I guess I do," she replied. "I'm going to get a job tomorrow, you know? I think . . . I'm supposed to go to the employment agency tomorrow."

"Crazy . . ." His eyes bored into her face, purposely trying to out-stare her. Laura was a pushover. "Lend me five bucks when you get your first pay check, okay, baby? I'm broke lately."

"Hey . . ." she quipped, a vague smile on her face, trying to capture the humorous note she didn't feel. "I didn't even get it yet. Take it easy, hanh?"

"How's everything these days over at the Club Lisa?" he asked insinuatingly.

"Oh, I don't know," she said hesitantly, dropping her vague smile. "I haven't been there in a while."

"What's the matter, baby, lose your taste for the girls?" He chuckled.

Laura frowned guiltily as her dark life was layed bare.

"I just figured to cut that crap out," she explained. "It's crazy stuff. I don't even know how I got mixed up with that shit." Laura's honesty was painful to her. She felt incapable of successful lies, however, and detection, she knew, could be more painful.

"What are you doing now, hanging in Santo's with the gay boys, the fags?"

"No, . . . I been trying to get my head back on right." Her voice was very soft, almost inaudible. "Rita and Jeannie have been helping me . . . and like that, you know? I've been listening to them, and they put the Lisa down real bad. So, . . . I don't go."

"You got two great advisors there, baby."

"It's better than nobody," she snapped in defense. "Better than everybody that ever tried before . . . supposed to have tried anyway."

Gene shrugged unconcernedly.

"Hi, Laura. Hi Gene," said Dick, one of the guys who always hung around in Johnson's. "How're all the good people in Johnson's tonight?" He smiled, revealing crooked, pointed teeth. His face was thin and sharp-featured, rat-like.

"Hi, Dick," said Laura, glad to change the subject of conversation.

"Dick . . . how's the boy?" Gene slapped him hard on the back.

"Okay. What's happening, man?"

"Nothin'. You?"

"Ehh . . ." Dick shrugged.

"You guys want anything to drink?" asked Raoul Johnson, walking to their end of the bar. With no women around to interest him, Raoul was catering to his other love—money.

"Yeah, I'll take a beer," Dick said, smiling his thin smile.

Raoul pulled a bottle of beer from the cooler.

"What's happening?" Raoul asked.

"Nothin'."

They were all silent. Raoul leaned forward, his elbows on the bar. Dick sucked his beer out of the bottle. The others looked around the cafe. The other patrons were murmuring quietly. Gene glanced at Laura, then slowly smiled a leering, secret smile.

"I was just telling Laura that the word's gotten around that she gives a mean blow job," Gene remarked to the other two men. "I mean, I heard when she goes down, like she really goes down." He watched from the side of his eyes to see if he had hit his mark. He had. Laura began to squirm on her seat.

"Is that right?" Raoul asked, accepting a part in the jibe, noticing Laura's discomfort.

"I heard the same thing myself," Dick chimed in. "Is that the truth, Laura?"

"That's a hell of a nasty thing to say about me," Laura complained mildly, calmly, knowing they purposely taunted her, wanting her to be terrified. "No, sir, man, that's one thing I'd never do. Not me." She held onto the bottom of the stool with both hands.

"I heard you did it great. What the hell, there's nothing wrong with doing something and doing it well." Gene sneered, discontent with her calmness. "Isn't that right, Dick?"

"Sure is . . ." Dick was a superb agreer. He reveled in being considered part of a theory, part of a group, part of anything. "And you should share your talent with the rest of the world. You know, like maybe you can take the three of us on." He leered. His eyes slid to the corner of their sockets to see the reaction of Gene and Raoul. His forced smile rippled into a genuine smile of relief as the others laughed. He threw his head back, his mouth wide, chaotic noises escaping.

"You bastards. That's rotten, filthy rotten." The crude rib began to shatter Laura's forced composure. She wanted them to stop, but she didn't know exactly how to stop them without saying something childish at which they would laugh, or something sarcastic at which they would become angry. She was surrounded and trapped.

"You look like you could do a real great job," Raoul snickered. His supercilious, professional-Negro air was coming through. He enjoyed taunting this little white ragamuffin. "Let's see you open your mouth. Come on. Open."

"You guys are terrible. What a thing to say to me." She began to tremble inside. "I never did that, never, agghh . . ." Her head shuddered in revulsion.

"Think you could handle this?" asked Raoul, who had gone to the other end of the bar and brought back something under his apron. "Think you could handle this?" He revealed a long piece of rubber hose that had been painted flesh color to resemble the male organ. "What do you think?" He dangled the rubber hose in front of Laura.

"Yow . . . Get that thing out of here," she screamed, pushing back on her stool in alarm. The stool fell backwards. She screamed again as she fell.

Gene grabbed her under the armpits as the stool fell to the floor. All the guys laughed as Gene held Laura in midair, returning her to the conversation. Laura managed a scared smile as she stood and righted the stool.

"I could introduce you to a very good friend of mine that size," Raoul suggested, his eyes narrow, a thin smile on his face.

"Here I am," Dick exclaimed, outspreading his arms, a sneery smile twisting his mouth.

"I guess you don't want to know me," said Raoul. "I'm a lot bigger than that."

"Come on you guys. Like, you know I'm the champ when it comes to that," Gene boasted.

"How about this size," Raoul suggested, further taunting Laura. He brandished a shot glass, moving it near Laura's mouth to see if she could fit the rim into her mouth. "Think you can handle this size?" He laughed.

"Come on now. You guys are awful." She shuddered with revulsion. "Who could ever do a thing like that?" She wanted them to stop now, but it was too late. Anything she said or did would be laughed at. She gritted her teeth angrily, searching for an opportunity to escape without being mocked.

"Baby," said Gene, "there's nothing wrong with going down on a person. Man, like I dig it myself."

"I'm hip you do, man," Raoul injected with a sly snicker.

"I'm talking about women, man, . . . women. Only someone like you who goes down on guys would think of something like that. When I go down on somebody, man, like all they got between their legs is hair." He stared fiercely at Raoul.

"I dig that kind of action myself," Dick leered boldly.

"I didn't hear any cat mention goin' down on a guy. I guess you just got that on your mind," added Raoul.

Gene glared at the smirk on Raoul's face.

"It keeps you healthy, you know?" Dick released through his rat mouth, enjoying the pleasure of hearing weird words bandied about. "It's good for everything. Makes hair grow on your chest."

"I got hair on my chest," said Raoul. "I need something to part it."

They all laughed loudly, boisterously, enjoying the evil release. The pace of their evil feast was increasing, reaching a frenzy pitch.

"How about we have a contest to see who can eat Laura the best, and she'll go down on the winner," Gene suggested laughingly. The others laughed and howled their approval.

Laura's smile sickened further. How could she get out of there, she wondered? She didn't care where she went, how cold it was, how alone she would be.

"You guys are crazy." She was stunned, unable to say more. If only Sammy would come to her end of the bar, she thought. He'd protect her. She could escape then.

"Man, I'll eat her so much she won't be able to stand it," Raoul boasted.

"Are you kidding, man?" Gene said dismissing Raoul's statement. He began to say something. The words described something he would do to Laura. It was so revolting, so degenerate, so physically, humanly inconceivable and fantastic that the rest of his statement was blotted from her ears as her insides wrenched. Her stomach began to pull up toward her throat.

The group laughed raucously at Gene's comment. They reveled in this ribald horror and taunting.

Laura's smile was rancid as her insides swirled.

"I'd crawl bare-ass over a mile of broken beer bottles just to hear her piss in a canteen cup from a telephone pole," Dick added irrelevantly, not to be outdone.

The group snickered.

Laura steadied herself on her seat. She readied herself to leave but she felt faint. She felt she'd fall on the floor if she stood up.

"I'll see you later," Raoul said as he began to walk to the front to greet some well-dressed people who entered. He smiled at them, pointing gallantly to a table.

"You guys are awful, really awful," Laura said seriously, too upset to protest more. "You make somebody feel awful. I don't mind talking like that and kidding around, but don't keep it up like that."

"Aww, we were only kidding you, baby, you know that," Gene said placatingly, not wanting her to leave yet.

"Yeah, I guess so," she apologized, not caring one way or another.

They all stood quietly, looking around the bar. Laura was trying to edge off the stool.

"I'm going to cut, man," Dick announced. "I've got to git. I'll see you around."

"Okay, man. Take it easy."

"Which way are you walking?" Laura asked.

"I'm going to Pandora's. You going over?"

"Yeah, I'm going home. I think I'll go now. See you, Gene. So long, Sammy."

Sammy didn't hear her weak voice through the noise and the music in the background.

"Sammy!" she called louder.

He looked up.

"So long."

"So long, take it easy." He smiled.

Raoul leered condescendingly as she followed Dick out the door.

"What are you doing these days, Dick?" Laura asked to start a new subject as they walked toward the Avenue of the Americas. She wasn't enthralled by Dick's company, but where else could she go? To whom could she speak? She couldn't go to the apartment, and every place else was dead, empty.

"I'm taking pictures now. Remember I was working for Joe Turner a while ago. Well, like I saved some bread and bought me some equipment, and like I started on my own. Now I'm my own boss."

"That's pretty cool. How're you doing?"

"Paying my rent, and like that. You know, I'm not knocking down any doors, but I'm keeping going."

"That's great."

"You're getting a job tomorrow, hanh?" he inquired.

"Yeah. How'd you know?"

"I was standing right behind you when you were talking to Gene, wasn't I?"

"Oh, yeah, that's right. Yeah, I might get the job tomorrow. I need the money."

"You're still shacking with Jeannie and Rita, aren't you?"

"Yeah, but still, I have to pay rent and buy myself some clothes and things."

"Tell your old man to send you some loot."

"Yeah . . . Fat chance of that. Christ, they're always complaining about money. You know, there's so many kids and all . . ." *What a lousy, lonely world*, she thought. If only people would listen to her once in a while. If only they'd stop taunting her.

"You have a lot of brothers?"

"Only one brother, but I have four sisters. They're all older than me. Everybody's older than me. By the time I'd get any money from them I'd be walking in the street with no clothes on."

"Listen, baby, if you find yourself without any clothes, you don't have to walk the streets. You can come over to my place." He fluttered his eyebrows.

"Thanks a lot," Laura said curtly, looking ahead.

"What does your old man do?"

"Works as a longshoreman and gets drunk."

"Those longshoremen get good money."

"So do bars and crap games and shylocks and all the rest of the working man's sucker traps." These revived thoughts angered her. She was tired of being abused, stepped on.

"You know, I never heard you say so much at one time."

She didn't look at him. She was talking to herself out loud, looking straight ahead.

"I can talk. I can say a lot of things. Of course, where I lived, Christ, you couldn't say anything out of the way. My old man is the kind of guy that believes in hitting women and children. Everybody was a threat to him, everybody was a stranger. He'd come home rough and tough all the time, always showing he was the boss. He used to beat my old lady and the kids, and get drunk and gamble. He was a gem. After a while, my old lady, with nothing else to do, got on her own booze jags, . . . and then all the kids really had to shift for themselves. One of my sisters got picked up for prostitution."

"No kidding?" That was keen to Dick.

Laura didn't answer. She couldn't bring herself to say offensive things.

"I was the youngest. Instead of that being in my favor, that was my tough luck. I wasn't only helpless, but abandoned. I had to take care of myself."

"How about your brothers and sisters. Didn't they help you?"

"They were so busy working, keeping their souls and bodies together, they could hardly be bothered with me. What the hell, I was only a skinny kid. I don't mind that they were all worrying about themselves. Everyone had it tough. My old man might have been poor, hard working, all that crap—although he wouldn't have been poor if he didn't gamble and drink so much—but that didn't mean he should have five kids. That's the trouble with poor people; they're poor because they're ignorant, too God damn dumb to get out of their rut, to do anything about it. They're so God damn dumb that they keep getting themselves further and further involved, drinking to forget they're poor, gambling, hoping that they'll make it the easy way because they can't figure any other way to get out of the hole. Ever go to a race track?"

"No, I can't afford to get into one."

"My old man gave me a big day out once. Took me to Jamaica with him. All you see around there are these sleasy characters trying to make the big time the easy way. All they have to do is hit one big one, a few small ones—too lazy to figure out something that'll really get them out of the hole. They want it the easy way, without thinking. I can't forgive him, say he was too dumb to realize the difference. He should have been able to realize the difference. Either that or have been sterilized. I wasn't unhappy when I wasn't existing. I didn't know the difference. And some idiot who couldn't control his loins, who had to have an emotional release from the hell he continually intensified for himself, had five kids. He doesn't know a fucking thing about kids . . ."

"He must have known a *fucking* thing," Dick remarked jokingly.

Laura flickered a momentary smile. She was fuming and spuming anger now. "You know, I think that ignorant people shouldn't be allowed to have kids."

"Hey, . . . that's a coukie thing to say. How are you gonna say to someone you can't have kids?"

"As easy as they can say to someone, 'Get into that electric chair, Charlie.'"

Dick was silent. Laura fumed quietly, her mind racing inside herself.

"Don't you get along with any of your brothers and sisters?"

"The only one I got along with is my sister Joan. She's the youngest next to me. We tried to take care of each other once in a while. The rest of them bother me, or give me a pain, or something."

"What do you mean they bother you?"

"Ahhh, . . . they call me skinny, or ugly, or stupid things like that. You know, they think it's a big joke," she said quickly, not wanting to talk about it any longer. "I wouldn't ask them for the right time."

"I don't think you're skinny or ugly, baby." Dick patted her rear end.

"Hey, . . . you son-of-a-bitch. Watch your hands."

"Oh, what the hell, a little goose won't hurt you, will it?" Dick said, wanting to again enjoy the sound of his salacious words. It was pleasureful for him to talk these words aloud.

"Why don't you just leave me alone," Laura pleaded. "Don't start any crap with me, hanh?"

"What do you mean, don't start any crap? What did I do?"

"Nothin'. You didn't do a thing. And like don't bother, . . . okay? I don't want to be bothered."

"Come here," Dick said with sudden determination. He pulled her into the darkened doorway of a closed store. "Come here, you little bitch." He pulled her to himself, held both her hands in one of his hands, thrusting his other groping hand between her legs. He squeezed her femininity viciously.

"You bastard!! You rotten, filthy, dopey bastard," she screamed as she struggled, trying desperately to jerk one of her hands free from his grip. The pain of his grip between her legs was excruciating. "Leave me alone," she screamed in agony.

Her screams excited Dick more.

Laura finally pulled one of her hands loose and dug her nails frantically at his eyes.

"Why you rotten little bitch," he burst with pain, his grip loosening as her nails sank into the flesh. He shoved her away as he felt the warm stinging stiffness of wounds spread down his face.

Laura fell backward, landing hard on the sidewalk. She scrambled to her feet and began to run.

"Come here you little bitch," he yelled, running after her. He ran as fast as he could, his teeth bared and clenched.

Laura could hear his footsteps falling just behind her. Slowly, he closed the gap between them. Laura tried running faster, terror mounting within her. The gap remained constant for half a block.

Then, the bulk of his weight started to slow him down. The gap started to open as he could summon no more speed from his body. He made an all-powerful lunge at her, kicking his foot. He missed and stumbled into the street, hobbling to catch his balance.

"You little bitch," he screamed as her fleeing, running image diminished. "I'll kill you."

Her footsteps echoed throughout the street as she ran desperately from her enraged suitor. The sound diminished as she turned the corner. Laura sobbed, tears streaming down her cheeks, as she ran frantically across Seventh Avenue toward the quiet, dark, warm apartment, where, she hoped, she could escape the people who beset her.

10

THE COLD, QUIET DAWN filtered yellow through the drapes which sealed Tom's apartment from the outside world. The loud, rude noises of the world were stilled, the pounding footsteps of walkers had vanished, the shrill voices of women calling their children from the street were silenced. The clangor and clamor of the past was only a memory. Now, its inhabitants hidden, the world seemed pure and clean, majestically poised to blossom with the beauty of a new day. It was like the respite after a violent battle, after the attacker had come for a long time, and now an eerie stillness, a serene magnificence, pervaded everything.

Ever so slightly, the claws of a street cat rummaging hungrily through a garbage can, scratched the air. In the distance, a boat, whistling to the river, greeted the new morning. In the street below, a lone car engine growled, then roared with life. The crescendo of engine blended with motion, at its zenith a fender rattled, then the sound was absorbed into the oblivion of silence.

The room was again abuzz with the static and pressure of quiet. The silence existed and was ever the same and undisturbed, an intermingling with eternity and nothingness.

Suddenly, a rattle ushered a golden, gleaming brightness into the room. Rita clamped her eyes closed more tightly, drawing her head back and away from the sudden burst of incandescence. Her hand shaded her eyes as she squinted toward the source of the light. Tom, shirtless, was outlined before the window. He had pulled back the drapes, allowing shafts of sunlight, just risen above surrounding buildings, to sear the room. Through the shafts floated a myriad of dust particles. Tom, risen, washed, had opened the curtains to let in the day, to awaken Rita.

Rita watched Tom's back. One of her arms lay outside the covers. Her other hand held the blanket to her chin. Only her head, floating on a spray of long, black hair, contrasted against the whiteness of the sheets.

Tom peered through the windows, absently rubbing his hands in a towel. He watched the street below intently. Now he turned and walked toward the bed. He noticed the glistening reflection of Rita's open eyes.

"Morning, baby . . ." His face rippled with a smile. "Hope you don't mind getting up so early? I have to go to work."

"That's okay," Rita's voice rasped shakily as she stretched one arm into the air, then wiped the sleep from her eyes. "I have to go to work, . . ." She stretched her shoulders, her head trembling, her voice straining out. ". . . too, this morning."

"Man, it takes you a long time to wake up," Tom chuckled. He tossed the towel toward the bathroom which was through a door near the side of the bed.

"How long have you been up?" Rita asked, looking around. She sat up holding the covers about herself.

"I don't know—fifteen minutes or so." He looked at his watch, then sat on the side of the bed.

"What time is it?" Rita stretched her free arm over her head. When the muscles were taut, she lowered the arm and began to stroke Tom's neck.

"Seven fifteen." Tom nestled his head further into her hand so she could stroke it more firmly. "Mmmmm, . . . that's nice," he purred. "A beautiful woman stroking your head early on a beautiful morning—great!" He raised his arms straight over his head and stretched them, letting himself sink backward slowly so that he lay across Rita's legs. She lay back on the pillow, still holding the covers in one hand, stroking Tom's head with the other. They stared absently at the ceiling.

"I was just looking out into the street," Tom said, twisting to gaze toward the window. "And there was this cat—a real one, that is, to be differentiated from the swinging kind." He smiled. Rita laughed in crinkly-eyed enjoyment. "And he was digging in the garbage pail for his breakfast, or dinner. I don't know what hours this cat keeps."

"Probably going home from a night on the town. He's picking up breakfast."

"Yeah. Well, I'm looking at this cat, and I said to myself, I wonder where his woman is? Then I thought of me—us—and I thought how much nicer it is to be here with you than out there."

"Thanks a lot. You're real cool with your compliments."

"Aww, you know what I mean." Tom twisted toward Rita, appealing.

"I know," she said softly, smiling, nodding her head slightly. As lovers sense each other's mood because they are *sympatico*, close, almost one, so Rita could sense Tom's thoughts. The closeness they shared dispelled fears, opened the way for a deeper mutual understanding.

"I mean, it's so alone and cold out there," he said intensely, "and somebody's liable to come along any minute and shoo him, or put the lid on the can, or throw a rock at him, or something. You know, like he's all by himself, all lonely and all, and maybe he got in a fight last night and some big cat came and took his girl away, and now he's thinking of his girl, and how it used to be, and how the big cat is prob-ably making it with her, and like that. You know what I mean?" he asked hopefully. "Like, it's real tough to be out there all alone." Tom's head twisted back toward the window.

"I guess I know how the cat feels." Rita was grave and pensive.

"Yeah, you know what I mean," Tom agreed. "Now all the little God damn cat wants to do is get himself some chow. Nobody else is going to take care of him. He probably sees Mary's cat in the window—Mary is a chick that lives across the street—and like the cat in the can looks up and sees this cat inside the window, all warm and fed, and taken care of, and as he looks up over the lip of this greasy garbage can, he gets to wish he had some place warm with somebody to take care of him."

"Yeah, I know, and like maybe it's been that way all his life," Rita added, "running and jumping, and he wants to stop but he can't. He was probably born in a back alley one night, and his old lady took off right away without even saying 'hello'—just left him there to shift for himself. And all people ever do is throw rocks at him or chase him because he wants to eat. Probably that first night some guy came along and saw kittens, all newborn in his alley, and gathered them up, because it was dark and no one could see him, and threw them in a garbage pail so he wouldn't have to bother keeping them."

They lay silently on the bed, gazing up at the ceiling, the mood and quiet infusing them with thought. Time passed slowly. Tom lifted himself up on one elbow and twisted toward Rita.

"That's what I mean about being so much nicer here with you than in the garbage can. And yet, maybe we're both in the garbage can right along with him, and like, maybe that's where we'll stay, and . . . ahh, . . ." Tom exclaimed hopelessly, "I don't know what the hell I'm talking about." He twisted back toward the window, propping himself up on both elbows.

Rita sat up and touched his shoulder. He turned, embraced her, and they clung to each other hungrily. Her bare body felt warm and soft in his arms.

"I know what you're saying," she assured him consolingly. "People are like that. They don't only treat cats like that either."

Tom snuggled his head on Rita's shoulders. She pressed her head against his.

"Maybe we only met for one night, but even for one night it's better than being in the garbage can alone," Tom murmured, not looking up.

They were silent, both aware that their brief warmth was over, not knowing if they would ever find each other or warmth again.

"It's as if we're cats and found a whole clean fish, and like we enjoyed it, and it was good, and we'll always remember it," Tom continued. "People should accept temporary pleasures and not grumble, or worry, or bitch, because life isn't better than it is. It's rough and rotten sometimes. It's cold and it's hard, like a garbage can."

"And the cats from the nice warm houses come out and want to pick at the garbage cans too," added Rita. "They don't have to. They do it because they're bastards, or because they don't have any sense, or they don't know why. But they keep coming out and eating in the pails, and when they go home they get cleaned and fed, and make believe they don't eat out of garbage cans. They never had to feel the cold. They don't know what it's like; they just do it for a lark, . . . and they don't even know how cold it is when they get there, 'cause they can always go back. It's different when there's no place to go back to—tougher."

"I hope the cat in the pail downstairs will be lucky and find some good food for a change today. That makes it a little easier sometimes. When he finds it he won't worry about it, or hoard it. He won't worry about anything until it's all gone. That's what's good about animals. They find something, they enjoy it, and that's it. Like we found each other, and it was warm and tender for a while, and it helps you to forget the rotten times. Soon the real smart, normal people in those warm houses will start going to work and chase all the cats out of the cans as they go. They don't want to feel that anybody can use or enjoy something they can't—even garbage. They chase the cat because he's not working or something. They don't know why they chase him. They just chase him 'cause they're not cats and so what's the difference? They don't feel it."

"People are the most vicious, brutal things alive. An animal wouldn't bother anything unless he was hungry or frightened. People are jealous, envious, sneaky, rotten, treacherous . . ." She cut herself off disgustedly.

"It was real nice here in our garbage can, baby." Tom squeezed Rita to himself more tightly, desperately.

"Too bad it ended so soon," Rita added sadly. "But that's the way it goes. It would anyway. We should only remember it was nice."

"I know what you mean, baby, and like you're one of the only people I know that knows what I mean. Oh, they know all right, but then they don't know—they don't want to know! They don't want the burden of thinking about it. It's easier to go along without thinking. But underneath they really know." He became silent, staring at the ceiling.

"I wish this would never change, . . . that we could always be warm and happy. I guess because I know how cold it can be."

"Maybe that's why the cats with warm houses don't want to think, to know," Rita murmured. "They're afraid of the garbage can, and the cold—afraid they'll be in it. So they make believe it doesn't exist, as if that will make it disappear."

"Yeah. I'd like to be warm and happy too, . . . we, . . . you and me, . . . me and somebody. But it's better this way. Better to be happy once in a while, better to think about having been happy once, than to curse and be miserable 'cause you can't be happy all the time. Lots of those cats are unhappy living in a warm garbage can. They're unhappy, but too afraid to move. They'd rather be dead, warm and safe, than live by taking a chance."

"They're going to die anyway, . . ." Rita commented indifferently.

"Yeah. And they're getting fat and lazy, forgetting how to run. If somebody ever chases them, they die like a miserable pig. A cat's not a cat if he doesn't know how to run. Those house cats are just throw-pillows, not cats. You've got to taste life and remember the important things. The rest doesn't matter." He looked at his watch and turned to Rita. "I gotta get going. You can stay until later if you want to. Just shut the door behind you—if you want."

"Okay. I don't have to be to work until eleven thirty." She smiled, a deep sadness in her dark eyes.

Tom stood and began to button his shirt.

"I guess we'll just keep jumping from pail to pail, . . ." he added.

"I guess so, cat. And all my life, even when I die, I'll remember all the good things, and I'll remember you, and this, and I'll be happy again because I'll know I didn't waste it. I touched life."

"Don't talk about dying. There's not a cat alive more alive than you." Tom tousled her hair playfully, pushing her back on the bed.

She watched Tom finish dressing. As he put on his tie, he walked to the window and looked down into the street.

Below, a janitor in sooty clothes leaned on his broom, interrupting his sweeping to allow some people to pass on their way to the subway. The lids of the garbage cans had all been replaced. The janitor started to sweep again, his broom scratching the sidewalk.

"Well, the garbage can is covered, and the long hungry coldness begins again." Tom walked back from the window, slipping his jacket on.

"But he'll remember and it won't be so bad."

"No, . . . it won't be so bad." He bent down and kissed her forehead. "I'll see you soon, okay?"

"Sure, maybe I'll see you tonight," Rita said perfunctorily, not sure that she would.

"No, I have to leave tonight, go home. Somebody in my family is getting married, so we'll all get together and say, "Isn't it a shame we only get together at weddings and funerals." He smiled.

"Be cool then." Rita lay back on the pillow. She was sad. The warmth was really over, and she was alone again. She pulled the covers tightly about herself.

"So long, baby." Tom opened the door. "Listen, be sure to shut this tight will you?"

"Sure."

Rita heard Tom's footsteps follow one after the other down the steps. She felt colder and lonelier with each step. She pulled the covers up over her head and cuddled tightly against the pillow.

11

THE FLAMES ENCASED BY THE FRONT WINDOW of the hamburger shop licked spectacularly through open grillwork at the oozing raw meat patties. Smoke swirled and funneled up into a bright copper flue hanging imposingly, open-mouthed over the grill. Droplets of moisture rolled paths through the steam which fogged the inside of the plate window. From outside, occasional human shadows filtered through the steam; anonymous eyes watched the leaping flames, the cooking meat, studied the menu taped to the window, then passed on to be engulfed in the all-encompassing light beyond.

Work was as usual for Rita this day, save that she was a bit tired. She sat at a back table sipping coffee and gazing absently at the people in the shop. Her customers, already served, sat upon the low, revolving stools of the counter and at the tables, eating and talking. Two girls, obviously from Uptown, unconsciously munched hamburgers as they giddily and voraciously observed and absorbed the sights and people about them. Boxes of new-bought clothing from one of the Village shops were propped against the legs of their chairs.

Unwont to move, her head supported on her palms, her elbows on the table, Rita turned her thoughts within herself, unhurriedly contemplating her work. Work began and ended and what was accomplished? Serving a plate of food, removing an empty plate, washing the plate, out again, in again, day after day. It seemed so useless, redundant, futile, working to maintain life, maintaining life to work, ad finitum. Rita's work, however, provided the funds necessary for Rita's acting class; it had a purpose, a reason, beside itself, for being.

Rita glanced toward the grill. The colored chef in his high, white, floppy hat, spatula in hand, watched his edible creations simmer. He was fat and jolly, constantly flashing a gold tooth in the center of his mouth. Chef possessed the enviable capacity for enjoying whatever he did, unworried and unconcerned about the revolutions of the universe, or the revolutions of anything in that universe, save, for the moment, the revolutions of meat patties on the grill before him. Rita thought of the millions of workers like Chef who had no ambition, no aim, no goal. Why bother to live? Why bother to work, then rest, then rise to work again, if nothing is accomplished except the sustenance of life, if there is no cognizance of one's personal existence save for the numbness of hunger and tiredness? Ambition springs from thought, and the unambitious, the thoughtless, the plodders merely exist, are not people, and a machine could replace them with less erring efficiency. The plodders only prolong the wait for inevitable death. And when the waters of life close over their grave, they shall be forgotten, and it shall be as if they had never existed. And what shall it have mattered if they never had? Life was a rotten trick, Rita thought. Work and eat and sleep and push plates, and wash them, and go to the movies, and go home and go to work and eat and sleep and nothing and more nothing. It was horrible!

It was horrible, however, only for the plodders with no ideas, no semblance of ambition, who, without their desire were born into a strange world of which they knew nothing, in which they were never afforded a chance to find out anything. Rita felt sorry for them because they were nothing, because they could be no more than nothing. How sad and lonely the plodders must be, those who mope along, waiting, wondering. How they must long for death and, when they wake each morning still alive, feel the dread of another day of life upon them.

That's why people feel so badly when they get up in the morning to face troubles; they're disappointed they didn't die.

Beauty alone, Rita thought, in its singular tabernacle within the soul of each man makes the waiting bearable, pleasant, happy. Beauty is the enjoyment of the present. It must come in this moment being lived, however; it can not be in the future. In this moment, there must be the enjoyment of this moment, not the worry about tomorrow. For nothing exists but the present moment blended with past moments by man's intellect.

And yet, Rita thought, all things lose their beauty because they are material, because they do change, must change. The most unchanging beauty is the ultimate beauty, the ultimate happiness. Only God is unchanging. God is true beauty and all beauty is true God, and nothing else matters, and who cares about anything but God all the time?

"Hey, Rita," a patron called impatiently as he sat at one of the tables toward the front of the shop. "Brew me a cup of tea, will you?"

Rita shook off the wraps of thought and found herself sitting with a cup of cold coffee.

"Right with you," she called. She stood and walked behind the counter.

A cold gust of air cut across the room as the door opened. The blast of air chilled Rita. She glanced up to see who was entering. Jeannie and Laura smiled toward Rita, then sat at the counter near the front door. Rita brewed tea and walked toward her customer's table. The two Uptown girls, regarding Laura and Jeannie in their Village casualness as curiosities, nudged each other giddily. Rita noticed this, but dismissed it as she made her way to the front.

"Here you go." She marked the customer's check and turned and sat on the stool next to Laura.

"Where did *you* go last night?" Jeannie inquired, a knowing inflection in her voice.

"I went out," Rita replied factually. "How come you didn't go to work today?"

"I called up and told them I was a little ill. I was too tired to go in this morning," Jeannie replied equally matter-of-factly.

"How's that? Stay out late last night?"

"No. Just felt tired this morning."

"I missed you last night. It was cold alone in that bed," Laura remarked, chuckling unhumorously.

"I'm sorry I wasn't there to keep it warmer for you. You know how it goes though. How come you're not out on that job you were supposed to start?"

"Oh . . ." Laura's eyes swept past Rita and focused on the counter. "I didn't think I'd like the place." She tried to be unconcerned. "I didn't feel like going, that's all."

"Okay, baby. It's your job. You girls want something to eat?"

"I'll have a burger and a coke," said Jeannie. "Make sure it's cooked well. I don't want to get sick."

Rita nodded then looked to Laura.

"I'll have the same thing—medium—and a lemon in the coke."

"Two burgers! One medium! One well!" Rita called to the cook. "I'll be with you in a second," Rita said to the girls. She walked to the back to draw the cokes.

"That's absolutely the most ridiculous thing I've ever heard. Art?" scoffed one customer sitting at the counter to another customer sitting next to him. The first fellow was colored, with a beard. His friend was white. Rita hesitated to listen, wiping the counter in front of them as an excuse to hesitate.

"That whole damn school of abstraction and non-objectivism is boring nonsense," continued the colored fellow. "Take my painting for instance. I put into it what I see, how I see it. I give it a life of its own, apart from and yet concurrent with reality. That's what art is, the interpretation of life by an artist. And art, I don't care which art we're dealing with, it's merely the interpretation of life by the artist, capturing life."

"So then, actually, you agree with the abstractionist so long as what he paints and his art is an, or rather, is *his* interpretation of life?"

"*If* his painting is an interpretation of life, yes. Art doesn't necessarily follow exactly and minutely the renderings of nature or life. It has to be a subjective interpretation, and is worth something only if the artist is able to convey his meaning—an inner meaning, the meaning that *he* gets out of life—to the audience. It can be fire, thunder, horror, or gaiety, . . . but always life."

"So then there's nothing wrong with the abstractionist and his interpretation of life?" baited the white fellow, upholding his point.

"Certainly not. But, like I said before, his interpretation must be really an interpretation of life. Some of these guys splatter paint on a canvas, and the more indistinguishable a canvas is, the more it's accepted. It's this God damn pseudosophisticated bunch, these phony bastards who walk around with a copy of *The New Yorker* under their arm, just for the sake of carrying *The New Yorker*. They figure this makes them. They're the ones who come to the Village and feel they're not really tourists 'cause they're really with it—they just don't have to prove it by wearing dirty clothes. Anyway, not to get carried away— this phony audience feels it's *the thing* not to understand a painting. So anyone who can paint anything that is utterly un-understandable is great. You see, these creeps don't understand art, so they cover it up by letting people think they follow a new school. It's like everything else. These psuedo-sophist creeps set their own limited standards within their own limited ability or desire—after all, *who can really say what's right and what's wrong,*" the colored artist mimicked viciously. "And when you set your own standards, it's very easy to achieve what you say you want to accomplish. Either that, or like 'Big Brother' in *1984* you change your standards to fit what you attain. But the standards of nature which you have to interpret in art have been pretty well set for quite some years. Man and the flaura and fauna don't change."

"But in the new schools of abstraction, those paintings are the author's interpretation of life, and, as such, are art, and are perfectly valid," the white fellow added earnestly. "Some of these guys put a lot of thought into their work and actually interpret life in their canvas. Just because you don't understand it, doesn't mean it's not good or not art."

"That's right. But, wait a minute. If interpretation of life and con- veyance of that interpretation is art, then the master artist is the guy who can create such a real, vivid, and universal meaning in his work— such feeling—that it reaches all people, everyone, everywhere, and means the same thing all the time to everyone. No, . . . wait a minute. Not the same thing all the time to everyone. I mean, that to different generations, the painting still retains a deep inner meaning, even if that meaning is altered by the alterations in life itself. This is mastery of an art form."

"All right, I guess so. But what the hell does that have to do with what we're talking about?"

"A lot. That stuff they're putting, or throwing, or scratching on canvas, is not necessarily art, nor is it necessarily an interpretation of life. It doesn't even mean anything to anybody now, in the era of its creation."

"Two burgers ready here," intoned the cook from the front of the shop. His call interrupted Rita's wrapt attention to the conversation.

"Okay," Rita called in answer. "Would you fellows hold it for a second while I deliver these burgers?"

"Sure thing," the white fellow chuckled. "Hurry up."

Rita drew two cokes from the machine, and rushed to the front of the store. She put the cokes and hamburgers down in front of Jeannie and Laura, looked at the rest of her customers—they were content—then hurried to the back again.

"Go!" she said, resuming her elbows-on-the-counter position.

"Where was I?" the Negro asked.

"You said that the abstract isn't necessarily interpreting life, nor is it even conveying art."

"Right. Okay. Now, many of these guys, feeling that they want to paint and not wanting to be conventional or anything as bourgeoise as that, you know, really rebelling and all that—perhaps because they can't paint a straight stroke—start throwing crap on a canvas, or a piece of burlap, or whatever. What are they interpreting? They put a piece of red tape and blue cord on white paper, and they call it *Composition 16*. They don't even pretend to give it a name. It's just something, a thing. One thing it's certainly not, is art. But that doesn't matter, 'cause people don't buy it for its feeling, but because it matches their drapes. Bums!" Anger flashed in the artist. "There's my point. Most of the guys I've come across just like to make designs. That's fine, but it's not art. And as nice as some of this stuff may look, it's not art. And don't come and say it's a new school. It may be, but not a new school of art."

"I wouldn't say that about all of it," injected Rita.

"Neither would I," agreed the colored fellow. "I said it wasn't necessarily so. You know, like the song, 'It ain't necessarily so,'" he sang a little off key. "But it happens all too often. I just like to keep the nonsense on a nice steady, low pitch, you know? And I'll give you another clue. A lot of these non-art artists sell this stuff at good prices, because they have a non-art audience who want to be chic, but don't know what the hell they're doing. You know, like they're scratching each other's back. One paints crap, the other hangs their crap paintings, and they put guys like me down cause I do square, arty stuff, you know, old-fashioned. People don't admire anything that toes the line today. They don't like to toe the line, and they don't want things around that remind them how far off they are. Not like my painting is great, but I'm trying," he said playfully.

Rita glanced at the two girls from Uptown sitting next to the colored artist. They had been listening to the conversation. They looked at each other, their mouths rippling into mocking smirks, nudging each other, their eyes looking up at the ceiling. They noticed Rita looking at them, and both of them turned their heads to the front as if they were glancing out the front window, their heads shaking with laughter.

The artist noticed Rita's glance and turned and looked at them. He turned back to his friend and Rita with a dismissing, deprecating shrug.

"Anyway . . . I'm with you," said Rita. "But what the hell . . . as long as you enjoy your art."

"Yeah, but you can't eat unsold paintings. Sometimes you got to give in just to eat," he said, harshly realistic.

Rita was struck hard by the leaden, compromising remark. She studied his face.

"But don't worry, baby. I'm with you too," the colored fellow added enthusiastically. "I'm just kidding."

Rita smiled.

"You've proven your point for today," the white fellow added, also smiling. "I can't argue with you."

"Some of these guys are supposed to be great because they started a new school of this or that. So what? Who the hell knows what they've said on their canvas? But they're accepted because some other people say terrific things about something they don't understand either, only they don't want to show their dumbness," concluded the Negro.

"Hey Rita," called a customer who had just come in and sat down. "How about a burger?"

"Just a minute. Be right with you." Rita pushed away from the counter on which she had been leaning. "One burger," she called to the cook. "How do you want that?"

"Rare."

He was a heavy man of about fifty years. He dressed the way most most of the people in the Village dress—casual shoes, a sweater, and heavy wool pants. On him, they looked out of place and sloppy. His clothes looked baggy and hanging and were wrinkled and without a crease. Thoughts of the futility of life and about fat people who spend much time eating flashed through Rita's mind. The more time occupied with trivia, the less time there was to think about the life passing by. If one was occupied enough, one could almost forget that life was being wasted.

Eating—sitting down in one place for an hour, three or four times a day, almost one day a week—at least eating took care of one day a week, and a person had only six other days to tolerate.

"Burger ready."

Rita gave the burger to the customer. "Anything to drink with that?"

"Coffee," the man said, chomping a huge bite out of the burger. He ate in big, smashing chews, his mouth agape, so one could see the ground food inside his mouth. Rita shuddered in disgust and walked away. She put a mug of coffee in front of him without looking at him and walked to where Laura and Jeannie were sitting.

"What were you doing back there?" Laura asked.

"Oh, just a couple of fellows talking about art."

"What're we doing tonight?" Jeannie asked.

"I don't know. What's happening?"

"Nothing."

"As usual."

"Maybe we can scare up a party or something," Jeannie suggested. "We gotta find something."

"That'd be a cool idea. Who do we know that wants to have a party at their place?"

"Why don't we have one at our place," suggested Laura. "We haven't had one in a long time."

Rita and Jeannie looked at each other inquisitively.

"It's all right with me," Rita said shrugging.

"Me too."

"Well, crazy. We'll have a little blowout at our place. Wait a minute," Rita said painfully, remembering something. "What are we going to drink? We only have a little vodka left."

"We *had* a little vodka left."

"So, . . . everybody brings a little to drink, and we supply the place," Laura suggested, smiling hesitantly.

"Okay. If it's okay with them, it's okay with me."

"Crazy. You two go home and put the breakables away. I'll be there as soon as I finish here." They stood. Rita winked at them meaningfully.

"Okay. See you later," Jeannie said casually. She and Laura 'opened the door and left. Not having a bill, they didn't pay for the food, and this made living a little easier.

12

"SAY, MAN, WHAT'S HAPPENING?" Frankie the Mexican asked Josh Minot when they met on Fourth Street. His inflection denoted true curiosity rather than casual greeting.

"I don't know, man. I think there's a blast coming off over at Jeannie and Laura's place."

"Crazy. You going?"

"I don't know, man," Josh regretted. "Like you gotta bring some juice 'cause they haven't much over there, and like I don't have much loot."

"So let's swing over anyway; we'll split some beer. *I'm* no John D. either, you know."

"Crazy. That's a cool idea." Josh took some change from his pocket. "Here's mine. You buy the beer. I'll meet you in front of the place in about fifteen. I have a little errand first."

"Okay, man." Frankie smiled wryly. "What's her name?" Josh returned a sly smile, then began to walk toward the Avenue of the Americas.

"Hey, what's the address?"

"Eighty-seven Christopher," Josh called, twisting back. He turned forward again and walked hurriedly away.

Frankie turned toward Sheridan Square and the delicatessen. Just then, Jim Panar stepped off the stoop leading up to Pandora's Box. He turned toward Frankie.

"Say, man, what's happening?"

"Nothing much. There's something going on over at eighty-seven Christopher if you want to go."

"Eighty-seven Christopher? Whose place is that?"

"Laura's."

Jim's forehead furrowed.

"You know Laura. Little skinny girl, always wearing pants and a boy's jacket."

Jim shut his eyes, searching his memory for the girl that fit the description. He shook his head, unable to place her.

"You know Laura, man," Frankie insisted. "We were talking to her one night at the art show on Sixth Avenue. Remember, she was with two other girls. She has short hair, . . . remember? You said she looked like the little Dutch Boy."

"Yeah, yeah, . . . now I remember," Jim exclaimed, shaking a finger in the air. "Over at her pad, man?"

"Yeah. Only thing is, you got to bring some drinking water over. You know?" Frankie ended abruptly, letting the statement speak for itself.

"Yeah, but like I'm a little low on scratch."

"Listen, man, do what I'm doing. Like split a pack of beer with somebody."

"That's pretty cool. How about I come in with you?"

"You better find somebody else. Josh is in on this six-pack already with me, and like we can't spread this brew out too thin. Man, like we can hardly get high unless we drink a gallon of it anyway. No sense springing for loot if we're not even going to get a bit high." Frankie laughed.

"I dig, man. That's okay. I'll find somebody and bring him, or her, I hope, over. Like I'll see you there. Eighty-seven Christopher, hanh?"

"Right. Crazy. See you later." Frankie continued toward the delicatessen.

Each of them walked in a different direction. As they passed people they knew, according to how friendly they were with that person, they'd mention the party and the address. When the time for the party arrived, more than thirty people were spreading news of a party among the wandering searchers of the Village streets.

"Come on in," exploded from the front room, carrying across the span of the entire apartment.

Two fellows stood hesitantly in the doorway. A blast of music sailed out to them on air fragrant with smoke and beer and women's perfume. The entire panorama before them was alive—people were everywhere, all different people, jam-packed, wearing all colors of clothing, standing, sitting, drinking, talking, laughing—and behind all this was the hollow pounding of music.

"Come on in!" exploded more insistently.

The two stepped in, looking about warily. They were not dressed in the fashion of the Village, but in the fashion of the outside; they were tourists. Their clothing was the everyday Uptown styles seen in every store in the Uptown world, worn because they were accepted everywhere and no decisions or excuses had to be made for them—living made easy, made to order. The villagers run fast from this uniformity, showing in visible reality, by clinging to another, an off beat, conformity, their external distinctness, and, by inference, the internal.

The two fellows walked self-consciously through the mass of people in the middle room.

One of the female guests was squatting, digging in the refrigerator. She stood erect, hungrily sucking a whole tomato.

The two tourists stepped over the legs of a male guest who lay full length on the floor, smoking a cigarette. They made their way toward a vacant space in a corner of the front room. One of them carried a brown paper bag. As he placed it atop a low bookcase, beer cans clunked together.

Music blared from the phonograph next to the bookcase, filling the room with a rhythmic background din, accenting the atmosphere. The tourists looked about unfamiliarly at the people in the apartment.

One girl was dressed in a red dress, long black stockings, and black high heels. Her hair was black and long, outlining a thin drab face. She looked like a Charles Addam's character.

The two tourists had come from Louis', having learned of the party from a conversation overheard at the bar, deciding to attend though they knew no one, wanting to sample a mad Village party. They were party crashers, but at this party they were, to their surprise, most welcome.

As at many Village parties, whoever arrived was welcome; the more who arrived, the better the chances of a good party. It is the unknown and ever-different aspect of Village life, compared to the normal, routine, everyday sameness and drabness of life Uptown which makes the Village alive and exciting and alluring to the Villagers. People at the party may not even know whose party they're at, but they and their potential exuberance are welcome indeed.

The tourist with the bag uncovered a six-pack of beer, punctured two cans, handed one to his partner, and started to drink. They both leaned against the wall, their eyes absorbing the party.

The Villagers were spread all over the apartment. Some were drunk and tottering; others just sat quietly, others were loud, walking around, talking aimlessly and drinking. The room in which the two tourists were standing was jammed with people. Two men and a girl sat on the couch. One of the men was propped against the back of the couch, motionless, as if in a stupor. He stared straight ahead, immobile, his hands balancing a can of beer on his leg. Next to him sat a short, red-haired artist, frantically, tongue-bitingly drawing the face of the girl seated next to him. The girl had short black hair, and wore Bermuda shorts, a pair of dirty, beat-up tennis sneakers, and a sweater. It was Jeannie, in clothes that were a vestige of her college days.

Directly opposite the two tourists, a colored fellow slouched, abandoned to relaxation in his chair, his eyes closed, one hand clamped around a can of beer, a lit cigarette smoking between the fingers of his other hand.

On the floor, between the colored fellow's chair and the tourists, a homely blonde girl, in slacks, and a Negro fellow sat leaning against the wall, their legs bent in front of them, forming a tunnel, under which stood two cans of beer. The fellow offered the girl a cigarette. They lit up together and just sat, their backs against the wall, their heads thrown back in utter detachment from the rest of the party, puffing on their cigarettes occasionally, slowly detaching themselves from the rest of the world.

A shoeless girl draped in an orange cotton dress with a blue sash bound about her waist danced wildly in the center of the crowd with a white fellow wearing jeans and a faded green T-shirt. She kicked her leg and almost kicked the head of the colored guy sitting on the floor.

A fellow from the middle room staggered through the crowd and opened the window, leaning out to look at Christopher Street. He yelled drunkenly at some people walking in the street. He laughed, then threw an empty can out the window.

A tall colored fellow walked from the rear bedroom into the middle room. He was very dark, and very tall, and very thin. He had a supple, flexible, smooth dancer's body, except he bounced when he walked, as if he had springs in his heels. He wore slim clothes and dark glasses. He opened the refrigerator, bending from the waist, looking into the storage compartment. He stood erect, slamming the refrigerator door angrily, forlornly, looking around the room for some beer. He snatched a paper bag on the tub cover, but it was merely puffed up by things long past rather than things now present. His hands anticipated resistance, and the empty bag flew up easily, quickly in his hands. Its unexpected emptiness caused him to grimace, and he smashed the bag into a round ball and flung it under the sink. Several beer cans stood on the tub, a triangular black mark of opening on their tops. He started to shake them. His eyes widened with delighted discovery as he felt the weight of one can. He put it to his lips, tilting his head to drink, and happily walked back to the bedroom.

The girl who had been sucking the tomato opened the refrigerator again, searching around. She came up munching a slice of white bread.

In the back bedroom, there were six people. Besides the tall Negro fellow, there were two couples lying on the bed talking with Rita, who was standing. Josh Minot was lying next to a white girl he had just met. The other girl, also white, was lying next to a white fellow. The girls were from the Bronx and came to the Village almost every night. In their own neighborhood, they were considered real wild, racy chicks because of their Village association. The white fellow was a student at New York University.

A very skinny, gaunt fellow, dressed in unmatching pants and jacket, entered the bedroom. He was about six feet in height, and his hands hung to a point just above his knees. He looked cadaverous, and his tattered clothes made him resemble a scarecrow. His long thin fingers were clamped around a beer can like a claw. His face was smeared with disdainful acceptance of the party, as he viewed it from beneath half-closed eyelids. He was in another world. His lips moved in silent self-discussion. His thin, bony face surveyed the bedroom, his square jawbone protruding forward. He frowned, turned about, and left the bedroom, returning to the middle room. Rita followed him out and stood in the middle room looking around at her party.

On the roof, almost but not quite part of the party, sat Laura. She had left the party and climbed to the roof, feeling crowded and nervous, wanting fresh air and quiet. Now, bundled in a coat and sweater, a scarf around her head, she listened to the distant, removed voices of the people below. It was odd and fun. The voices and the things overheard were so out of place on the roof. They were parts played in a movie; they were unrealities, absurd unrealities that lost their meaning as they floated up to the skies. She was a spy, and she could see and hear them, but they could not see her. She leaned over the edge of the roof and saw the back of a man's head as he sat on the floor, leaning against the wall, just under the windowsill. She saw a man's legs walk past the window, and she saw feet pointed at the figure sitting under the window. The feet moved and another person sat down. Laura recognized the close-cropped, curly head of Frankie the Mexican. He had a funny-shaped head, she thought. It was sort of bony and bumpy in the back.

Jeannie was still posing for the red-haired artist. The gaunt scarecrow who had poked his head into the bedroom now sat next to the redhead and, with a pen dispensing red ink, drew on a piece of paper. The red-headed artist thrust his hand into his pocket. He withdrew a fresh drawing brush. He dunked his used brush in a glass of water—the ink turned the water black—shook the surplus water off the bristles, stuck it in his mouth, and wrung it out through tightly held lips as if he were pulling a shirt through a squeeze dryer. He placed the cleaned brush in his pocket, wiped his hand on the couch, and started to draw with the new brush.

Rita, walked into the front room and stood by the side of the phonograph, next to the window, near the two tourists. She glanced over and noticed them staring at her.

"Hi," she said, smiling. "You just get here?"

"Yeah," replied the taller of the two, his insides jumping nervously with excitement. They were at a party in the Village, and the excitement of anticipated madness was overtaking them. The guys on the block where they hung out would die with envy when they told them; they'd tell them how brave they were and what a screwy bunch of jerks were at the party—how some goof was drawing a picture of some broad—she wasn't bad either—and another guy that looked like he hadn't eaten in years was drawing, and all the faggots, and the niggers. They envisioned each girl as a nymphomaniac, and each of the guys seemed a weird combination of queer, artist, and lover. Each of the movements of the Villagers were altered and vivified and intensified in the tourists' imaginations.

"I've never seen you two before," Rita remarked with friendly curiosity. "You live around here?" *They could,* she thought, *even if they dressed as they do. They might be new.*

"Yeah, . . . yeah, . . . we live over on the East Side though." The tall, skinny one lied, smirking naughtily, pleased with himself for his quick thinking. His eyes snapped down hungrily to Rita's bust and then, feeling conspicuous, began to search the floor innocently. He pretended something was wrong with his shoe. He bent his knee, scratched his foot, and glanced self-consciously at Rita again.

"Oh? Over by Cooper Union?"

"Yeah," replied the other fellow, a pleading look on his dark, diffident face, "over by Cooper Union. Nice party you've got here." He pointed his beer can at the room and the people. He was smiling, wanting Rita to like him.

"Yeah, . . . it's not bad," she said, "but we don't have enough to drink. We're starting to run out."

The skinny fellow's eyes darted quickly to the side, enveloping the package of beer protectively. His eyebrows grouped thoughtfully.

"Here, . . . have one of our beers." He offered hesitantly, realizing he and his friend had only three each.

The skinny fellow was tall, with an ostrich-like appearance. Perhaps it was the way he acted that really caused him to resemble an ostrich. He was nervous, quick moving, like the ostrich—an unsure person who didn't do anything daring on his own, acting only when forced to, or when it was safe. His furtive, nervous glances and the obscene way he laughed indicated he not only interpreted the Village as being a licentious place; all life was like that for him. He was sure sordidness and evil and hot times existed everywhere and he was looking for them. He gave the impression of dirtiness, of sneakiness. He was the kind of guy who thinks all women are burlesque queens, or just the same as burlesque queens, only not in show business. He'll probably expect his wife to bump and grind for him on his wedding night, before they get down to do the *dirty* deed. Sometimes you feel sorry for people like that because they're weak and unsure, but sometimes you hate them because they're sneaky and dirty.

"Thanks." Rita smiled as she took the beer.

The skinny fellow looked at his buddy with a signal of success. He smiled a thrilled little wince of a smile. The second fellow winked boldly to show Skinny he was with him.

"Here, I'll open it for you," the dark fellow offered. He took a can opener and pulled the end up until the point punctured the can and a little burst of air came out. He made another hole on the other side.

"Thanks," said Rita. "I'll tell you what. The guys have been drinking a new drink tonight. It makes the beer last longer. Wait a minute."

The two watched Rita walk to the middle room, reach under the sink and walk back with a bottle of coke.

"What are you going to do with the coke?" asked Skinny.

"Mix it half and half with the beer."

He grimaced. "What kind of a crazy drink is that?"

"What's crazy? It makes the beer last longer. Besides, three of these and you don't care what's happening. You can drink anything." She laughed hilariously.

The two guys laughed too. Skinny's laugh stopped short. He

was all for Rita not knowing what was happening. He winked at his friend.

Rita snared three paper cups from the top of the bookcase. The dark fellow mixed the beer and coke, pouring both simultaneously.

The two fellows drank the first sip warily.

"Hey, this is good," exclaimed Skinny.

"Sure. Just 'cause you never tried it before doesn't mean it can't be." She drank more of her drink.

"This your place?" the dark fellow inquired.

"Yes." Rita sipped from the cup. She nodded, not really for any reason save that she was a little drunk.

"Nice place." The dark fellow nodded too, looking around. He nodded his head to assure her of his good thoughts of her home. He was very serious and sincere. His movements were quick, and he watched people after he did something, to see if they noticed him, to see if they would mock him. It made one nervous to watch his nervousness.

A howl burst from the bedroom. The tall colored fellow who had been looking for beer earlier, came laughing, running, and jumping out of the bedroom, stopping at the end of a jump in the center of the middle room.

"Good grief," he shouted laughingly to the whole apartment. "Who is that mother fucker in there." He indicated the bedroom over his shoulder. A deep-throated laugh gripped his body, doubling him over. Many people ran to the door of the bedroom. Inside, the red-headed artist who had been drawing Jeannie was talking to the two couples lying on the bed as he drew one of the girls.

"Certainly," he continued to jabber rapidly, not noticing the crowd at the door. "The most important thing is to bring the balance between the smooth fine lines and the thick hard lines that you can find if you look very carefully at my drawings. See . . . that's the most important thing. It gives a very special, weird effect. And yet, underneath, the meaning, the warmth, . . . the depth comes through." He was talking, or rather chattering almost insanely, to no one in particular about nothing intelligible. The speed with which he spoke varied with the rate at which he drew, according to the stroke that he was putting on the paper. He slowed when he came to a difficult line, and when he was drawing quickly, easily, his voice became a chattering, rapid drone. The gaunt bedraggled scarecrow sauntered through the crowd and watched for a moment, a pouting frown on his face.

"Frank, . . . give me the green pen. This one has no more ink," the scarecrow said gravely to the red head. "Besides I think I need a little green in my drawing." In his hand was the drawing he had been working on. It was a mass of red lines—nothing more—intertwining, crossing, spiraling, zigzagging aimlessly across the paper.

Frank stopped drawing and slid his hand into the inside pocket of his jacket. He pulled out a box of pens, but the one he wanted wasn't there. He put his hand into the outside breast pocket and pulled out two brushes and a Japanese bamboo pen. He opened the pen, fitted the top on the back of the pen body, and jabbed a couple of lines on the side of the page on which he was working.

"Here. What's the matter with the other pen?"

"I don't know," the scarecrow said gravely, as if pens were beneath him and he was loathe to speak of them. As he spoke, his eyes were either closed or rose to the ceiling. He spoke with the deep-throatedness of a man deciding the fate of the world.

The redhead looked to his model and began to draw again. The tall colored fellow who had first run out of the room came back and stood next to the redhead. He was still laughing, watching.

"What was that you said about the thin lines, man," the Negro asked laughingly, looking at the crowd.

"I was saying that the thin lines have to blend . . ." The redhead began to drone again aimlessly.

Many of the people who had rushed to see the attraction rejoined the rest of the party which hadn't bothered answering the colored fellow's call.

Jeannie sat on the floor in the front room, next to a dark-haired white fellow who was sitting on the edge of his chair, bending toward her, talking. He put his arms out and caressed her head. She put her head against the side of his leg while he stroked her hair.

"Who's that?" the skinny tourist asked Rita. He was interested in what was happening, and what he thought was going to happen, considering the proximity of Jeannie and the fellow on the chair. Skinny's eyes gleamed evilly and he wrinkled his nose. He was almost giggling with delight.

"A friend of Jeannie's," Rita answered phlegmatically. "What's your names?"

"Paul . . . Paul Macklin," said the skinny fellow slowly, making it up as he pronounced it. This is Johnny Rivers."

The dark tourist looked at her pleadingly again.

"Hello," said Rita by way of greeting, the way people always greet someone they've spoken with for a long time while not actually knowing their name. Men often shake hands at this point, even though they may have been speaking together for hours.

One of the male guests returned to the apartment from the outside hall. He had been to the toilet in the hall. He stood in the doorway, his hands on his hips, his eyes half closed from alcohol, his bottom jaw jutting out involuntarily. His lips pursed fleshily together in surveyance. He just stood, swaying slightly, staring angrily at Jeannie and the guy stroking her head. He stomped over to a chair and pulled his coat from the back of it. Someone sitting on the chair was unwittingly sitting on the sleeve. The drunk swung his arms, yanking the coat, and the sleeve was pulled from under the rear end of the scarecrow artist.

"I beg your pardon," complained the scarecrow indignantly, looking up with surprise. He stared for a moment, then eased back into the chair, gazing at the opposite wall, his eyes resuming their half-closed position.

The drunk put his coat on and made his way toward the door. Jeannie stood and ran over to him.

"Where you going, honey?" She grabbed his arm.

"I'm going, that's all. What the hell is this? I stand around and watch some guy pawing you." His head jiggled involuntarily.

"Oh, come on, silly. I was just sitting talking."

"Well, go ahead back and talk."

"Don't go yet," Jeannie pleaded. "Stay!"

She grasped his arm and turned him around toward the party again. They walked to the couch and sat down together. Jeannie still held his arm and now she leaned her head against his shoulder.

Frankie and Jim Panar were still sitting on the floor, drinking beer under the window in the front room.

"What the hell is that chick doing?" Frankie asked, referring to Jeannie.

" I don't know. Looks to me like she's playing games."

"Yeah, lots of them." The two men sat and drank, dispassionately watching Jeannie leaning on the shoulder of the drunk.

The tall Negro from the bedroom now wandered into the front room and looked around. He saw Jeannie and signalled to her with a jerk of his head. The drunk on whose shoulder she was leaning was facing the other way so that he didn't see the colored fellow. Jeannie excused herself tactfully and walked into the middle room. The colored fellow pulled Jeannie aside and started talking. The fellow who had been stroking Jeannie's hair when she sat on the floor next to his chair now stood up angrily.

"God damn bullshit, . . . that's what," he exclaimed loudly, looking around the room for something. He fell back into his seat. He was still looking around the room from his seated position when Jeannie, hearing his loud complaint, rushed over to him.

"What's the matter, baby?" she asked solicitously.

"Nothing. I'm just tired of your bullshit. Where's my coat?"

On the couch, Jeannie's other erstwhile lover just sat and watched the scene, completely detached by his drunkenness.

"Come on, . . . don't go," Jeannie urged the fellow in the chair.

"Shut up! Where's my coat?" He squinted around the room. He pulled himself to the edge of the chair to see better.

"Is this it?" Jeannie asked, picking up the sleeve of a coat hung on the back of the chair on which the fellow was sitting. She afforded him a glimpse of the sleeve, then dropped it and unconcernedly walked back to the couch.

"Yeah, . . . that's it . . . Gimme," he said as he pulled the coat angrily from around the back of the chair. He had trouble getting one of the sleeves over his arm. Finally, he thrust his arm desperately, angrily, through the armhole. The sleeve straightened out and his arm slid through.

"So long . . . I'll see you around," he called out generally as he swayingly made his way to the door. He banged against the tub on the way out, knocking a couple of glasses off the top. He stopped, looked poutingly at the fallen glasses for a moment, then waved his hands at them. The motion caused him to stagger backwards. He caught his balance and walked out the door.

Jeannie looked at Rita and shrugged uncaringly. Then she sat on the couch again and rested her head on the shoulder of her friend sitting there, having completely forgotten the colored fellow.

"I like these old apartments," exclaimed the scarecrow, standing limply in the center of the front room. He extended one hand toward the ceiling, clutching a can of beer with the other. "They've got something . . . These apartments they give you today, you pay a fortune for them, . . . and the ceilings . . ." He grimaced, bringing his hand down to a level just over his head. "No room . . ." He shook his head disgustedly, then walked to the tub and began shaking the abandoned beer cans, hoping for one with some fluid still inside. Now and again he would raise a can to his lips and let the few dregs of beer drip into his mouth. "Fine vintage, . . . fine vintage," he announced seriously. But the vintage in one can wasn't so fine; he spit ashes and cigarette butts out of his mouth.

"Can you just see that guy paying a fortune for a new apartment?" Frankie whispered to Jim.

"Yeah, . . . just about."

"What the hell?" Frankie exclaimed incredulously. "Jeannie's got a new one now."

Jeannie was now standing in the doorway between the front room and the middle room with a tall, blond, white fellow who had just wandered into the party.

"Who's the guy?" asked Jim.

"Don't know. Never saw him before."

Rita and skinny Paul were now sitting on the couch. Johnny, Paul's friend, was sitting on the floor a bit away from Frankie and Jim. He was just sitting, watching the others around him. He noticed Jim Panar looking at him and smiled weakly.

The red-headed artist and the scarecrow began packing their sketch pads and art supplies. They had pads, and racks, and rags, and inks, and were stuffing all of them into two plastic Pan-American Air-line overnight bags.

"See that red-headed guy?" Jim asked Frankie.

"You think I'm blind?"

"I saw him about two months ago, you know? It was early in the morning. I was down Washington Square Park and I see a guy sleeping in the fountain. It was empty, no water or anything. That's the guy who was sleeping there—right in the middle of the oval—on the cement. He used one of those bags of his for a pillow."

"I believe it. What'd'ya say we cut, man? There's no more juice."

"Oke, . . . this place is beginning to drag. Not enough chicks either. Where the hell's Laura been?"

"I think she split out of here about an hour ago with some cat. I don't know where the hell she is."

They stood and walked toward the door.

"So long, Rita," called Jim.

Rita turned from talking to Paul and said good-night to both of them. Paul flickered a wince of a smile.

Rita turned back to Paul.

"I don't get over here much. I should though. This is a crazy place," said Paul. He was completely thrilled by his own boldness and daring, the excitement of this adventure. He looked at his buddy and smiled, lifting his eyebrows.

"It's all right," replied Rita dryly. She was feeling a little reckless and high.

"You've got some crazy parties here, hanh?" His face wrinkled evilly.

"Yeah, . . . once in a while." Rita sipped at her drink. "There's always a party somewhere, . . . something anyway."

Paul watched Rita drink. His eyes were like hot coals burning through his head as he stared at Rita's Adam's apple bobbing with the drink inside her throat. His mouth twitched a little with excitement. He searched for a place to put his hands. He was conscious of his body; he looked at his feet, his hands. He put his hands under his knee joints. He reached into his shirt pocket and pulled out a single cigarette and lit it; he folded his arms, smiling. He liked to watch Rita drink, 'cause if she were drunk . . .

"I heard about them parties," he said with a leer, his eyes darting down to her bust and then over the smoothness of her skirt, pulled taut by the fullness of her thighs. He looked to her face again. "Heard they were kind of wild."

"Yeah. Got a cigarette?"

He took out his pack without taking his eyes from her and reached it toward her.

"Heard there was a lot of . . . fucking . . .?" He articulated the word with a special pleasure and relish. His eyes glistened, studying Rita as he thrilled with naughtiness.

"No more than anywhere else," Rita replied flatly. She gazed at Paul from under wrinkled brows as he lit her cigarette. There was a wrong note, a clinker, in the way he had said that.

Rita's outer unconcern heightened Paul's lustful excitement.

Rita was beginning to feel the tired letdown after a high soar. She thought that Paul ought to go home so she could go to bed. Most of the other people had already left.

Paul impulsively put his drink on the floor and slid his arm across Rita's stomach, jerking her roughly toward himself. She bolted with surprise, then twisted her shoulders and head away, wedging her arms desperately against his chest, holding herself away from him.

"C'mon, baby," he hissed through passion-gritted teeth. "Let's get out of here, . . . I'll show you a good time."

"Get . . . the hell . . . out of . . . here . . . you creepy bastard," she screamed, struggling, . . ."Go on . . . get out, you dope." She was no longer tired or high.

Paul, having begun, pulled her more firmly, more desperately. He wrenched her, trying to bear-hug her to break the lock of her elbow that was holding her away.

"Get out of here, you dirty bastard. Help! . . . You bastard!" Rita screamed frightenedly as she felt her body being forced, pressed, pulled, closer to Paul's hot, beery breath. He was puffing and snorting, his eyes satanically agleam.

The two fellows lying with the girls on the bed in the bedroom scrambled into the middle room. Their heads pivoted rapidly, looking for the source of the screams.

Johnny, the other tourist, had run into the middle room and now cowered in a corner, hoping the two fellows wouldn't turn around and see him.

Jeannie and two drunks were sitting on the floor of the middle room, looking puzzled, helplessly toward the front room.

Rita gurgled another scream. Paul was audibly straining and panting to get her closer to himself.

The two fellows ran into the front room. They saw Paul and pounced on him, grabbing him by the neck. Rita was struggling to pull away, but Paul held both her hands by the wrist. She twisted from him, and her watery, shining eyes appealed and pleaded with the two fellows. The college kid hauled Paul backwards off the couch by the shoulders while Josh loosened his hands from Rita's wrists. Paul was reaching a climax of ecstacy.

"Don't, . . . don't," he pleaded raspingly with the fellows as they dragged him off the couch. His eyes were sealed with lust.

The college kid propped Paul into a standing position. Josh swung his fist viciously into Paul's groin. Paul gasped convulsively for air and toppled to the floor.

Rita, crying and screaming, ran into the middle room. She fell to the floor, her head in Jeannie's lap. Jeannie and the two girls from the bedroom comforted her. Jeannie's two drunken friends watched helplessly.

Josh and the college kid lifted Paul bodily. He was doubled over, gasping for breath, trying desperately to pull some breath in over the pain that didn't allow him to move his lungs or stomach. He couldn't draw a breath. He only rattled a gasp. The two fellows carried him to the door which had been left open when Johnny ran out, and flung him to the floor of the hall. He lay there groaning and squirming.

A door at the end of the hall opened and a man's head stuck out. His hair stood awry where it had been disarranged by a pillow. He peered down the hall through sleep-laden eyes, trying to make out what was happening. He saw Paul lying on the floor and started cursing in Italian. He bit his own finger in anger and slammed his door.

The fellows looked at Paul with loathing, then shut the apartment door. Rita was cursing and moaning and crying. The two other girls stood around, trying to console her. Jeannie had her arms around Rita. The drunks opened the refrigerator, looking for some beer.

"Come on. What the hell? Let's call it a night," Jeannie announced looking around.

The drunks shrugged. The two couples put on their coats and started to leave.

"Nice party. Thanks," said one of the drunks as he followed the others out the door.

"Come on you. Let's get out of here before I kill you," Josh said viciously, bending over Paul who was groaning and rubbing his groin. Josh pulled him to his feet, and helped him walk to the stairs. At the top of the staircase, Josh gave him a shove.

Rita and Jeannie could hear a noise as someone's feet hit the steps, and then there was a crash and a thud, . . . and then the footsteps of the party-goers as they followed down the stairs.

13

JOHNNY HAD DASHED FROM THE APARTMENT. He had scaled the steps directly in front of the door, his feet falling lightly on the metal edges so that no one at the waning party could hear him escaping. His only thought had been flight—the roof leading away. He hadn't bothered to consider his next move from the roof.

A scream of pain froze him still as he opened the roof door. He turned and, through the unlit gloom, watched the door of the apartment below. The door was open. He could see only a small section of the floor, nothing more. He heard more screaming and then crying and a man groaning. Two pairs of legs walked toward the door. Johnny's hands perspired nervously; he grasped the handle of the roof door, ready to bolt if anyone from the apartment saw him. He stared, terror-stricken, as two men carried Paul to the door and threw him to the floor outside the apartment. They returned to the apartment and Paul lay on the floor writhing in pain, holding his groin.

Johnny wanted to go down, to help Paul, but the angry voices mixed with crying and cursing in the apartment, and the fear of discovery and a thrashing riveted him to the spot. He stood as still as the walls, even conscious of the sucking sound he made as he cautiously drew in his breath.

A door at the other end of the hall below opened. Johnny's head automatically drew back further. He heard a sleepy voice curse in some foreign tongue—it might have been Spanish or Italian—then the door slammed closed.

Johnny desperately considered the best method of getting out of his precarious situation. His head nervously twisted from side to side, his eyes searching his perch, looking for a means of escape. Suddenly, to his utter horror, the door behind him swung backwards, opening. Johnny felt a frigid, paralyzing, horrifying, fear flash through him as the door swung open. He stood petrified, afraid, awaiting a blow on his head. It did not come. He twisted about to face whomever it was. The figure of a girl was silhouetted against the light of the moon, which appeared as a spotlight contrasting against the ebony blackness of Johnny's hiding place. Johnny forced himself to move rapidly, yet falteringly, out onto the roof.

"Shhhh . . . ," he begged Laura, who had been on the roof all this time and who was descending to see what all the screaming was about. Johnny shut the door shakily but carefully, lest the slightest noise should summon the avengers of Rita's virtue.

"What's the matter?" whispered Laura quizzically. "What's happening downstairs?"

"I don't know . . . I don't know . . ." His eyes darted over Laura's countenance, trying to fathom her disposition toward him.

"Well, what are you running up here for? Something wrong downstairs?"

"I don't know," he insisted. "Some guy is getting a beating or something." He could hardly control his nervousness. His mouth seemed dry and his mind thought frantically. "I just ran up here. I wanted some air."

"Are they after you too?"

"I don't know . . . I don't know . . . I just ran up here."

Laura walked toward the door to look down to see if anyone was coming up the stairs. Johnny bolted to the door, and pressed his back against it, bracing his feet against the roof.

"You're not going to tell them I'm here? Please?"

Laura's sympathy, born of an understanding of fear and loneliness, was aroused. She couldn't betray this fellow and be the cause of someone hurting him.

"I was only going to look if anyone was coming."

Her childlike simplicity assured him. He relaxed a bit; fright engulfed him now like a wave. He felt limp; his stomach felt hollow and down in his feet.

"Oh, God, they almost killed him," Johnny related, terror-stricken.

Laura melted with sympathy. "Don't worry, I won't tell them you're here. Come here." She motioned Johnny to follow as she walked to the low retaining wall separating the roof of this house from the roof of the next house.

The retaining wall extended from the back to the front, opening at the center into an elongated narrow polygon-shaped shaft four feet wide and twelve feet long.

"This is the shaftway," Laura explained, sitting on the edge of the opening. "There's our apartment down there." She indicated a window on the side of the black bottomless pit inside the polygon.

"*Your* apartment?" Johnny stared at her, perplexed.

"Yes, . . . I live there with Jeannie and Rita."

Johnny stood up nervously, upset by being with one of the members of that outraged group from which he had run.

"Don't worry." She smiled weakly to disarm his fears. "I'm not going to tell anyone you're here."

Johnny sat again slowly and gazed toward the lighted window just below. He could see nothing but some of the rug on the floor, the light playing on it, and part of a table. There were no noises from within.

"I wonder what's going on down there?" Johnny whispered.

"I don't know. I can't hear anything."

They both spoke in slow, quiet, mysterious whispers.

"I'll go to the door and see what's going on." She walked toward the door leading down.

Nervously, Johnny rose from his sitting position, studying the neighboring rooftop. He could make out the shadowed images of thin poles standing upright and the strands of clothesline sloping lazily down from the top and reaching up again to the top of the next pole. Chimney pipes stuck up on the sides of the buildings. Beyond the next roof, Johnny saw yet another low wall separating that building from the next one.

Laura pulled the roof door open. It squeaked once, sharply, metallically.

Johnny mounted the wall, ready to bolt over to the next roof. He trembled with expectancy of danger, of betrayal as Laura's head disappeared into the doorway. He held his breath fearfully. She stretched onto her tiptoes, her head penetrating the inside of the house more deeply. After crushing seconds of fear, she pulled her head back and shut the door quietly, holding one hand on the door frame to guide the door into position easily. She tiptoed back to Johnny.

"Well?"

"Your friend is laying on the floor outside the apartment, . . . and there are still some people inside."

"What's going on?"

"I don't know. They're just talking."

"I hope they don't come up here. How the hell will I get out of here?" He searched the surrounding roofs.

"I don't think they'll come up." She wanted to reassure him.

"If they do, I'm sunk." His eyes darted to the doorway of the stairwell, which stood out as a huge, black shadow on the bluish-whiteness of the moon-bathed roof.

"What did you do?" Laura asked curiously.

"Me . . .? I didn't do a thing, not a thing, . . . honest. That's my buddy though. You know, they'll probably figure to give me a beating too. That'd teach him a lesson."

"I don't think they'd do anything to you. You didn't do anything. What'd your friend do?"

"I don't know. Is there any way off this roof besides that doorway?"

"No, just the other roofs, . . . but they're all locked. Come on." She stood erect and stepped onto and then off the other side of the retaining wall.

"Where we going?"

"There's a little spot over here where they can't see you, even if they come up."

Laura led Johnny over two roofs. The third roof was higher than the others, but Laura mounted it with the aid of a milk box there for that purpose. Johnny followed. They walked to the front of that roof. A high, wide chimney stood outlined against the sky. Laura sat at the base of the huge chimney on the side away from the doorway of her own building.

"I come up here a lot. This place has heat, the chimney is nice and warm, and they can't see you from over there."

Johnny looked around cautiously and sat down. The chimney sent a comfortable warm feeling through his back.

"This is nice," he remarked.

They sat silently for many minutes. He wondered why she didn't betray him. His attention was drawn away, however, to the sounds of the roof. Wind whined over the stretched clotheslines; the poles snickered and creaked, but no other sounds were heard.

"What's your name?" he asked after several minutes of silence.

"Laura. Yours?"

"Johnny. That guy tried to fool around with one of the girls down there. Rita, . . . you know? I guess she's your roommate. She started to scream. That's when I ran out. He's crazy, that guy, sometimes. You know, he does some crazy things."

"Oh? You live around here?"

"No. We're from New Jersey. We just came over to look around. You know, have some fun maybe, that's all. I didn't come over to rape anybody, you know? We just came over to Louis' for kicks. My friend is a little strange. I mean, it wasn't my idea about your friend and all . . ."

"Don't worry. They can't find us here."

"Wheww . . ." Johnny blew out his breath in relief. It was pleasant to be safe and to breathe deeply after all the half breaths to which he had rationed himself during his escape. He looked up to the sky. The night was clear, and the moon shimmered a silvered light from its full, pock-marked surface. The stars were gleaming, and as he turned his eyes from the brightness of the moon, he saw the stars shining brightly like little holes in the dark blanket of night letting in sunlight.

"What are you looking at?"

"The stars. Ever look at the stars? I'm not good at it or anything, but I like to look at the stars once in a while, you know, when I'm alone . . . ."

"Do you know anything about them? I mean scientific stuff?" Laura wondered.

"Only a little. Like I said, I'm not good at it. See that line of stars up there?" He pointed over his shoulder to a spot behind them. Laura twisted toward him, looking to where he pointed. Her mouth agape, she searched the heavens.

"Where? I don't see it."

"Right there." Johnny drew his finger back a couple of inches and shot it out again to indicate which stars he meant.

Laura squinted, straining her eyes, but in the mass of little dots of light she couldn't pick out a line of stars. They all looked like a jumble.

"Where? I can't see them."

"Right up there." Johnny moved closer to Laura so that he could focus on the same level as her eyes. His face was almost touching hers, and he was very conscious of this. He watched her from the side of his eyes. Her profile was very close to his face, gazing at the sky. He moved closer to her to point out the star, extremely careful lest their faces should touch and she think he was trying to rape her. She smelled lovely, fresh and clean, he thought, sort of like soap and scented powder.

"See . . . There are three bright stars right in a row. Up there, . . . see," he said, using his outstretched arm and finger as a guide. "See them?"

"Yeah, . . . yeah. I see them now," Laura said excitedly, a straight line appearing in that mass.

"Well, that's the belt of Orion. See off to the right and up. There's another real bright star."

". . . Yeah?" Laura answered, unsuredly, searching. Johnny watched her little face furrow momentarily, then became calm again as she found what she was looking for.

"Well, that's Orion's arm. Now, see out to the right further. There's a curving line of stars . . . They sort of curve up and down?"

Laura studied the sky again. Johnny watched her. He felt pleased that he was being helpful, that someone was listening to him because he knew something, and that someone wasn't laughing at him and his nervousness.

"Yeah. What are they?"

"That's Orion's shield," he said more confidently. "If you look more to the right of that, there's a big bright star. See it?"

"Yeah . . . yeah . . . I see it." Laura was really excited at being able to discern something up there out of the jumble of little dots.

"That's Taurus's eye. Taurus the Bull's eye."

"Taurus the Bullseye?"

"No. Taurus's eye. Taurus is the bull." Johnny laughed Laura laughed too.

As they laughed, Johnny gazed steadily at Laura. He became conscious of his staring and his laugh became hollow and unreal. He stopped laughing and just gazed at Laura. She looked at him too, and they both looked away, so as not to stare at each other. After several minutes, Johnny looked back at her. He became conscious of being alone with a female. It was a rare event in his life. He was nervous and didn't know what he was expected to do.

Johnny looked at Laura and believed she was returning his look with one of expectancy, as if she was waiting for him to do something. *Maybe she likes me*, he thought. It was always like this, the girl expecting him to do something, and he never being able to do it. He was self-conscious about it. He didn't know just what he should do. All the guys on the block always kidded his shyness. Perhaps he could just extend his hand and hold hers. That would be a start. All he needed was a start; and, if he were wrong, that's all there was to that. She wouldn't get angry if he tried to hold her hand. But he couldn't put his hand out. She was probably sitting there waiting for him to start, sitting and wondering what was wrong with him. She was probably thinking he didn't know what he was doing, probably laughing. Probably thinking what a chicken he is. Thoughts were engulfing Johnny—*here I am on the roof and we could have some fun together. I might put my arm around her and just kiss her.* A big lump was in his throat and he swallowed and felt his Adam's apple go up and down, and he made a little gurgling noise which he felt sure she heard. Now she could be sure he was nervous. If he didn't do something soon she probably would go home. She might be getting tired of waiting. "What are you thinking about?" Laura asked.

"Nothing . . . nothing."

Maybe if he mentioned that it was cold, she would agree with him and he could put his arm about her. That's all he wanted to do, because then he could tell if she was interested in him, and it wouldn't be so hard. He'd know what to do then.

"I think it's kind of cold."

"It is. It's a little chilly. But it's not too bad by this chimney."

Her ambivalent answer threw him off balance. He wasn't sure if he should make his advance now.

"Are you cold?" he asked, trying to get a more positive statement from her.

"A little, . . . but it's okay."

He started to reach his arm out toward her. The gulf between them seemed interminable. His arm just stretched out and out. He felt as if the whole world was a witness to his action, and that everyone was laughing at his shyness and slowness. *If anyone ever saw me they'd laugh*, he thought. *Any other guy from the block would've been making out with her already.* His hands finally spanned the chasm between them, and his fingers touched her jacket and he skinned his knuckles on the chimney as he slipped his hand behind her head.

"What are you doing?" she asked, startled. Her words seemed derisive.

"I'll keep you a little warmer," he stuttered, trying to be gay. His remark seemed to him to have come out too weakly, too flat.

"No, . . . that's all right," she said nervously, trying to take his arm from around her shoulder.

She is only playing games. This is only the playfulness of woman, he thought. You can't give up like that. She's just trying to give you a hard time, to see if you stick to it.

"Oh, come on, my arm around your shoulder won't hurt."

Laura was bewildered, too shy herself to be brusque. She suffered his arm on her shoulder. For precaution, however, she clutched his hand as it dangled forward over her shoulder.

The fact that she was holding his hand strengthened Johnny,

assured him. *She is interested in me*, he thought. He tried to do the next thing that he thought he should do. He thought he should kiss her. They sat there silently for what seemed an eternity to the two. Each second passed slowly, and they were both conscious of their own presence as well as each other's. Johnny felt little specks in the cement of the chimney digging into his wrist as her back pressed it into the wall. Laura felt only the ponderous weight of his arm on her shoulder. Johnny leaned toward Laura to kiss her.

"Don't, . . . please don't," she pleaded, leaning away.

"Come on," he urged, feeling that she was just being playfully shy. He pulled her closer to himself, trying to be manly. He was afraid to be timid. "What's a little kiss?"

"Please don't." Laura's head squirmed away from his mouth.

"Oh, come on," urged Johnny, nervous and confused, now that she was refusing so vehemently.

"Stop!" Tears started to well up in her eyes. "Don't make me yell for the people down in the apartment. Please leave me alone."

Johnny was not quite sure any more. His grip loosened.

"Just leave me alone," Laura pleaded, single tears running down each cheek. "I'm going down . . . You can wait here, and leave when you want."

She stood, walked to the edge of the roof, lowered herself to the milkbox, and then to the lower roof. Johnny heard the stiff tar bubbles crack under her feet as she walked quickly toward her own building.

He sat with the warmth of the chimney still against his back. He was humiliated. He felt rotten and cheap. He felt as if he had tried to seduce a nice girl. Yet he felt as if he weren't a man because he couldn't get her to make out with him. How often he had heard stories from the guys about being with girls, and how easily they started fooling around with them—and he failed, he failed miserably. He put his hands on his bent knees, and put his face in them, . . . and he was sobbing, and cursing, . . . and he sat on the cold roof with the moon lowering through the heavens.

14.

THE BLUSTERY, TORTUROUS WINTER WIND continued its siege of the Village, restricting the activities of the Villagers within doors. The weather was neither extremely frigid, nor unseasonably warm for any marked length of time. It was a confused sort of winter with mild weather lulling the city for a few days, then a sudden attack by ripping, biting cold wind. Heavy snow did not fall often, but flurries constantly found their way to earth, only to be trampled instantly into nothingness by the hundreds of thousands of feet and cars constantly traveling the streets.

When snow did, on occasion, fall heavily, it remained on the streets for a long time. Piles would be shaped along the curbs and at the corners by the city's orange snow plows, and the soft, white snow became filthy piles of ice shale, mixed with garbage which had been surreptitiously abandoned because the snow forced a discontinuance of the sanitation service.

Walking was terribly difficult, the only paths being the narrow ones fashioned by pounding feet. Old people constantly slipped and fell. One felt sorry for the old women; when they fell helpless and confused in the snow, their dresses swirled up around their thighs and one could see their dark stockings, and their shriveled, skinny legs, and one thought sadly about the days recently past when these had been as young as the children now scampering to the top of the snow heaps on the corner, and then their legs exciting not pitiable.

Children happily climbed atop the eight-foot snow hills formed by the snow plows, and beat their chests rapidly with mittened hands, and slid down on the seats of their pants or on dismantled corrugated boxes while their mothers waited patiently, resignedly, as the children enjoyed winter in the city.

It was difficult for cars, too. Drivers were forced to park almost in the middle of the streets, four-foot furrows of snow lining the curbstones. The street surface was often extremely icy, and wheels became lodged in the ice, whirring violently but impotently to free themselves. When cars could move, they were forced into ruts that had been melted out of the ice by other cars. Sometimes the drivers couldn't turn their cars out of the ruts when they wished, and they passed their turns and tied up traffic as they tried to back up. Many car owners didn't mind the storm's covering their cars with snow, however. The burial afforded them a parking space until the city could dig out the streets, which task always seemed more activity than result.

Scooters were becoming a popular means of transportation in the city, and often one would see the raw redness of an intrepid scooter rider's face as he blew steam on his hands, waiting for a traffic light to change.

Through the winter, Rita and her roommates continued their rather hectic, futile, biding way of life, as did the rest of the people in the Village. The Villagers bided their time, waiting for something to happen, something to break, a big chance to come along. They waited for the world to blossom into a beautiful place. They waited and waited, amusing themselves the while.

The Village and its inhabitants are considered strange, off beat, but in all its sad ugliness, it is not so strange as the conceptions the people outside harbor about it. Sadness—a hollow, gnawing sadness—and loneliness is the quality which permeates much of the activity of the Village, not gaiety and abandon. The actors, the actresses, the painters, the poets, the sculptors, the writers, the lonely, the unaccepted, all find their way to the quiet streets, where at night one can walk alone and hear the lamentation rising out of the streets and buildings, swelling from every bar and cafe and coffee shop. Dreams of success are replaced by temporary respites of love and affection, of acceptance and friendship.

And just as the Village is strange, so, very often, is the acceptance found there. There is a great deal of mixing of Negro and white people. Not that this mixing of Negro and white is so strange, only the terms on which it is arranged, and the great profusion of it in this one tiny area.

This integration is only another manifestation of rebelliousness, the expression of hidden needs and desires on the part of the mixers, a purposeful, visible railing against Uptown society and all its preachings and doctrines.

Here is a place where both races meet on equal terms, thereby demonstrating, revealing the hollowness and ignorance of Uptown. Here, brotherly love blooms, thrives; but it bears only bitter fruit. The beauty of the love affairs and friendships is not the primary concern. It is a façade which shows to the world in the case of both white and black that the people so engaged are noble, fine, better than the ones outside who are not magnanimous enough to accept each other. This mixing then is not an acceptance, a solution. It is an unhealthy atmosphere, through which some people ostentatiously attempt to create about themselves an aura of dignity, nobility, worthiness, independence for the rest of the world to note. This integration, taken in the light of a desire to impress the world, being a means to personal aggrandizement, not an end in itself, is not a pretty picture. It is a sad, visible demonstration that there is still a great gap between the two groups.

The coffee shops and cafes continued to be filled with the usual crowds each night, and people came and sat about, talking the talk of people in the Village, all the while waiting for something to happen. They talked art, or acting, or life in general. They talked of every subject that interests the curious intellectual mind, although in many cases the curiosity and the intellectualism is feigned, is a sham and a show. Everybody wants to be intellectual and arty, but some people are just phony author's-name droppers.

Marriage and God are the two favorite subjects of the Villagers because they are the two subjects which cause them the most grief. One prevalent theory is that God has forsaken the world. He allows people to exist without any seeming support, allows them to be miserable, and wretched, without so much as consoling them. It flies against the Village-tempered mind to believe in Him in this unmerciful role. Besides, not believing in God is indeed a rebellion against the ordinary practices of society. So too, talking about art, loving Negroes and most every practice indigenous to the Village.

Marriage is the foundation of society, and society has forsaken these people. Through marriage they were brought into society, in it they have seen much misery, and because of it they have suffered pain and discontent.

God and marriage are the stable things which are so pat, so sure, that the unsure person can not grasp them fully for any length of time. To one who can not find the answer to problems within himself, it is impossible to reach out and permanently hold onto something without to solve problems. God does not exist in the material, and for those who need a present salve, the promise of a future salve is of no benefit. People who can not be happy with themselves can not be happy with others, nor can they make others happy. The circle goes round and round, and the talk follows a certain, almost predictable, path.

The parties continued through the winter, as did the idyllic evening or week affairs, and the restless prowling of the people hungry for relief.

In April, the evenings started to darken the city later, and the promise of warmth, and sun, and life, and spring, and new things, was in the air.

15

THE AIR WAS SOFT AND GENTLE AT LAST. The growing within the earth, life, could almost be heard in a song of joy, of liberation. Softening branches speckled with small buds of green swayed gently in the evening breeze, casting forth a faint fragrance. Evenings now embraced the city slowly, the western sky glowing with orange-redness, outlining billowed, purple-tinted clouds, silhouetting shimmering-eyed buildings.

Johnson's was livelier and gayer. It, too, as the earth, seemed more vital. Swaying music floated through doors outspread to welcome the warm, fresh breezes, filling every crevice of Minetta Lane with a happiness and an exuberance it had not known for many months. People were shedding their darkly frigid winter features, rejoicing with the reborn smiles of jubilation.

As Rita, Jeannie, and Laura approached Johnson's, three people stepped off the front step and disappeared out of the bare light into the sudden grey-blackness of the surrounding night. The girls entered. The large, exposed overhead fan was rotating, circulating the smoke. As it revolved from a hub attached to the ceiling, the fan and the hub throbbed and vibrated. Those below glanced overhead every few minutes, nervously anticipating being chopped to bits when it fell.

Sammy was behind the bar pouring a drink for someone already a little drunk. The customer hung limp-legged from the bar, propped up on one elbow, his free hand fumbling with his glass. Staggered down the length of the bar were other patrons, some of whom the girls knew, all talking and drinking. At the rear of the bar, bathed in the rotating, polychromatic light from the jukebox, stood a chattering huddle of five fellows, Josh Minot, Jim Panar, Frankie the Mexican, and two fellows the girls had never met.

The girls took seats at a table opposite the bar, near the front door. Dick, who was now Johnson's waiter and whose past bold advances Laura deigned to ignore and forget rather than suffer the embarrassment of bringing them to light, took their order. The girls sat quietly, watching the others in the cafe.

Between serving customers, Sammy was sponging the shelves behind the bar. The bottles which usually stood on the shelves were spread like sentinels along the bar. Sammy wiped each bottle with a damp rag before replacing it on the shelf.

"Man, I'm going to have to start giving this shit away," he exclaimed to no one in particular as he wiped a long thin-necked, square-bottomed bottle.

"What is it, man?" asked the drunk, forcing his limp head up inquisitively.

Sammy squinted at the label for a moment. "It's Greek wine."

"Oh. Those Greeks . . . Boy they've got some women, those Greeks . . . But they put them chastity belts on . . ." The drunk pointed a swaying, admonishing finger at Sammy. "Remember in the time of all those gods and everything?"

"You know when I'd like to live, man?" mused Sammy, stopping his shelf washing. "Back in the days of Venus de Milo and all them cats . . . you know? Man, that was a lotta woman to like."

"You're not kidding," the drunk replied enthusiastically. "Those women were all right." He stuck out his bottom lip in conviction, nodding his head.

"Yeah, man. If I lived in those days, man, I'd be making it in the street. You know, like they didn't care about that stuff."

"Yaaa." The drunk disapproved. "They put them chastity belts on the women, and they'd leave them on for so long . . . the women'd smell so bad, nobody'd go near them anyway." The drunk laughed convulsively, staggering, almost falling away from the bar. Sammy laughed too, then resumed putting the bottles on the shelf.

Johnson was now standing in the back, contributing his chatter and laughter to the group of fellows at the end of the bar. Johnson laughed loudly at the end of a story, turned and jaunted toward the front of the cafe. He removed from his pocket a Balero, a Mexican toy. It was a pipe-shaped piece of wood to which was attached by a string, a ping-pong-sized white wooden ball. There was a small hole in the ball. Johnson stood in the center of the cafe swinging the ball into the air, trying to catch it on one of the concave, bowl-like sections. There were actually four catching areas on the Balero. Two, one smaller than the other, on the crosspiece which resembled the bowl of a pipe; and two others on the stem of the pipe. One of the catching surfaces on the stem was another, even smaller, scoop; the other was actually a short point with which to spear the hole in the ball. Johnson was swinging the ball on the string and pushing the largest of the scoops under it. The little ball arched in the air, descended, and bounced off the lip of the scoop. Johnson swung it up again. Occasionally, he caught the ball on the scoop, and he'd stand watching it quiver to a stop on the end of the stem. Then he'd sneer, and wag his head with self pleasure and look cunningly out of the side of his eye at a heavy-set girl propped between the wall and the bar just inside the front window. She returned a blank, wondering, vague smile. Then he'd wag his head again, and start the swinging ball into action.

One of the two fellows from the group at the back, whom the girls didn't know, walked toward Johnson, his attention focused-on the swinging ball in Johnson's hand. He stopped and watched with fascination as Johnson swung the ball, following each arc of the ball and its subsequent bounce off the lip with his head as well as his eyes.

"Hey, man, that game is real great," he exclaimed finally. "Man, we used to play that for hours when we were in Mexico. I don't even remember the name of it. What'd they call that, man?"

"I don't know, man. What's in a name?" replied Johnson as he kept swinging the ball out in front of the scoop. "I think they call it *flying balls."* Johnson chuckled snidely, looking up momentarily to the corner where the heavy girl was, then down again at the ball that bounced off the lip of the scoop.

"Hey, Marc! Marc!" the fellow called to the other stranger in the group at the back. "Marc, . . . look what's here. Remember this game? You used to be champ at it, weren't you, man?"

Marc stopped speaking to the group for a moment, looked up and angled his head so he could see Johnson. The others turned to look, too. Marc nodded to his friend and moved back into the closed group to continue the conversation. The fifth fellow still stood watching Johnson flip the ball.

"Ever been to Mexico, man?" he asked Johnson. "They play that down there all the time."

"Mexico?" Johnson looked at the fellow quizzically. "Man, I'm Mexican . . . are you kidding? I'm a champ at this sort of thing. See? It's easy. I'm not even bothering to catch the ball. I'm just letting it drop in the cup and knocking it right out." The ball bounced off the front lip again. "Did 'ya see that catch, man?"

"Let's see how many you can get in a row."

"You kidding me, man? What is this, a show? Later, . . . when the bar closes. You know, like now all the people are around, I'm just goofin' now. Stick around . . . stick around . . . . I'll show you later." Johnson wound the string around the stem and stuffed the Balero in his pocket and walked to the back.

"Hey, Raoul . . ." called the drunk hanging on the bar as Johnson walked past him. "How about buying me a drink. I've been buying here for a long time, and you never even bought me one drink yet."

Johnson smirked with annoyance. "I don't buy nobody."

"Come on, Raoul. You can buy me a drink."

"What for, man? I owe you anything?"

"I bought plenty of drinks here."

"That's what you come for, that's what you get. I don't owe you anything."

Johnson frowned disgustedly, walked back further and rejoined the group standing at the end of the bar. Marc was just concluding a description of a Village party to which he had been the evening before.

"Man," interjected Johnson, "I went to this party. I was in this room, you know? It was one of these real way-out parties, you know? . . . 'n I have about these ten chicks around, and I'm huggin' and kissin', and ballin' them. And all of a sudden this big fuckin' black guy comes in, and man, all these chicks take off for him. I grab my three chicks, and tell them, 'Come on, let's split, I don't like spades.' "Raoul laughed uproariously. The entire group laughed with him.

"Yeah, man," Johnson continued, "those chicks on the Concourse, you have some real balls with them. Jump in the bed and they all jump in with you." He cocked his head, and with a smug little smile, his eyes half closed, he nodded in time with the music. He began to snap his fingers.

"Let me tell you about a party, man," said Jim Panar. "I was standing right here the other night and there were these two white guys at the end of the bar with this colored cat. Man, he was a nice looking guy, you know, chocolate color, with real smooth skin, heavy eyelids; he kept them half fluttered all the time like it was real sexy."

"You mean Louie?" asked Johnson.

"No, not Louie Jackson."

"No, I know, man. There's another cat comes in here sometimes, a little guy, a swinger . . . His name is Lou."

"Well, that was his name, if it's the same guy. Anyway, you know, we're standing here talking, and one of the white guys is drunk, and starts shooting off his mouth. The other white guy is trying to shut him up, but the little colored cat doesn't care. He tells the white guy, 'See if I care you get your head knocked off . . . I couldn't care less, baby,' he said. Well, they take this drunk cat out of here before he does get his head knocked off. He was kind of high. And then, like as they're going out, this other white guy tells me, 'Come on, we got a party going.' So like I wasn't doing anything, you know? I figure I go to a party. The little guy was a screaming fag, but I figure the other two for straight Joes. They were truck drivers. Pretty tough-looking guys, with tattoos and all, you know? So we walk down a couple of blocks with this drunk guy strung between us, me and this other white guy, and the little colored cat's flying along in front of us, swinging his little hips, and like we go to this pad. I think it was the colored cat's place, you know, all swinging fag doodads around. And the drunk is walking around the pad slobbering about how he didn't give a shit, he was tough and could knock the shit outta anybody. The other white guy is sitting next to me bein' real nice, social, you know, pouring drinks for me and all. And the sweet one starts cookin' steak. And the drunk keeps talking, and I'm wondering where the rest of the party was."

"You didn't know you were the party," Josh remarked chidingly.

"Yeah . . ." Jim laughed. "Well, anyway, the colored cat keeps telling the drunk he don't care, and that they should have let him get his head knocked off, it would teach him right. And the guy sitting next to me keeps filling my glass, and telling me not to bother worrying about them and he gets me sandwiches and asks me if I wanted anything else."

"He probably wanted you to tell him you wanted to make him," Johnson said, chuckling.

"Yeah. Then I had these real fine steak sandwiches, and they were great, . . . and this guy next to me is treating me like I was a king."

"Or a queen," Josh added.

"Yeah. Jesus, will you guys let me finish. So, this guy starts feeling the muscles in my leg, and my arm, and makes this sucking noise like he was flipping, and he tells me he wants to blow me. The other two guys disappeared into the bathroom—the colored guy wanted to straighten the drunk out and sort of talk to him, and wanted to leave us alone, he said. Well, they go in there and there's not a sound. And this guy sittin' next to me wants to blow me or just hold it or something. But I kept putting him off, and telling him I don't dig the action, and all the time I'm eating the sandwiches. You know, I didn't want to cut out on such fine sandwiches. Soon the two guys from the bathroom come back, and the drunk is hoisting up his fly and not saying a word, and the colored guy ain't sayin' a word, and Jesus, now I start really worrying. I figure I was going to have to knock my way out the door. You know, they started giving me the creeps—this guy next to me purring on my shoulder, and the other two looking at me, wondering why I'm giving their friend a hard time. So I get up and say I gotta go somewhere, you know? The guy next to me says, 'No, no. Don't go.' But man, like I bolted for the door, and man, did I cut out of this place. Man, I haven't run so fast in years."

The group all laughed at Jim's story; one of them poked him in the ribs, and everybody got red from laughing. The laughter began to ebb. Frankie, Josh, Jim, together with Marc and Joe, the two new fellows, began to glance around the bar for something new to talk about. They ordered another beer apiece and stood at the bar waiting to undertake a new conversation.

Rita, Jeannie, and Laura were still at the table sipping at glasses of beer. Johnson now began dancing to the blaring music. Josh was looking around the cafe when Rita caught his eye and motioned him toward her table. He went over and sat down.

"Who's the cat up there with you, the new one?" Rita asked interestedly.

"Which one, baby?" Josh looked up.

"The dark one with the red shirt."

"That's Marc. I met those two cats at Dani's the other night. The little guy is Joe, and the one in the red shirt is Marc. He's a school teacher yet. You interested, baby?"

Rita raised her eyebrows, signaling, "could be."

Josh smiled. "Wait a minute. I'll introduce you." He stood and walked to the back.

"That's my idea of a nice-looking guy," Rita remarked to the other girls when Josh left.

"We could swing pretty together anytime," Jeannie agreed.

Laura just smiled.

Rita watched as Josh began speaking to Marc, turning toward the girls' table as he did. Marc turned and looked toward the table, exchanging glances with Rita. Rita smiled almost imperceptibly.

Marc smiled at Josh and walked toward the table. He was medium in height, with long dark hair, a few strands of which curled over his forehead. His eyes were dark—darker, Rita thought, than any she had ever seen before. His eyes mesmerized her with a sort of inner warmth. Rita glanced downward to break away from his penetrating gaze. She noticed he wore tight, well-pressed, black slacks and black slip-on Italian shoes. Rita smiled inwardly. She had a theory about people and their shoes.

From a person's shoes she could tell the sort of person with whom she was speaking. Since stylists concentrate on the main clothing, leaving shoes to the discretion and taste of the wearer, Rita could gain a candid, penetrating insight into a person's character from his shoes. The style and condition of the shoes reflect the taste and personality of the person—scuffed, uncared-for shoes indicate a sloppy, careless person; bland shoes, a bland personality; common shoes, a common personality. Marc's shoes were of a very soft leather, and were soleless, that is, the sole was just a continuation of the upper shoe and not a separate piece of leather.

Marc reached the table. Rita looked from Marc's shoes back to his face. She was smiling. His eyes were warm and gentle, just as she knew they would be.

"Hi. I'm Marc. Josh said that if I came over and said that, you might let me sit down with you." He smiled broadly. He had a long dimple in his cheek when he smiled.

"Sure, sit down. This is Jeannie . . . this is Laura . . . and I'm Rita." Rita couldn't repress her smile.

"Hi, Marc," said Laura. Jeannie nodded and smiled.

"I like your shoes," remarked Rita. "I don't always come on like this, but I've never seen a pair of shoes like that."

"I bought them in Italy. They really swing, don't they." He was pleased.

"I'll say." Rita looked into his face. Their eyes held each other's for a moment. Rita felt he was looking right down into her soul. She looked away.

"You girls live around here?" asked Marc, turning to the girls.

"Yeah . . . you?" asked Jeannie.

Rita admired him as he spoke to the others. She couldn't keep her eyes from him.

"I've just gotten back to town. Matter of fact I just came back from Italy. Wish I had stayed there," he said reflectively, looking at the travel poster depicting Rome on the wall. His eyes fell upon Rita and gazed intently. He wrinkled his brow and smiled. "Maybe not."

"Why do you say that?" asked Jeannie, whose eyes and mind were not on the same level of communication as Rita's and Marc's.

"I don't know," he said meaninglessly, not caring if she understood, knowing Rita understood. He was unmindful of the words he spoke to Laura and Jeannie. How was Italy? Fine. Beautiful this time of year—Taormina—swimming—wine—Rome—The Appian Highway—Ponte Vecchio—Provenza de Laurenzana. Where did his people come from?

All the time he was talking, his mind was preoccupied with one thought—Rita. Not Rita as she was physically sitting next to him, whose eyes he would catch looking into his at various points during the conversation; but Rita, the girl, the woman, the idea, the person. He felt he knew her, what she was, what she was like. They had never met before, but he knew. All the women who had ever attracted him looked like Rita. Not really, not physically that is. They were all different physically, but they all shared an aliveness, a vitality, an inner force that struck him the moment he looked at them. Suddenly, out of a room full of people, as his eye blurred past odd-shaped heads, he could pick out the one woman in the room that he knew he would like. And Marc liked Rita!

Just then, Tom, the fellow Rita had stayed with at his apartment a couple of months before, entered Johnson's. With him was a colored girl. She was dark complexioned and very intriguing in the way that many colored women are. It is a mystique, a fascination perhaps born of the perversity of man, his desire for the forbidden—the intrigue of intrigue for intrigue. Tom saw Rita and smiled. She smiled back, warmly and affectionately, and they both remembered the cat in the ash can.

"Hi, Rita, how've you been?" asked Tom, smiling broadly. He was holding the colored girl's hand. She stood next to him, looking on amiably, with that half-smile of vague friendliness for people she had never met.

"Okay, how're you?" Rita looked to the colored girl inquisitively, as women are prone to look at other women. The colored girl returned the look amiably.

"This is Barbara," said Tom, introducing the girl, having noticed them look at each other.

"Hi. This is Marc," said Rita, turning to Marc.

Every time they looked into each other's eyes, a little light went on.

They gazed and were held by each other's eyes, smiling warmly outside and in.

"This is Laura and Jeannie," Rita said, continuing the introductions.

"Hi," said Barbara to all.

Rita looked at Marc again, and their souls began to speak silently. *Perhaps it would be fun to see each other more, soon.* Rita was fascinated.

Tom stood next to the table, looking around the cafe. One hand was to his chin, and he craned his head, looking into the remotest depths of the place.

"You didn't see Stan, did you?" he asked, looking back at the girls.

"No. I haven't seen him since that night we all were here," said Jeannie.

"Listen, I've got to shove. If Stan comes in, tell him to meet us at the pad, will you?" Tom asked Jeannie.

"Sure."

"Okay, see you. So long, Rita," he said, smiling the cat smile, which was nice and warm and friendly and meant that he would always remember the cat, and would always have memories of that night. "So long, Marc . . . So long, girls."

"Bye," said Barbara, as they stepped out of the doorway and disappeared into the night.

"Gee, I even forgot those guys existed," said Jeannie.

"Yeah, it's really been a long time since we saw them," said Rita gazing reflectively at the door.

"Hey, . . . come on back," said Marc, shaking her head delicately by the chin.

"Oh, . . ." Rita exclaimed, returning to the present to find Marc looking at her curiously. She smiled.

"I'm going to Dani's for a while," said Laura, standing up. "I told Fran I'd see her there."

"Who the hell is Fran?" asked Jeannie.

"A friend of mine."

"Okay, honey, see you later," said Rita.

Laura smiled because Rita seemed to worry about her. Then with her awkward, stiff-legged walk, which gave her an up and down bounce, she walked out. Her walk was like a laugh. Not a happy laugh, but the laugh people laugh when they're embarrassed, laughing at themselves in order not to appear to be serious and therefore ridiculous. Laura walked in a ridiculous way in order to let people know that she wanted them to laugh, and if they did she wouldn't mind it so much.

"She's an awfully lonely-looking thing," Marc commented as he watched her go out the door. "What's with her?"

"She's just bugged a little. Like everybody else, she's got her problems, too," replied Rita.

"Yeah, everybody has problems," agreed Marc. "I wonder what normal is. Everybody's sick. You know, not like just us, but everybody, outside and all. I don't know one person that hasn't got something bugging."

"Smile and laugh at it all," said Jeannie. "Just like they say in the song, *Just smile and laugh at it all.*" There was a note of hopeless bitterness in her voice.

"Smiling can get awful boring," said Marc. "I'd rather be sick and have fun, and like that. If you were normal, like you'd be awfully lonely."

They all laughed.

"Hey, Marc, come on, boy. We got to get uptown, man. Like, it's eleven-thirty already yet," said Marc's friend, Joe.

"Okay, okay," he said resignedly. "We've got to split; maybe we can make it some other time," said Marc looking at Rita intently, not wanting to leave.

"Sure, why not?" She smiled. "We're here all time time."

Marc started toward the door. "So long." He waved, looking at Rita once again.

Jeannie and Rita waved.

When Joe and Marc had gone, they looked at each other, Jeannie pursing her mouth and nodding her head in contemplative approval.

Rita looked at her and smiled with an inner warmth.

16

LAURA HAD LEFT RITA AND JEANNIE as they spoke with Marc, walked out of Johnson's and turned toward MacDougal Street and Dani's. Minetta Lane, on which Johnson's was located, was a dark, crooked lane about one hundred yards long, sloping from the Avenue of the Americas up toward a well-lit dead end at MacDougal Street. At the center, the lane was bisected by another alley which extended for fifty yards, then, with the typical insouciance of a Village street, curved in a 45-degree bend and continued back toward the Avenue of the Americas. This was Minetta Street. The houses on Minetta Lane and Minetta Street were all small private houses of different heights and shapes and colors. Even the windows of the houses varied in shape. They reminded one of the houses bordering a crowded Italian quay.

Laura was absorbed into the circle of light from the street lamp at the center of the lane. Her shadow was now cast just beneath her; she stepped on it. Ahead, shadowy figures were silhouetted against the backdrop of clashing neon lights and the confusion of people on Mac-Dougal Street. They walked toward Laura. Footsteps came toward her, and two unknown, indistinguishable shadows passed. As she reached the spot where a driveway made the sidewalk slope down steeply into the basement of a building, one approaching shadow stopped. Laura's insides leapt in surprise. She continued walking, ignoring the shadow, yet watching its dark substance from the corner of her eye. The shadow's eyes followed her every step. Laura walked down into the driveway, leaning to maintain her balance on the slope, and passed the stationary figure.

"Laura?" a voice inquired.

Laura stopped and looked around. She could not recognize the voice, and could see only a vague shadowed face. She stepped to the side, letting the greenish neon lights from the Minetta Tavern on the corner of MacDougal Street fall on the shadow. It was a man's face.

"It's me! Johnny!"

"Hello," Laura said apprehensively, remembering the night on the roof. She edged toward a path of direct escape.

"I've come down here a couple of times since that night." He looked to the ground embarrassedly, reflecting on his past deeds. "I've never been able to find you, though."

"Oh, . . . I've been around."

They stood looking at each other, wordless and very conscious of their own presence and silence.

"Well, so long now," said Laura turning to leave, not knowing what else to do. "Nice seeing you again."

"Laura!" Johnny blurted out imploringly. He walked to her, his eyes looking into her's for a moment, then focusing on her forehead. He was still cast in the eerie green light from the bar sign. He wanted to say something; his lips moved, but stopped abruptly; his hand waved awkwardly in the air. "I just wanted to say . . . well, you know. I didn't mean anything . . . that last time . . . It's just . . ."

"That's all right," said Laura, somewhat embarrassed at Johnny's embarrassment. "I don't care about that anymore."

Johnny gnawed his lips nervously. He smiled weakly, half from embarrassment, half in friendliness. He watched her face. *She looks so scared, so lonely, so weak,* he thought. If only he weren't so scared, too. *Why don't I ask her to have coffee with me; she wont mind that. Maybe she would, though?* His imagination conjured up all sorts of refusals and embarrassing rejections or retorts from which he recoiled frightened. *What the hell . . . . She can only say no. I'll ask her to have coffee with me. I'll say, "Laura, do you think you . . . ."* No, that's not right. *"Would you like some coffee?" "Sure," she'll tell me, "but not with you!" No. What the hell, I'll just ask her . . . .* The words began to slide up his throat like red-hot pellets. His mouth grew dry, and he felt his Adam's apple bob. He swallowed hard. *Damn Adam's apple*, he thought, *always bouncing like a jumping bean in my throat.* He felt more embarrassed because Laura was probably amused by his embarrassment. But he still wanted to ask her, now more than ever, and yet, now, now he felt more ashamed of himself because he couldn't get himself to ask.

"Well, . . . I've got to go now. I'll see you." Laura again turned to leave.

"Laura!" he called, summoning his nerve more from impulse than volition.

"What?" she asked softly.

Johnny was caught and had to say what he wanted. But he found it almost impossible.

"What?" she asked again, nervously, impatiently.

Johnny walked over to her. "I wanted to buy you some coffee or something—unless you're busy. I mean, we could have it some other time if you want. But if you've got nothing else to do, I don't either, . . . and maybe we could have some coffee together."

She studied his nervous face pleadingly looking into her nervous face. She too was sure her features revealed amusing nervousness.

"I guess we could," she replied. She was surprised, and more than that, now that she realized fully that Johnny was asking her to go for coffee with him, pleased.

Johnny was relieved. He smiled weakly, thankfully.

"I don't know where to take you. I don't know much about the Village."

"There's a little Italian coffee shop right next to Dani's. It's nice there—quiet."

There was something pleasantly sincere about Johnny, Laura now thought. He wasn't trying to be a wise guy now. He was nervous, but warm and gentle too. He seemed to really want to go for coffee and be with her. And she wanted to go too, because he didn't have that look about him, the one that most people had, the hard look, the one that seemed to want to devour her, to step on her. Suddenly, he looked like a friend.

They walked to the Continental Espresso and entered.

The flicker of small candles encased in red glass cups atop each table gave a half-reddish, half-yellow hue to the walls and the faces of the people seated about the tables in the Continental. Small oval tables lined each side of the aisle that cut down the center of the shop. Classic-styled oil paintings, intermixed with contemporary photographs taken by local photographers—probably customers—hung on the walls. On one wall, a huge canvas of Moses and The Chosen People at the rock of gushing water hung in darkness. In one front corner of the shop was a large square, marble-topped table and an ornately carved bench of black wood with climbing flowers and angels' heads cut into it. Soft red cushions adorned the seat. Silken cords held the pillows on the seat and hung down the side of the bench, ending in fringed tassels.

No one was sitting at the large table. Johnny motioned Laura toward it. He indicated a seat facing the interior of the shop, and Laura sat down as quickly and unobtrusively as possible. Johnny pushed her chair in from behind and sat down on the bench.

"I'm sorry," he said, standing hurriedly. "Maybe you want to sit down on the bench?"

"No . . . no This is fine."

They sat silently, watching the flame flickering on the walls and table. Johnny twisted himself toward the counter in the back, behind which a short, heavy man was making coffee. As he looked to the back, Johnny's eyes had passed quickly over Laura's face. He saw it only for a second, with the reddish tint on it. He saw her big eyes gazing intently, blankly at him. The man behind the counter saw Johnny and he smiled and bowed slightly so that Johnny would know he saw them. Johnny felt incapable of turning back to look at Laura, or even turning back to look at anything, feeling that his eyes would be drawn to see if Laura was looking at him, and he would seem foolish and obvious.

The man from behind the counter walked up the center aisle and over to their table. He had a friendly smile.

"*Buona sera*. What would you like to have?"

Johnny reached for the menu and looked at it for a moment.

"What are you going to have," he asked Laura and then looked up. "Oh . . . I thought you had a menu," he apologized handing the menu to her.

Without looking at the menu, she said she wanted coffee cappuccino. Johnny ordered the same. The man who was surely the owner of the shop went back to the counter. The espresso machine hissed in a sudden burst of effort.

"That was kind of a crazy night, that last time." Johnny began to absently lift and close the hinged top of the sugar bowl. "My friend Paul was black and blue for two weeks."

"Yeah, it was kind of crazy. And then you coming on like a crazy man yourself."

Johnny didn't understand her words exactly, but he knew what she was referring to, and he was embarrassed. He looked down.

"Oh, don't worry about that. It's all been forgotten."

The owner brought the two cups to their table.

"Anything else? We have some nice cheese. Pastry?"

"I don't want anything," said Laura.

"Nothing for me either."

The owner returned to his counter, leaving the two white cups steaming on the white table top.

"Well, let's have a toast," Johnny said as jovially as possible.

"What to?"

"To us, I guess. To forget the last time."

"Okay." She raised her cup. Somehow she didn't feel nervous with Johnny. They just sat and didn't say much, but just being there, smiling occasionally was all that was needed. It said so much. She knew that Johnny felt the same way she did. Johnny was someone to whom her feelings wouldn't be foolish. She knew he wouldn't make fun of her. It was an overwhelming relief to be with someone like herself, someone who understood as she understood, who wouldn't belittle her. She felt strangely happy, goose pimply, as she looked at Johnny. She felt sort of giddy. She felt like jumping up and down and smiling. She could see herself in a green pasture running and skipping and humming, with the green grass under her feet and a big smile on her face.

Johnny put down his cup and they looked at each other and smiled simultaneously, spontaneously. They were big smiles, so big that they surprised themselves and each other. They were real smiles, ones they hadn't used in such a very long time. They were smiles of discovery, of relief, of realization, of happiness.

"Are you going anywhere after this?"

"I was going to Dani's—that's the place a couple of doors down—to meet a girl friend, . . . but I don't have to," she added quickly. "I've had my coffee."

Johnny smiled as she smiled. "Maybe you'd like to go to a late movie—if you don't have anything else to do?"

Her neck tingled. "Okay . . . That'd be nice," she said, her eyes feeling aglow. She sat on the edge of her chair, her elbows on the table, and smiled her newly found warm smile at Johnny.

17

"OH COME ON, do me a favor will you?" Rita implored as she and Jeannie walked downtown along the Avenue of the Americas.

"That God damn place is going to be packed tighter than . . . ," Jeannie chuckled. "Tight as hell anyway. And with all the lousy people I know, it must be pretty tight down there."

"Look, we only have to go over for a minute; if he's not there, we'll cut right out. Come on."

"No! I won't get caught in that mess. There'll be a million tourists there. Look at them." Jeannie's arm indicated the throngs of people, obviously not from the Village, milling on the sidewalk ahead of them. "Jesus, how I hate this place on Friday and Saturday. Nothing but tourists and drunken sailors."

Surrounding the girls were throngs of outsiders parading in their Uptown raiments, having descended en masse to have a wild time. Girls in twos and threes window-shopped, hoping to be picked up by some swinging Bohemians. Fellows from outside stood on the corners or traveled from bar to bar looking to pick up some wild Village chicks.

On Friday and Saturday nights the Village takes on a strange aspect. Many of the Villagers retreat to private haunts, leaving an insipid, deserted place to the invaders—leaving the Village a throbbing, lively, glaring, washed out place crowded with tourists milling in droves, looking for the excitement that they have scared off with their garish, sacreligious, meddling march. The only exciting thing in the Village when tourists are there is the thrilled reaction of the store owners and cafe keepers to the continuous ring of their cash registers.

Ahead of the girls, some soldiers stopped a fellow to ask directions. The fellow was dressed as a Villager. He turned and pointed toward Third Street; he was directing them to the strip joints. They probably had asked him where a soldier could have some fun. That was a hard question to answer, since the wild girls for whom the soldiers were looking didn't think of the soldiers as much fun—just tourists. The soldiers started toward the strip joints with a "whoop" of anticipation.

"Look at this place," Jeannie said disgustedly. "And you want to go to Johnson's? You're out of your coukie mind! Even if Marc is there, what are you going to do, hang from the ceiling and hold hands?"

"Oh, stop being a crab apple and come on. It won't kill you. We're almost there now." Rita increased her pace, taking hold of Jeannie's arm.

"Wait a minute," objected Jeannie, shaking Rita off. They stood near the edge of the sidewalk facing each other. "Listen, I'm not going. You go ahead by yourself."

"Hi, girls," remarked a collegiately dressed fellow sitting in an open convertible which was parked at the curb. Two fellows were sitting in the car, "How about you two girls coming to a party. There's plenty to drink, and we'll have a lil' ol' ball." The college boys looked them up and down.

"Take off and have your ball all by your lil' ol' square self," Rita remarked curtly, turning away from the car.

"Now girls," admonished the driver as he got out and skirted around the car to approach the girls. "That isn't nice. Really . . ." He strode next to them as they began walking away. "We have this apartment down on Hudson Street, and there's plenty of booze and music, and us. Come on."

"You want to go, Rita?" Jeannie asked enthusiastically.

"No. You know where I'm going. You go ahead, if you want to. I'll see you later."

"Oh, come on with me," Jeannie insisted. "I don't want to go by myself."

"Yeah, come on, Rita," urged the other college boy who had driven the car to where the girls now stood. He leaned out the window. "What the hell, there're plenty more people there if that's what's bothering you. It's going to be a ball." He used the word ball as if it were a special word from a foreign language.

"No, I've got somewhere to go. I'll see you later, if you're going," Rita said to Jeannie.

"Sure she's going," insisted the fellow standing next to them, putting his arm under Jeannie's and turning toward the car.

"Oh, okay," Jeannie said, slightly annoyed at Rita. She walked to the car arm in arm with the college boy. "Let's go," she smiled. "Boola, boola."

The collegians laughed. The fellow in the car opened the door and let Jeannie slip into the back seat.

"So long," called Jeannie smiling, waving, as the car sped off from the curb, disappearing down the Avenue.

Rita frowned, then crossed the street and walked quickly toward Johnson's. Somehow she had to go to Johnson's; a feeling inside told her Marc would be there. She wanted him to be there.

Across the street from Rita, sailors began yelping in an affected, feminine way.

"Yoo hoo . . . yoo hoo . . ."

One of them had rolled his pants to the knee and was holding one of his arms poised in the air, his hand hanging limply from the wrist, as his entire body, especially his hips and shoulders, snapped exaggeratedly as he walked. His friends were hysterical with laughter over their buddy's imitation of a faggot they thought they had just passed.

Rita walked more determinedly toward Johnson's. She thought it cruel for these sailors to torment someone they didn't know. But then, wasn't this society's normal reaction to something strange or different? If the strangeness or differentness is allowed to exist, is accepted, that from which it differs is not absolutely correct; society likes to be absolutely correct in order to abolish confusion, the need for thinking, even at the price of suppression. If the strangeness can be dismissed with a laugh, if a joke can be made of it, then somehow, psychologically, its threat is lessened. Homosexuality is a sickness, an affliction caused somewhere along the life path of an individual, frightening him into a state of terror, a state of fear so strong that, for need of human kindness and understanding, the person turns to the only path where protection and perhaps acceptance seems available. Where the humor in this affliction lies is hard to ascertain. For the most part, however, the laughter is hollow, the hatefulness too intense and unjustified to be merely a normal reaction of humor or dislike. Deep inside, the intense mocker or hater of homosexuals has a cold knot of fear, almost an overwhelming, consuming one, which is temporarily allayed by the ostentatious mocking of that thing which causes the chill.

Johnson's was jam packed; people were wedged from one end to the other. This was usual on Friday and Saturday night. Rita knew the Negro fellow stemming the tide of humanity at the front door. He smiled and let her squeeze in, then shut the door behind her. Despite the rotating fan overhead, the place was stifling. Patrons standing in the aisles were so tightly packed from one wall to the other, from the bar to the tables, that one had to climb over people in order to move. They all clung together, each leaning against the other. Those seated at the tables could not stand because of the crowd packed around their tables. Arms and backs and sides and legs, white and colored, in all varying shades between the two extremes, were pressed together—a hand with a drink in it here, a red shirt there, a grey sweater near the bar, suits from Uptown at the tables, a blond girl, a beard, a colored Villager, a laughing mouth, two colored fellows in suits looking around at the sights, silver earrings, four more girls, more heads, arms, flashing teeth, legs, mouths, ears, eyes, noses, smells, laughter, teeth, chatter, tongues, yelling, and drinks and much noise and shouting, pulsating in the air, everywhere. The background overflowed with bouncing jukebox music.

Rita squirmed between people, making her way toward the back. A fellow was making his way toward the front. His arms and shoulders were thrust in an interstice between the mob, while the lower half of his body, fighting its way forward, was still wedged behind. He looked up and saw Rita struggling toward him and stopped where he was resignedly while she squeezed sideways past him.

"Excuse me . . . excuse me . . . pardon me . . ." she repeated over and over, shuffling toward the back, squeezing between people, watching the faces surrounding her as she went, feeling their breath and body heat as she passed them. She was looking for one in particular. As she edged toward the back, she stepped on feet, felt legs push against her, suffered hot breath of alcohol in her face, was prodded by stomachs, backs, rear ends, thighs, hands, elbows, knees . . .

"Hi, Rita," called Josh. He was standing at the bar with a white girl. He was laughing while the girl, who looked as if she came from Uptown, was cooing as she touched his gold earring. Rita was separated from Josh and the girl by a row of chattering people.

"Does it hurt?" Rita heard the girl ask.

"Only a little at first." Josh burst with laughter.

The girl snickered awareness.

"Hi, Josh," replied Rita. She continued back, and was jostled and pushed out of the way by people who wanted to get through.

Near the jukebox, the wall was lined with men drinking from beer bottles. Rita reached the space at the end of the bar. Here the crowd was spread a little thinner.

Someone in the third row from the bar was lifting a bottle of beer from Sammy's hands over the heads of the people in the other two rows lining the bar. The fellow with the beer reached a hand with a dollar bill in it up into the air; the bill was snatched from his hand by one of the people behind the bar.

Another fellow, in the second row of people, was just putting his drink to his mouth when someone from the bar, clutching four drinks between his hands, stepped backwards in an attempt to return to his table. They collided. The fellow in back jumped back choking, beer dripping on his shirt and jacket sleeve.

"Sorry, man," the fellow who had bumped into him said over his shoulder, his hands wet where the drinks had spilled.

The victim, beer dripping from him, just glared and wiped the beer from his suit with his hand, flicking it onto the floor. Someone from one of the side tables stood up, bumping into him from the other side.

"Hey, come on, knock this shit off!" the sopping one blurted angrily.

"Hey," called Sammy from behind the bar, looking disapprovingly over the heads of the people at the bar. "Take it easy there, man."

"God damn it. You get pushed around here and you got to pay for it too."

"Listen, man," Sammy said in his quiet way. "Nobody sent for you. I didn't ask you to come here, you know? If you don't like it, like you can split anytime."

The fellow, unconsciously continuing to rub his wet shirt, became quiet, feeling the eyes of the people around the bar on him. Sammy, satisfied that the fellow would be no more trouble, began to mix some drinks.

"Hey, come on. Get your Louis Burgers right here. A Louis Burger is good for you," shouted Louis Jackson from behind the grill counter in the back. Louis was a tan Negro with long, black, curly hair, who always wore faded jeans low on his hips, the material gathering in baggy folds at the seat. He had named the special burger made with lettuce, tomato and onion, after himself.

"Here you go . . . They're delicious," he called, as smoke and spattering grease intensified the stifling atmosphere.

Rita saw Frankie the Mexican sitting at a table against the wall. At the same table was another fellow Rita had seen around and three girls that she had never seen before.

"Hey, Rita, here's a chair for you," called Frankie, pointing at an empty chair at the table.

"Okay, Frankie, I'll be there in a minute. I'm looking for somebody."

Rita was standing log-jammed in the middle of the gap between the tables and the jukebox. She scanned the faces around the cafe as people on all sides of her pushed and touched shoulders constantly. Others kept squeezing past Rita, making their way to the rest room in the back.

"Hello . . . ," said a white fellow as he squeezed his way toward the front of the cafe. His face was inches from Rita's and he stared at her as he squeezed past.

"Hey!" yelped a girl at the bar alarmedly as the staring fellow bumped into her, spilling part of her drink over her dress.

"I'm sorry," he said, turning to the girl. "See what I did on account of you," he said playfully as he turned back to Rita.

"I didn't make you do anything," she said curtly, moving away from him. "Don't blame me if you're sloppy."

The fellow shrugged and continued worming his way toward the front.

Louis came from behind the grill and squeezed next to Rita.

"Listen, baby, come over here." He took Rita by the arm and led her up to a fellow she had never before seen in the Village. The fellow was dressed in a three-button suit and a tab collar and striped tie. With him was a girl dressed in a very ordinary Uptown fashion. She wore a light-blue dress and hanging silver earrings. Her hair was a tinted reddish affair outlining a face with a small nose and brown eyes. Her dress was cut deeply in front revealing a heavy portion of chest fat.

"Talk to this cat," Louis whispered to Rita from the side of his mouth as they stopped in front of the standing couple.

"Bill . . . Bill, I want you to meet Rita. Rita, this is Bill and Audrey. They just came down to the Village and I thought we could make them feel right at home. Rita is my girl," said Louis turning toward Rita. She noticed a brilliance of amusement in his eyes, while his mouth and face remained calm.

Rita knew this bit. It was Louis' specialty. He would introduce a fellow to another girl, under the guise of friendship, and while everyone was talking, he would try and take the fellow's girl away from him— even for a short time.

"Do you live down here?" Bill asked Rita, whom Louis had stood directly in front of Bill. Louis stood next to Audrey. Rita felt rotten and low as she began talking to Bill. Out of the side of her eyes she could see Louis talking to Audrey. Now and again, Bill would say something to Louis, and Louis would answer quickly, unconcernedly. Then his conversation with Audrey would continue. Louis was monopolizing

Audrey, and Audrey, thrilled by the perverse, savage, sinful feeling of flirting with a Village Negro, liked the situation.

Bill talked to Rita about acting, and the Village, and his college, and the new motion pictures that each had seen. Bill bought a round of drinks. Louis accepted readily. The whole bit made Rita feel a little lousy.

Every once in a while, Audrey would glance out of the corner of her eyes to see if Bill was watching the conversation between Louis and herself. When she looked, Louis too would look, reverting his eyes to her when he was satisfied that all was going well. When the girl's eyes would return to Louis, they would take on a playful glow. She passed her tongue over her lips, perhaps to moisten them, perhaps to show Louis her tongue.

In the Village, in order to manifest a differentness from Uptown, people have no taboos about talking with or asking another fellow's girl for a dance, even if they don't know either of them. Usually the man wouldn't say anything, because he figured, *In the Village* ... and this was it. Rita had often seen a Villager giving a girl the eye while her date had his back turned. Often she had seen a fellow innocently ask another if he could dance with his date, and when they did dance, he would hold her close to himself and she would cling to him as her eyes had indicated she would even before he had asked her. People came down to the Village to allow things to happen to themselves, and when they'd go home they'd say it was the people in the Village that had done it all. The girls went down and looked for the mad, captivating lovers that they'd heard about; the fellows came down for the nymphomaniacs they'd heard were around, and when they left they would bring stories of seduction or near seduction home with them for the ears of the soon-to-follow sensation seekers of their neighborhood. What boring lives these people lead; what shallow minds, to think that this little plot of ground on Manhattan Island is so intriguing. It's not the place, it's the people ... and not the people who live there so much as the people who go there, who use the place for an excuse to do things they want to do anyway.

"Let's get a breath of fresh air," Louis suggested innocently to Audrey, ignoring Bill.

"Yeah . . . . whewww, . . . it's hot in here," Audrey said unconvincingly, moving her hand across her forehead. Louis' eyes riveted questioningly on Rita.

"I'll wait here for you," Rita said by rote. "I don't want to go through that crowd again."

Louis and Audrey started toward the door. Rita remained.

Bill shrugged. "I guess I'll stay here then. You get some air. I'll wait here."

"Okay, honey, would you mind my bag? I don't want to carry it through this crowd." Audrey handed Bill her handbag.

Rita watched them start to make their way through the crowd, then turned to Bill.

"Anyway," she said, trying to catch Bill's interest again. Rita knew that once Louis and Audrey were caught up in the crowd Bill was powerless to recall them.

Bill watched the two make their way through the tiderace of people gushing against the sluice gate at the front of the bar.

"Bill, Bill, you're not listening."

"Hhmm, . . . oh, I'm sorry, Rita; what were you saying?"

"I was saying that it seems the abstract painters today don't really have an art, but more a technique."

"I don't know, I think a lot of their stuff is interesting."

Slowly, Bill became engrossed in the conversation; and Rita knew she had succeeded. She felt nauseous.

Rita had been speaking to Bill for many minutes. Suddenly, as they spoke, Bill stared toward the front of the bar. Rita turned. A small colored person, dressed in slacks and a man's sport jacket had entered the cafe. It was really hard to decide if the person was a girl or a boy. It had short black hair, cut in a man's style, but the face was soft, and sweet looking, and had a smooth, made-up texture. Bill said it was a girl. Rita said it was a boy, . . . no, a girl. She couldn't tell if it were a Lesbian or a fag.

The indistinguishable individual came quite near to where Bill and Rita were standing, and looked about the cafe. Johnson, just then, came in from the outdoor garden; Rita hadn't known the garden was open. Now as she looked back, she noticed the door open and the lights in the garden shining. Johnson stopped short, his brow furrowing as he saw this unknown quantity standing near the jukebox. Johnson studied the person searchingly.

"You a boy or a girl, man?" asked Johnson.

"A boy."

"Well, get the hell outta here. I don't want you guys in here. Go on, get outta here." Johnson twisted the little fellow toward the door, and gave him a little impetus.

The fellow started to make his way back through the crowd.

Johnson snickered. "Got enough trouble around here without him."

Johnson turned and started to make a selection on the jukebox. He pressed several numbers, and the little green light that signals when a selection can be made went out. He reached behind the machine, tripping a device, and the little green light on the selection board lit up again.

"Hey, yure Raoul Johnson, aint 'cha?" asked a white fellow standing against the wall with several other white fellows. All of them were dressed in a style that was popular in the hood neighborhoods of the East Side. They had long hair, combed high on their heads and ending in a D.A., pegged pants, and sport shirts with the collar turned up. They slouched near the wall in a semi-circle, looking at Johnson as if he were a demi-god. They stood off and admired this romantic figure whom they considered a really exciting personality. After all, he owned this bar in the Village and was a sharp guy, and his photograph hung on the wall . . . .

"I seen you in pitchers, ain't I?"

Johnson was looking down at the jukebox listings. His eyes flitted over to the fellow quickly, a slight smile playing in them, then he looked back at the listings.

"Sure," said Johnson pressing another button.

The fellow looked at his buddies and nodded to check if they had heard.

They nodded in reply.

"Who's dis guy here?" the fellow asked Johnson with the rapidity of trepidatious humility, pointing to a picture of Louis Jackson which hung on the wall.

"That's Louis Jackson. The guy that's in the back by the kitchen," replied Johnson, still pushing buttons on the jukebox.

"He's a actor, ain't he? I tink I seen him in pitchers too. He was in pitchers, wasn'e?"

"Yeah, man. He was in lots of pictures, sure he was." Johnson finished selecting and started to sway with the music, snapping his fingers. "The last picture he was in was Jungle Safari, man, a swinging Tarzan picture." He did not look at the hood, fabricating the story easily, without concern.

"Yeah, yeah," the hood remembered, his face lighting up, as he forced his memory to conjure up the picture that never existed. "I tol' ja," the hood said to his friends as he walked back to them. "He was in Jungle Safari."

All the hoods gathered around the one that had been talking to Johnson. They were stealing admiring glances at Johnson, searching the back for Louis so that they might see another movie star.

Johnson was snapping his fingers, and laughing and smiling with the melody of the song. Actually, he was smiling at his own smugness, and the stupidity and gullibility of these hoods, to whose dreary lives he had just added some of his glitter. Johnson winked at Rita whom he knew had seen and heard the entire bit.

"Hey, . . . come on," Johnson shouted in rhythm. "Let's drink up. This is the Village, . . . Bohemia . . . . Let's be Bohemian," he yelled mockingly, because he knew the people at the bar had come to see Bohemia, and they thought it was great, even though Johnson was making it up as he went along. "Let's spend lots of money," he shouted. The people liked this coukie stuff because they expected it; Johnson liked it because it made him feel big.

"My God, this place is crazy," Bill said to Rita.

"Sure is, Bill, sure is. I want to look out in the garden for a minute. I'll be right back." Rita walked toward the door in the back and out into the garden.

Many little, round, white tables gleamed in the glare of the yellow and white bulbs strung on wires overhead. In the middle of the garden was a twisted tree, its gnarled, calloused arms reaching in all directions.

Rita looked around at the faces, still searching for Marc. A fellow rose from a side table and walked in her direction. She looked past him, searching. The fellow stopped in front of her; her eyes focused inquisitively on him. It was Marc's face. Her breath caught in her throat.

"Where you been, baby? I've been waiting for you all night." He took her by the arm and began to lead her toward a table. Rita hesitated, remembering Bill alone and forsaken inside.

"Kind of sure I'd be here, weren't you?"

"I'm here! I was hoping you'd come too. I didn't know where else you might be. Come on, sit down. What's the matter?" he asked, sensing Rita's reluctance to sit at the table.

"Let's not stay here, Marc. I don't want to stay. If you do, I'll come back in a while. I just want to get some fresh air away from this place. I'd like you to come too."

"That's okay with me." He picked up his jacket from behind a chair, left some money, and started toward the door leading inside.

Rita saw Bill, still standing on the side, now talking to a colored fellow at a table. She stopped.

"Bill, I'm leaving now. It was nice talking to you. I'll see you now."

Bill was surprised and confused. Rita passed on quickly before he could ask her about Louis or Audrey. She and Marc began squeezing through the crowd. Rita looked back and saw Bill looking lost and befuddled, standing alone with his drink in one hand and Audrey's handbag in the other. Rita turned forward and followed behind Marc, who was cutting a path for her through the human reeds that choked the aisle. Marc looked back at Bill with curiosity, looked to Rita, then turned and continued making his way through the crowd.

The fresh air seemed cool and free and fresh and relaxing after the physical struggle to get out of Johnson's. People were as jammed in as before, and more people were coming in. Even the street was crowded. Cars were parked half on the sidewalk to leave room in the narrow street for other cars to pass.

Marc and Rita stood in front of Johnson's for a moment, Rita waiting for Marc to decide in which direction they would walk. They crossed to the other side of the street, out of the glare of the light over

Johnson's and turned toward MacDougal Street. When they reached the right angle of Minetta Street they turned and walked along the quiet alleyway toward the Avenue.

"I like to walk on this street," said Marc.

"So do I."

They could see the houses ahead curve with the bend in the street. The houses, with their darkened windows and untrespassed steps, bore witness to the quiet of the street, in contrast to the bedlam around the corner. They passed silent arched doorways and shuttered windows. As they passed one doorway, they heard a rustling noise and a slight groan. They turned simultaneously. Inside the doorway, leaning against a wall, was a couple. The girl wore a light blue dress, and her back was against the wall. Her reddish hair caressed the side of a light Negro's face, mingling with his black curly hair. The Negro had on jeans, and he leaned against the girl, pressing her against the wall. The girl's arms swept up and around the Negro's back as if she were pulling him down as well as close to herself. They were kissing, and their heads moved from side to side together as if they were trying to rub their lips until they fused.

"Man," said Marc offhandedly as they walked past the doorway, . . . "somebody's having a ball. But in a doorway? Why don't they go to a pad or something?"

"They can't. That guy inside that I talked to as we were leaving?"

Marc nodded, indicating that he remembered the fellow.

"That's his chick."

Marc's face rippled with a cynical smirk. He shook his head slowly as they continued to walk toward the Avenue.

18

ALONG THE BEACH, as far as the eye could see, even past where the beach curved seaward, hiding the rest of the shore behind the promontory, white, rolling foam glistened against the dark blue of water, leaping on the crest of a wave, thundering down bouncingly to the surface of the sea, gently caressing the breast of the beach, seducing all the land toward its dark mantle. Interspersed between the roaring waves was the whispering, tinkling chorus of sand and foam and pieces of shell churned together in the backwash.

The sun simmered the white stretch of beach. Rays of heat wavered from the flat, footprint-pocked sand toward the heavens. Only a few shadowy places, where weeds grew thick and green and wild on the dunes, could be seen. Here and there, a piece of driftwood lay land-locked. Near one piece of driftwood, there was a sparkling; the sun reflected off a washed-ashore bottle.

From behind the curving promontory of sand, a black shadow of a rock jetty broke the surface of the water, jutting seaward for a great distance. At its tip, a tower with a shack, just visible in the shimmering glare of the sun on the water, stood quietly guarding the fortress of the beach.

The sun baked Marc as he lay next to Rita on the blanket. He was face down, asleep, his head turned toward Rita. One arm lay folded against his side; the other was stretched past the edge of the blanket, his hand grasping a soft pile of sand. Filter butts stuck out of the sand near his hand. Beads of perspiration lined his forehead; a few drops slowly coursed the length of his nose.

Rita watched him as he slept. Her feet, stretched past the end of the blanket, slowly worked a hole into the sand. Her arms were folded under her body, her hands just under her chin. She watched a drop of water roll on the tip of Marc's nose as his head moved with each breath. She reached one hand out and with the tip of her index finger carried the little drop away. Marc stirred. He wrinkled his nose. Rita tweaked his nose again. He flicked his hand at the disturbance. Rita caught his hand in mid-air and held it. He struggled momentarily to get free, and then relaxed as his eyes slowly opened. His eyes were streaked with red sleep lines. He smiled lazily.

"Oh, . . . are you awake?"

"No, I always sleep this way . . . with my eyes open."

"Oh, that's wonderful."

"What's so wonderful about it?"

"I don't know, but nobody else I know sleeps with their eyes open."

"Nobody else you know does a lot of things I do—including giving you a good slap on your rear once in a while." Marc stretched his arms into the air, making a straining noise as his chest muscles were pulled taut. He lowered his arms over Rita's shoulders.

"That's the truth," she smiled, moving close, snuggling against him. "I mean about you being like no one else."

Marc smiled. They kissed. Then Marc twisted onto his back, gazing at the expanse of blue overhead.

"Look at that seagull," exclaimed Marc, sitting up, shading his eyes with his hand, looking toward the ocean.

Rita twisted around and sat up, looking to the area toward which Marc was gazing.

In the sky, the motionless wings of the white bird arched against blue. The round body ending in the yellow beak, suspended between the wings, rose softly, motionlessly, silently in the air. Suddenly, the bird dipped, diving straight to the sea, flapping its wings, slowing itself as it neared the water, only its talons hitting the surface. Then, with the strong beat of its outspread wings, the bird pulled itself up into the air again.

"What a graceful bird," said Marc as they watched it glide sideways with the wind, its wings motionless again. The white bird began flapping away from them.

Rita stood, brushed sand from the seat of her suit, and walked toward the sea. The slick of darkened sand at the edge of the beach was cold and hard and wet under foot. As she stood frozen on the cold sand, a sheet of water slid in over the shore, covering her foot. A chill passed through her body and subsided as she stood ankle-deep in the foamy surf. Directly in front of her, a sheet of water reared up, arched gracefully, and snapped toward her, crashing on the surface. Rita gazed at the shoreline that stretched away from her. Waves stretched parallel with the beach along the entire length of shore. A tingle gripped the back of her neck and behind her ears as she watched the superb grace and harmony, the sheer power and majesty of nature. It was a new, strange, and pleasureful sensation for her to thrill to the mere world about her. The world had suddenly begun to blossom. Her senses were now more acutely tuned to the changing moods and subtle, unmatchable beauty surrounding her. Rita had never taken pleasure in her surroundings, nor ever noticed the world about her. Now, through Marc, the world itself had become warm and endearing. Marc was understanding and knowledged. He could explain nature, life, to her. He was opening a new world for her, a world that had never been opened before. And that curiosity about the nature of things that had been stifled in the past, rushed to the surface now, and Rita was reveling in discovery, in the pleasure of being alive. Her pleasure was increased by the presence and companionship of Marc who understood and enjoyed being anywhere, because life was everywhere, because life came from inside. Rita too was beginning to understand that life was all around her, inside her, not restricted to coffee shops in the Village, and wearing coukie clothes.

Rita laughed at the thought of clothes, turning to see Marc walking toward her from the blanket. He was clad in a skimpy red bikini.

"How's that water?" Marc's feet sank into the soft sand, leaving their imprint. His smile evaporated instantly as his feet hit the slick of water at the edge of the beach. He hopped on one foot. "Wow, . . ." he blurted, surprised by the cold, which he felt more now that the sun had warmed him completely. "It sort of gets you when you're not used to it."

"Come on, you chicken." Rita lifted her foot through the water as if to kick water on Marc.

He shrank back a few steps, raising his hands defensively. "Come on now—don't fool around."

Rita pulled her leg back, smiling. Marc walked toward her.

"Man, this is some beach," Rita remarked. "How'd you know about it?"

"Man, . . . man, . . . is that the only way you can speak? Come off it!" Marc complained.

"All right, . . . all right. God damn it! Once in a while I slip. Don't jump down my God damn throat."

"Okay . . . I'm sorry, baby." Marc regretted his hasty remonstrance. He put his arms about her waist. "Let's go in the water." He gazed down at the top of her head as she peered, head down, at the sand.

"No . . . I don't want to go swimming." Her voice sounded hurt.

"Oh, come on, don't be an old party poop."

"No, . . . I'm not an old party poop," she said seriously.

Marc laughed at her expression. Even Rita begrudged a smile. Then she became serious again.

"I only made one mistake. You didn't have to get so damn nasty."

"I wasn't nasty . . . Ahh, I'm sorry I was nasty. I just wanted to remind you of that cool talk. Now come on." He grabbed Rita's arm and started running toward the water, pulling her with him.

"Stop! Let go," Rita screamed playfully, trying to dig her feet into the sand to stop her forward motion.

Marc ran, then swung his arm, dragging Rita forward, and threw her into the embrace of an oncoming wave. He followed after her and dove in. They surfaced in the trough of two waves. Water ran off their heads and down their faces. Rita blew water from her mouth.

"You bastard," she said playfully, laughing.

"What do you mean, bastard?" He pushed her head under the water. She bobbed to the surface gasping. She watched him for a second, then her hand lashed out and grabbed his nose, held it, and squeezed it.

"Let go . . . let go . . ."

"No . . . no . . ."

Marc pulled his head back quickly, electing to suffer the sudden burst of pain rather than be held prisoner by the nose. As Rita's fingers slipped from his face, he dove quickly beneath the surface. He saw her legs in front of him through the green mass of water. They were black, vague shadows, churning little bubbles as they pumped up and down, moving away from him. He stroked forward, one stroke pulling him even with her running legs. He grabbed her legs and, twisting himself, caught the bottom with his own feet, and lifted Rita upward. Rising to the surface still lifting, he threw her into the air. She flew a few feet, then sank beneath the water. Marc was laughing as she bobbed to the surface, her long black hair hanging against her head in a wet mass, water streaming down her face. She was blowing water away from her mouth and gasping for breath in the same motion. Marc laughed louder as she began to cough from swallowing water. Rita gritted her teeth and started toward him angrily. Marc turned and began to run toward shore, his legs churning against the impeding mass of water. The level of the sea decreased and his speed increased, and he quickly found himself free of the water. He sprinted across the beach to the blanket, turned, and waited for her to join him. She ran to him and stopped, laughing.

"You rotten, . . . rotten . . . ," she blurted, gasping for breath.

"I know, so are you." He embraced her and pulled her down on the blanket.

They lay on the blanket laughing, holding each other. Marc took her head between his hands and kissed her.

"Marc, baby, it's so great, just so great."

"I know." He kissed her forehead. "I'm very pleased with you . . . by you . . . at you . . . just pleased and very happy." His hand stroked her hair. He suddenly squeezed her tightly, happily.

"When we first met I dug you the end," Rita explained, "but I never thought we'd be together as long as this, or as much as this, or as nice as this. You make everything seem great, grand."

She kissed the tip of his nose. Marc laughed and hugged her tightly. She kissed his mouth full, her arms encircling him tightly.

They lay on the blanket quietly, just enjoying the warmth of their embrace for a long time, as the warmth and the sound of the surf lulled their souls.

Marc squinted down the curving expanse of beach. The sun was low in the western sky. Only a few dark figures remained on the beach.

"It's time to get going, baby. We want to get home in time to eat and then to the show."

"I wish we could stay here forever."

"We shall stay here forever. In our memories, in time, this moment shall never die—it exists."

"Can we come here again?"

"We'll come back again. Maybe tomorrow—if I don't get stuck in school." He took a cigarette out of the pack, lit it, and sucked some smoke into his lungs. "Well, let's get started," he said in a strained way as he pushed himself up to a standing position.

He reached his hand down, took Rita's hand, and pulled her to her feet. They picked up their gear and started toward the car through the warm sand that sank beneath their feet.

19

THE LOWERING SUN BLAZED a brilliant, blinding, reddish gold directly through the windshield, making driving near impossible. Marc spoke little, concentrating on overcoming sunset's glare.

"I'm glad we got the radio fixed," Rita remarked, humming soft harmony to the tune drifting through the car.

"Uh humm . . ."

"I really like to listen to music while we're driving, don't you?"

"What?"

Marc had been conscious only of the road ahead; his concentration was instantly reabsorbed by the road.

"I said I like to listen to music while we're driving."

"Will you stop bugging me, for Christ's sake!" He didn't turn from the road. "I have to drive and I can't concentrate and listen to you."

Rita recoiled instantly.

". . . and shut the God damn thing off." Marc snapped the radio off. "How the hell can I drive with this sun, and you, and the radio?"

Rita brooded silently, peering through the side window at the houses which lined the highway, foliage entwined about their steps, bathed in the evening sun. She gazed absently at the other cars along-side of which they drove, passing each in turn.

"Wow . . . this sun is blinding," Marc said abstractly, pulling the sun visor down.

Rita remained silent. Though well initiated to Marc's inexplicable outbursts of temper and anger, she was not impervious to their sting. She spoke not another word until they reached New York—which to New Yorkers is Manhattan.

The city was hot and close with humidity even though the sun was setting behind the buildings. Rita and Marc began to perspire, their clothes beginning to cling uncomfortably. Marc pulled alongside a parked car and backed into a parking space.

"Wheww . . . I'm sure glad to be home. I'm tired," he exclaimed, turning off the ignition. "I wish the hell we were still at that cool beach."

Rita ignored him, hastily gathering her belongings from the back seat. She opened the car door and started angrily toward the apart-ment.

Marc remained in the car for a moment, watching her stride toward the building. He knew from her rapid, determined walk that she was still angry. Her face was set and she was probably cursing him.

"Hey, wait for me," he called, jumping from the car.

Rita continued into the building, ignoring him completely.

Marc locked the car, ran to the building, and started up the stairs. He heard a door slam shut on a landing above as he ran up the steps. *She is a fiery one*, he thought, laughing to himself.

"What the hell are you so mad about?" he asked innocently as he closed the apartment door behind him.

Rita walked into the bedroom and closed the door behind her. She began changing out of her swimsuit, which she had worn home under a sweater and jeans. She reopened the door and came out of the bed-room clad in her bathrobe. Without looking at Marc, she marched straight toward the bathroom.

Marc put down the glass of beer he had poured for himself. "Hey, come on now." He sprang from his chair and caught Rita by the arm as she stormed past him. "Come on, don't be so angry. I didn't mean to be curt with you. It was the sun and all."

"That's no excuse to talk to me the way you did," she said, refusing to look at him, trying to loose his grip.

"Aww, come on now . . . I'm sorry."

"That's just the trouble, you're always sorry. And the next time you'll do it again. I'm tired of being spoken to like I were your little servant girl."

"I didn't talk to you like you were my servant girl, baby. The sun . . ."

"The sun, the sun . . . I suppose the sun *made* you talk like that, hanh?" She tugged desperately, trying to pry Marc's hands from her wrists.

"Can't you forget it?"

"No, no, I can't forget it. You've been taking me for granted for weeks now and I'm tired of it. You don't own me." She succeeded in loosing Marc's grip. She bolted into the bathroom and slammed the door.

"God damn it! I said I'm sorry," Marc shouted to the closed door.

The water of the shower started to spray down against the plastic curtains. Marc twirled about angrily and walked to the kitchen table.

"God damn women . . ." He emptied the beer can into his glass. He cocked his arm to crash the empty can against the wall. As he brought his arm forward, he lessened the power driving it forward and deject-edly let his arm flap at his side without releasing the can. He glanced momentarily toward the garbage pail and lobbed the can at it. It hit the lip of the pail and rebounded to the floor.

"Can't even throw the God damned garbage away right." He lit a cigarette, took his glass of beer, and walked to the window overlooking the street. He rested his head against the window frame.

Below, someone had opened the fire hydrant. A powerful stream of water was gushing across the street. Neighborhood children danced in its cooling spray. One child ran through the spray with his dog in his arms. Smaller children in white cotton underclothes were gleefully running down the steps of the tenements across the street. When their underclothing was soaked, it clung to the pink skin of their buttocks. They were all happy and dancing in the water. One kid in the spray was fully clothed, and his clothes were soaked and flapping about his body as he danced. Older folks fanning themselves in apartment windows watched the cavorting children, probably wishing they could jump in too. One old woman, heavy and squat, had taken off her shoes and was dancing by the curb across the street from the hydrant, as the water skimmed there and then flowed toward the sewers. Her husband, in a strap undershirt, a cigar stub in his mouth, was laughing and clapping his hands. On the roof across the street from Marc's apartment some older boys and girls in bathing suits were leaning over the edge of the roof, watching the younger children in the spray below.

An old lady sat at one of the windows of her apartment in the same building where the kids were leaning over the roof. She fanned herself with a folded newspaper with one hand, covering her mouth with her other hand. Marc wondered why the old woman covered her mouth with her hand—perhaps to hide the spaces from which her teeth had fallen.

A car eased through the stream of water, the children screaming delight as the water pounded its metal side.

Marc pushed away from the window frame and sat in the over-stuffed arm chair which faced the window. He gazed up at the dusk-streaked sky and sighed, shaking his head. He sipped his beer, leaned his head against the back of the chair and smoked his cigarette.

They're all alike, he thought to himself. *God damn women. God damn women. Can't even ask them to let you drive the car, they start crying and bitching.* "God damn it . . ." he shouted through gritted teeth, twisting to stare at the closed bathroom door. "Wait till she comes out," he said under his breath.

His eyes scanned the apartment. It was a pleasant apartment in which they lived, he thought, his anger easing. The three rooms had been his alone before Rita moved in. The place wasn't elaborately furnished, but it was all that he could afford in the beginning, and in the beginning furniture and space do not matter—not at first, when all one wants is privacy. It had been enough for the two of them too—in the beginning anyway. But as reason through prolonged association supplanted passion, Marc began to see shortcomings, to realize the need for more than a communion of physical existence. Perhaps some paint? It was still his apartment, he thought angrily, and it was the way he wanted it; he refused to be pressured into a corner.

Marc had never before thought of the toll of living together, but he was at least mindful of it now. It was a nice enough apartment, he assured himself. It was convenient for him to get to school during the school year. It was a long haul, however, from his east-seventies tenement to the Village. That was why Rita had quit working. She still attended acting classes, although lately she had been attending less and less. She no longer had the time; she was now more concerned with the task of keeping a pleasant home for Marc and herself. Living together was great, Marc thought, except for times like this. He couldn't stand a woman's caprices. In the last weeks, they had been getting along real well, he admitted—just every once in a while they'd have a little conflict.

I didn't have to yell at her like that. I didn't mean to.

The bathroom door opened and Rita came out in her robe, a towel draped into a turban about her head. Contrary to what Marc had expected, she walked toward his chair and sat on the edge of the chair, slipping her arm behind his head.

"I'm sorry, baby," she said, kissing his temple. "I guess I was just a little hot and bothered before. The shower cooled me off."

"That's all right. I didn't mean it, you know? I know you didn't either."

"Okay, . . . let's forget it. We said we were sorry. I love you." She leaned forward and kissed him. Marc slid his arms about her waist and held her tightly against himself. They parted and he rested his head against hers.

Dusk was now enveloping the city and the room was deep grey and dark with shadows. Rita absently stroked Marc's head.

"It's kind of funny," she said.

"What's that?"

"Oh, the way I've changed since we've been living together."

"Me too. I'm a lot different than I was. Don't know how to explain it . . . but I can tell."

"I can't say either, but I know it's different," she explained. "Maybe it's that I understand."

"Us?"

"Us . . . and me—lots of things. Things about love and people. Things I never stopped to think about before."

"Yeah, I know. I guess when you're bouncing around like a Yo-yo without a string you don't give much time to thinking about other people, and how maybe they're unhappy or lonely or sick, too. I never gave two damns about anybody. If they bugged me, carried on the way I didn't like, I put them down, but quick. But you, with all your crazy tantrums and all, you drive me nuts . . . but, somehow, I don't mind it so much." He smiled a bit.

"Yeah, that's something like it. I would never have taken the things I take from you from a guy before. But now it doesn't matter. You know, what's the difference if you get a mad on once in a while—I know you don't mean it. I love you and you love me, and we need each other. Without you it'd be like living on the moon. I know you don't get angry because you . . . well, I don't know. You just get mad some-times—so do I—then it goes away, and everything is all right again. I guess that's the difference. I understand, like life is real, life is earnest. I guess love is really just an outweighing of human faults and hard times and old bitch Mother Nature by warmth and companionship. You know, you learn to accept the fact that everybody is a bit different, imperfect. We're getting to understand the things we don't like, aren't we?" she asked softly, smiling.

"Yeah. I feel that way too. Sometimes you think I'm putting you down and you get angry at me. And then I get a little angry 'cause I'm not really putting you down. But I understand you more now, and I don't mind so much."

"I'm getting better though," she suggested.

"Me too, I hope. I'm tired of being inside my doubting skull counter-punching myself. I want to relax. I'm glad we're together. It's good for us, for me."

Rita continued to stroke Marc's head.

"Do you think we'll get married?" she asked absently.

"I don't know." Marc shrugged. "Maybe . . . who knows?"

They remained where they were, Marc sitting in the chair, resting his head against Rita, Rita sitting on the arm of the chair stroking his head—the golden, purplish, reddish, harbingers of night rose high in the sky, pulling the veils of evening after them.

20

THE FINGER HOLES SPUN IN A BLUR over the letters and numbers on the phone dial as Rita's finger selected the desired combination. She sank back in the overstuffed chair, gazing through the window at thin strips of cold, fall rain winding out of the sky. Small clumps of transparent light-grey clouds, outlined against the dark grey of great rain clouds, floated on the wind, their fragile bodies torn out of shape, dispersed into vague nothingness. The room was overcast by gloom; no lights were lit. Rita sat half in shadow, her legs and hips obscured by dismal grey, the upper part of her body encased in ebon shadow.

In the earpiece, she could hear the steady bleating as the phone rang. She inhaled from her cigarette. The tip blazed orange, casting a pale light on her mouth and cheeks, then faded to a slight reddish glow. Rita spit out the smoke as the phone on the other end was lifted.

"Hello?"

"Hello, Mother . . . Rita. How're you?"

"Rita?" Mother exclaimed with surprise. "How're you?" She emphasized the "you" that had been lost so long.

"Okay. How's Dad and Randy?"

Rita was being sincere when she asked about her family. She

could now call and be sincere because through her life and love with Marc she was more securely a person, she was no longer plagued by the insecurity of being alone and unloved, and she could understand her parents' anxiety and insecurity because she now knew that they too were only human, plagued with human imperfections, fears, needs, anxieties, just as she and Marc were. Before—before Marc—she had never been so understanding as to consider that her parents might be doing what they were doing because they believed in their own way of life, because they had to be themselves, because they too were insecure in their relation to the world. She had not considered the fact that people differ in taste and intellect as much as they differ in appearance. Even if Rita had realized before, she would never have been forgiving. Why should she have been the one to accept rather than they? Why should she have forgiven them? Now she understood, and in understanding, she felt she must be the one to go forward with outspread arms. If she disagreed with them, she thought, she should try to indicate her disagreement gently rather than condemn them. How irrational the behavior of months past now seemed. It was wonderful to be with Marc, she thought, wonderful to be awakened to the world finally, after years and years of unending sleep.

"Fine, fine, everybody's just fine," Mother assured her. "But we haven't heard from you in so long. We were starting to worry. Poppa was going to call, but I told him, 'She's all right. If something is wrong, we'll hear,' I told him. So how are the girls, all right?"

"Oh fine, we're all fine too."

"That's good. What are you doing these days?"

Rita was disappointed that Mother's voice was the same. Somehow she had hoped it might have changed. She envisioned Mother at home, now by the kitchen phone, trying to dig into Rita's life, trying to tactfully interrogate her, to see if she was still a disgrace.

"Working a little . . . going to school . . . the same things," she lied.

"You're still going to that school, hanh?" Mother asked, a deep-seated disapproval ringing in her voice.

Rita drew in her breath. "Yes, . . . I'm still going to school."

A profound silence befell the conversation.

Why does knowledge impose understanding which ignorance and laziness can shirk? Must I be the appeaser, Rita wondered, the offerer, the one who must go to them, to offer gift tokens? Have these adults no obligation to me? Am I not a person?

"What else is new in the neighborhood?" asked Rita, making conversation.

"Nothing much. You know Mrs. Shoren's daughter, Betty? You should see the lovely engagement ring she got—five carats—and such a nice boy too, so respectful, and nice. It's such a pleasure for a mother to see her daughter so well provided. Ahh . . ." Mother sighed soulfully.

"Yes, really nice," agreed Rita, leaping agilely to the side of the thrust as it tried desperately, albeit lovingly, to tear into her flesh. Rita tried to justify Mother's obtuseness. Mother had been brought up in a different world; the rules that her grandparents had drummed into their children—rules inflexibly tied to the horsecart and Jewish persecution, were out of tune today. It is impossible to retain specific rules forever, because the old rules were made to cope with old problems, and now there are new problems, different problems, and the need for new rules. The world is bigger, and wider, and faster, and there are more things to do and enjoy, and more freedom, and more problems, . . . and though it's nice to have respect, it should help, not impede life as it exists. People must respect themselves first, before they can respect things that once were. Rita wondered what the ancients were like—the ones who made up the ancient rules. Were they so much more self-sufficient as to have been able to think for themselves? Why were people who were now alive so incapable of making rules, if not for themselves at least for posterity? Was it the age of automation and mass production which did not require thought, which reduced people to digits and cogs in a vast machinery? Or was it that the rules of life were always created haphazardly, by inaction and whim, evolving by themselves from the depths of indecision.

"You know," continued Mother ". . . your brother, Randy, he's getting so big now. He's going out on dates with a girl from school. What a big boy! He even wants to take Poppa's car, but I won't let him. He might hurt himself."

"I think he's a little young to be driving a car."

"Aww, he's only a boy. But he's getting big already," Mother crowed proudly.

Life is not breathing or eating, Rita thought. Life is change. And a thing that does not change is dead.

"So how come you called? I mean, you don't usually."

"I thought it might be nice if I said hello to my family."

"Oh, really? You mean, you're just waking up?" Mother was sarcastic in the way only ignorance can be sarcastic—like a dull hammer.

Rita held her breath, holding in her annoyance.

"Yes, I guess so," Rita replied resignedly. "Everyone has to wake up once in a while—don't they?"

"Why don't you come over for dinner. We haven't seen you in months, you know?"

Rita wasn't prepared for another visit yet. She just couldn't bear being trapped again.

"Yes, I know. Maybe I'll come over soon and have dinner one night. That is, if there's no plate throwing or any other nonsense."

"You know Poppa don't mean that. He's just tired from working and he gets upset right away. He don't mean nothin' . . ."

Understanding is wonderful, Rita thought, but it's difficult too. Difficult to accept and forgive misunderstanding and the ignorance of those understood.

"I guess he doesn't mean it, but it's terrible to come home and be greeted like that. You know, I can't live my life your way forever. I have to be able to think on my own . . . to think out my own life. I'm very happy now."

"Maybe. You're young yet . . . you'll see."

"What do you mean, I'm young yet. I can think. I can use my head now. Is there a certain gift that parents get all of a sudden when they become parents that makes them so much smarter than anybody."

"Are you starting in again?"

"I'm sorry," she said guiltily. She had forgotten to duck. "Can't you just let me live my own life, my own way, . . . and we can be friends . . . happy together because we just enjoy?"

"Sure . . . you know everything. Your parents are stupid. Such a smart girl."

"Okay . . . Let's not fight. I have to go now," she said quickly, feeling the need of relief after the first almost successful encounter. "I'll give you a ring next week, and come for dinner maybe."

"Okay, dear, . . . but listen, don't wear those black stockings. They make you look terrible. I mean, you know . . . they're not for you, dear. Believe Momma . . ."

"All right, Mother," Rita agreed in desperation. "Give my love to Poppa and Randy. And tell Randy not to be going out with too many girls. He'll get to be a playboy."

Mother chuckled appreciatively. "I'll tell him, dear. Goodbye now. Give Momma a kiss."

Rita puckered her lips and sent a short, audible kiss into the receiver.

"So long, see you soon." Rita took the phone from her ear and turned to replace it on the cradle. Just then she heard Marc behind her, closing the door.

21

"WHO WERE YOU TALKING TO?" Marc asked as he walked toward Rita.

"My mother." Rita walked toward him, her arms outstretched.

Marc lit the small lamp on the bookcase against the side wall and put his portfolio down on a chair. He removed his sweater, throwing it on the chair with the portfolio.

"Your mother?" He held Rita off, studying her face intently.

"Yes . . . why do you ask like that?"

"No reason, . . . no reason at all," Marc said calmly yet curtly. He studied Rita's face as he lit a cigarette. He snapped the cover of his lighter shut and blew out the smoke in a thin, steady stream before him. He walked to the kitchen and reached into the refrigerator for a beer.

"It's crazy, you know?" He took the bottle opener from the drawer under the table edge. ". . . the way people are, and like sometimes they don't like each other and refuse to talk to each other . . ." He popped the top off the bottle, lifted it, and took a long pull from it. ". . . and then they'll call each other on the phone and kiss and say, 'I'll see you soon.' Crazy, isn't it?" A hard smile split his face.

Rita winced, realizing Marc was starting in on one of his tirades about being deceived.

"Oh, Marc, . . . please don't start with that jealous stuff again. Jesus Christ, I can't even talk to anyone on the phone now."

"Who the hell are you kidding—me? You don't even talk to your mother! So you tell me it's your mother you're talking to when I come in here and you're kissing the shit out of the phone. Come on, baby, . . . this is Marc!" he yelled, tapping his chest with his thumb.

"I know who it is, . . . you jealous idiot," Rita said calmly, smiling to reassure and calm Marc. "Come on, baby," she tried to put her arms around his neck. "That *was* my mother. I'll call her back and you can talk to her if you want."

"I don't want to talk to your mother. I don't want to talk to anyone. God damn women! Can't trust them for a minute. Turn around once slow, and they're off making it in the closet with some other cat. What the hell's the use? It's always the same. Every one of you." He turned and walked to the bedroom.

Tears welled up in Rita's eyes. She had never loved anyone as she loved Marc; she had never been so fulfilled by anyone, and never before had it hurt so to be disbelieved. That he distrusted her fidelity was even more crushing. Through their love, the sexual act had become something more than a mere physical pleasure. It was a consummation, a blending, an embodiment of their love; it was warm and beautiful and sincere and harmonious. Thoughts of her past affairs didn't fill her with sorrow as much as wonder. How could it be that she had cherished those fleeting passions snatched out of time, compared to this eternal beauty and serenity? Only this was making love—this physical sharing of eternity for brief seconds. Even the phrase "making love" made her pity her promiscuous friends, her former self for her past life. How could she have called that making love . . . when all it was was a pilfered physical act.

Marc's jealous rages were beginning to weary her, however. She had been awakened to the beauty of love, of tenderness and kindness, but these were fragile, delicate qualities, new born in her, and easily crushed. And Marc seemed bent on a destruction of those feelings with his constant accusations and attacks.

Rita followed Marc into the bedroom. Marc was lying full length on the bed, his ankles crossed, his head propped up on the pillow. He held a magazine in front of his face with one hand, and the bottle of beer in the other.

"Marc . . . Marc . . . you stupid child. Can't you understand I'm not any other woman? I'm me. The other's, whoever they are, and whoever they go to bed with, don't count. You're persecuting yourself with straw-men possibilities; the Empire State building might fall tomorrow too, but worry about it when it happens. Can't you see—understand—that I love you, only you, baby? How could you even think that I'd be going with anybody else?"

"It happens all the time, baby." He did not look at her. "What do you mean, how could I think of it? It's easy if you've seen all the God damn tramps I've seen other guys married to."

"But I'm not one of them—not me, Marc. Can't you ever believe that? Won't you try to believe that? I'm me—Rita—and I love you and I don't want anyone else." She knew this mood by now. She knew she had to be gentle and warm, overly affectionate and demonstrative. He'd come off it shortly.

Marc finished his beer and put the bottle on the floor. Rita grabbed the bottle as it toppled and started to roll under the bed.

"There's deposit on these bottles," she said lightly, trying to change his mood.

"Fuck it! Who needs the two cents? Who needs anything?"

"Marc, baby," she sat on the floor, next to him, clasping him about the neck. "Marc . . . . Please believe me, baby. I could never be with anyone but you. Baby, I love you . . . . Don't you understand that? I love you . . . . " Her tears soaked warmly through his shirt.

Hesitantly, Marc slid his arms around her back and held her tightly. The sincerity of her pleading moved him. His hurt and suspicion were allayed.

"I want to believe in you, baby. I want to. Really. It's just that you see so much crap around," he exclaimed angrily. "Do you think I want to be this way? Do you think it's fun?"

Marc removed Rita's arms and stood up. He paced the floor, then stopped and stood facing the wall.

"God damn it, I wish I wouldn't get like this. I don't want to, believe me, baby. I know I get to be too much. Just think what a pain in the ass it would be to you if it was you who was racked by these nutty moods. It kills me to have to worry, to have to doubt you, but I can't help it, baby. I really can't! I just go crazy with jealousy sometimes. It's more than that too, more than jealousy. I'm afraid you'll leave me, afraid I'll be alone—and baby, I need you." He turned to face Rita. "Forgive me, baby, please forgive me. Help me."

Rita stood and rushed to him, embracing him.

"That's all right, darling," she assured him. "I want you to be able to believe in me. I love you—I love you so much."

Marc looked into her eyes, then kissed her needfully. His lips caressed her cheeks, her nose, her tears, tasting their warm saltiness. He smiled, his apprehension flying . . . as he clung to her desperately. They remained embracing silently for many minutes.

"Now come on; we're going to a party tonight," Marc exclaimed.

"Really? . . . Whose?" she asked excitedly, happy that his mood had changed and that Marc believed in her.

"I don't know. It's downtown. A couple of cats I met today are having a fling and asked me to come and like that. They said to drop down. So, we're going to drop down."

"Oh, good. You're not mad anymore? . . ."

"No."

". . . and you believe I love you?"

"Sure." He forced himself to smile.

She hugged him tightly, pressing her head against his chest.

"Now, come on," he said, patting her rear end playfully.

"Hey! . . . Aww, don't do that. You know I can't stand it."

"Okay," he smiled. "Come on. I'll take my shower and then you can have the entire washroom for the next two hours."

"Thank you," said Rita curtsying graciously low. Marc bowed and smiled.

22

THE PARTY WAS HELD IN A PHOTOGRAPHER'S STUDIO which had been fashioned out of an entire floor in a loft building. Its stone walls had been whitewashed and partitioned off into living quarters at the front, studio in the center, and darkroom at the rear. Two huge mobiles made up of the host's photographs twirled from the ceiling in the living quarters. Other photographs—deep textured, grainy photographs of the city, and beaches, and girls—hung on the walls. Props and backdrops and spotlights filled the studio portion. The dark room portion was shielded from the party by heavy drapery. The furniture strewn about was mostly odd pieces picked up inexpensively in second-hand furniture stores, re-finished and reupholstered by the photographer—coffee tables with legs cut down to give them a low effect, and brightly covered cherry-wood couches and mahogany-legged chairs.

The party was the usual Village party. All varieties of people kept wandering in and out. One fellow had long, unkempt hair and a straggly beard, and wore jeans and old, beat-up shoes. With him was a girl with long, blonde, unkempt hair that hung below her shoulders. She wore a full skirt, flat comfortable shoes, and a sweater which allowed her unhaltered breasts to sag and sway. She had huge buttocks which rose up, quivered, and dropped convulsively as she walked. They were quite the couple—a poet and his appreciative mistress. They were intensely Bohemian and practical to the point of being impractical for the sake of Bohemianism. They typified the people who are too creative to do any prosaic work and who sit in Washington Square Park reading poems to each other in some unintelligible poetic language and think the rest of the world is a dull place which doesn't appreciate the artistic ability of this bearded genius. She would probably carry their children strapped to her back in a gunny sack, or tied in a net sling around her side, so that she could shop and walk and not be impeded by the baby—nor be burdened with the obligation of purchasing a stroller carriage. They were the hiking type who'd walk from the Village to Central Park to save the carfare—besides, "walking is good for the body."

Calypso music floated through the apartment. The guests filled the rooms with an accompaniment of lilting, clipped accents of native singing. The chanting and drumbeat mingled amongst the drinking girls, the sketching artists, the laughing Negroes showing their rows of white teeth, the dancing couples, the small groups of people clustered in conversation. Some guests sat on the floor. Others stood about, drinking and talking. One couple was executing a slow dance. The two held their arms extended rigidly at angles from their bodies, their legs lifting one after the other. They kept their eyes on each other and circled without touching each other.

A few outsiders entered the apartment with one of the Villagers. Some outsiders were already at the party by themselves, but nobody bothered them as long as they didn't start any trouble.

The party had been going for some time and even the beer-and-coke combination was running low. Empty bottles were hoisted into the air several times every minute—eyes pierced their glass body— only to be dropped on the table or floor to deceive the next thirsty partier. The drink was scarce, but its effect was very much present.

Though Marc and Rita had pretty much satisfied their need for nocturnal wandering and searching in the maze of coffee shops and cafes of the Village, they continued to associate with the Village and its people for the sake of having something more to do than sitting in an

Uptown movie house or sipping a soda in a neighborhood luncheon-ette. At least something did happen in the Village; there was life in the Village; there were conversations to be had on subjects more compel-ling than the weather or baseball.

Rita sat on a huge, stuffed hassock, a bottle of beer in her hand. She had just ended a conversation with two girls who now began dancing with a couple of fellows from Uptown. She turned to scan the party for any new people and conversations. Through the crowd, she spied Jeannie and Laura. This was the first time in two weeks that Rita had seen them. Laura was with Johnny. Jeannie was just setting out on an expedition with a tall Uptowner into the inner reaches of the dark room.

Rita was delighted to see Laura vibrant and changed from the little shy Laura with whom she had lived. Laura was dressed in a skirt and sweater and wore black, knee-high socks and flat shoes. He hair was even fixed with a little sprig of a flower and she wore a bit of lip rouge. She was smiling and seemed very happy and sure of herself. Johnny too was certainly happy to be with Laura. They were two different peo-ple, the released spirits of two captives that had liberated each other.

Laura smiled as she noticed Rita watching her. Johnny and she walked over to Rita.

"I haven't seen you in weeks. Where've you been keeping your-self?" Laura inquired.

"You know, Marc, school, the house, all make Rita a busy girl"

"I guess so. Rita, you remember Johnny. He's such a great guy." She turned and grasped his arm, smiling warmly. "Johnny . . . this is Rita."

"Hi. I think we met once before, a little fleetingly—at the party at your place, Laura's place—remember?"

"Yes, you were there with a tall, skinny fellow with red hair—Paul—and you left rather suddenly, didn't you?"

"Yeah, that's it. You've got the picture." He looked down and laughed.

"You two seem to be having a good time. What makes you so happy?"

"Oh, Rita . . . you probably know how it feels . . . but it's like I've been released from solitary confinement inside my soul. Since Johnny and I have been going out, I feel like I'm alive." She became a bit embarrassed by her own enthusiasm.

"That's wonderful, honey. I know what you mean," Rita assured her, glancing around the room for Marc. He was standing at the other end of the apartment with one of his buddies who was playing the guitar. They were singing a folk tune.

"I guess Marc'll be off to school again soon, hanh?" Laura asked.

"He's already started. But we've had the summer off together. I took off from school and work for a while so that we could be together for the entire summer without interference."

"That sounds great. I wish we could've done that," Johnny remarked.

"That's all right, we'll be together plenty," Laura said smiling warmly. Johnny smiled too.

"What's up with you two?"

Laura smiled at Johnny again and turned to Rita. "We're going to get married."

Rita was dumbstruck. "Really? . . . Oh, man, that's great . . . that's wonderful. I'm almost knocked out. When did all this happen?"

"It's been happening right along," said Johnny. "We get along good . . . and like that." He smiled at Laura.

"That's great! It really is—just wonderful." Rita stood and kissed Laura and hugged her happily. Laura began to explain the coming event. She was more pleased and happy about this than about anything else that had ever happened in her entire life. At one point in the conversation, Rita glanced up and saw Tom the Cat enter the party. *Tom from so long ago*, she thought to herself, *so many years, so many ages ago*. It had seemed wonderful to be with Tom that night so long ago—yet now, it seemed so dull, so meaningless—as if it hadn't happened.

Tom saw Rita with Johnny and Laura. He walked over, swaying from drink that he had consumed before he arrived at this party. He was smiling broadly, with abandon, pulling a girl along by the hand.

"Hi, baby, how've you been?"

"Okay, Tom, how're you?" replied Rita smiling, amused at Tom's tipsiness. "You look like you've been doing all right tonight."

"Oh, . . . this is Joan." He turned to point at the girl.

"I didn't mean her. I meant you looked like you're already a little high."

"Oh . . . Well, anyway, this is Joan." He chuckled.

"Hi," said Joan to Rita, Laura, and Johnny. Joan was a brunette, short, a little heavy, but cute. She looked like a girl who liked to laugh. She had a happy, big smile.

"You remember Laura, don't you, Tom? And this is Johnny, her boyfriend."

"Hi, John, this is Joan. I don't remember meeting Laura. Hi. This is Joan."

Joan began chuckling.

Tom's face retained a constant, happy smile. "Whose pad is this?" he asked, looking around the apartment.

"Jimmy's," Laura offered.

"Jimmy? Who's Jimmy?" Tom frowned, trying to recall a face to fit that name.

"That fellow over there." Rita indicated the other side of the room.

Tom turned around and looked across the room, his eyes not focusing well.

"That one, with the little black beard on his chin," Rita explained, pointing across the room.

"Jimmy? His name is Tony. I know him, . . . but his name is Tony. I know him a long time."

"Well, you don't know him too well," said Laura smiling, "'cause his name is Jimmy."

"Jimmy . . . mmm . . . that's sure not what I call him . . . but anyway, . . . this is sure Joan." He pointed limply at his date and burst into a laugh.

Everybody laughed. Tom doubled over with mirth. Joan had a high-pitched, cackling sort of laugh that burst out of her mouth right at the start and just kept coming out. Joan's eyes were tearing as the laughter began to fade. Sporadically, she burst with a reminiscent chuckle, leading the rest of the group back into laughter.

"Tom, I'm going to the little girl's room. I'll be right back," said Joan.

"Okay, take your time. I'll be right here with the cat." Tom looked at Rita and smiled. "Hi'ya, cat . . . . "

"Hi, Tom. That was sure a long time ago."

"Sure was. How'd'ya like this chick?" He nodded in the direction in which Joan had departed.

"She's a nice girl. Where did you get her?"

"I met her in . . . the street," said Tom, laughing slowly and softly. He was happy to be a little out of this world.

"You're really gone, you know that?" remarked Rita.

"What's the cat stuff?" Johnny asked interestedly.

"Private joke," replied Rita.

"That's right." Tom walked toward Rita and put his arm around her shoulder. "We've got a private secret. Bet you didn't know we were so friendly, did you?"

"Congratulations," exclaimed Laura.

"Thank you. May I kiss the bride now?" Tom bowed, then kissed Rita's cheek.

"My goodness, Tom," Rita reproved him playfully. "You're too much tonight."

"No, I'm not, I'm just enough—as usual." He kissed her cheek again. Everybody began to laugh again. Tom smiled, his head rolling on his shoulder from side to side as he watched the rest of the room, his arm still around Rita's shoulders.

"Rita, . . ." Marc called sternly and curtly. He was standing just behind the group.

"What, Marc?" Rita asked turning around, still laughing.

Marc was standing with his arms folded across his chest, a hard, steady glare on his face.

"I want to talk to you. Do you mind?" he said, looking at Tom.

Rita took Tom's arm from around her shoulder and walked slowly toward Marc. He had that look—the jealous, angry, hurt look. Rita's stomach felt empty suddenly, and as large as a cavern.

"Not here. Come on." Marc turned and walked out of the apartment.

Rita followed him as the others in the small group watched, their faces blank.

"What are we being so secretive about?" asked Rita playfully as they reached the hallway outside the apartment. She pretended not to comprehend. A cool draught of air drifted up the stairwell, but failed to soothe the perspired brows of the two.

"What the hell is all that action with this guy that just came in?"

"You mean Tom—just now? You met him once before." Rita played dumb, trying to delay the onslaught.

"Oh . . . so that's Tom? No, I never met him before. I never even saw him. I've heard of him though. You two are turning on again—I saw that."

"Oh, Tom . . . I mean, Marc, what the . . ."

"You don't even know my name now," Marc screamed. "I'm Marc . . . Marc, baby. Tom's in there. I'm not the cat—he's the cat." Marc became more incensed and furious as he recalled the story of the cat, which Rita had related to him.

"Baby . . . I stuttered . . . does that mean something is going on?"

"No, not that alone. But you're standing in there and he's kissing you, and you were having a ball—laughing and talking, just like I wasn't even here. What the hell am I, . . . a dummy?" The color of his face deepened to purple. His anger was beginning to control him. "You're turning on with some guy while I'm in the same pad." He clenched his fists, his eyes almost bulging out of his head. "Am I some kind of idiot clown that you can pull that on?" His teeth bared.

The door of the apartment swung open. The noise of the party, which had been muffled, now flew out, over and around the figure of Jimmy, the fellow who owned the apartment.

"Hey, man, hanh? Keep it a little cool, will you?" Jimmy demanded. "Man, like just down to a slow roar. There's another cat living upstairs, and like he'll call the cops, you know?"

"Yeah, man, okay, okay, I'll take care of it." Marc stared impatiently at Jimmy, waiting for him to leave.

Jimmy returned Marc's gaze blandly. His eyes darted occasionally to Rita. He turned back into the apartment. The noise of the party swelled and faded as the door opened and closed.

"Be serious, Marc—Jesus Christ. Tom was a little high, and like he was kidding around. It doesn't mean anything at all, darling."

Marc glared at her uncompromisingly, his clenched fists turning white with the tension.

"Oh, come off it, baby," she yelped exasperated. She reached out to put her arms around his neck.

"Bullshit, bullshit. Get away from me," he said, grimacing, removing her arms from around his neck. "What are you, a sex machine, throwing yourself at every guy that gets near you? I didn't come out here to make it with you. I want to know what the hell is coming off? I know all about the cat and all that. And now what? You starting in again? Hanh? Making a fool out of me? Here . . . in front of everybody?"

"I know you know about the cat," she said slowly, deliberately. "I told you, remember? So the guy comes to a party and he's a little high, and like he's kidding around. Like, we're friends. He has a date with him—or didn't you bother to notice?"

"All I saw was the two of you balling."

"Oh, come off that trash. For Christ's sake, the guy gives me two little kisses on the cheek and you call it balling. Man, you're a couk, . . . you know that? You're a real, honest to God couk sometimes."

"Don't give me that line, baby. I don't dig the action here. I don't dig the dirty finger at all. He the "mother" you said you were talking to on the phone today?"

"Stop it, will you? . . . stop it, you idiot." Rita felt like crying, dying. "Are you trying to get rid of me? If you are, just say so. I'll go . . . all you have to do is say so. But don't persecute me like this. Didn't we have this out this afternoon? I don't want to go through it again. I told you what happened. If that isn't good enough for you, it's tough. What the hell am I supposed to say?"

"Nothing, nothing at all." Marc twirled and started down the stairs.

Rita did not stir. She watched him descend and set her jaw determinedly. Suddenly, she was resigned to the impossibility of Marc's ever being able to trust her, their love ever being able to overcome his fear. But he was leaving now; she'd be alone again right now. Terror gripped her. She bolted down the stairs after him. She caught him and threw her arms around his neck, clinging to his back.

"Marc, oh Marc, baby . . . Baby, I love you . . . Nobody else means anything to me. Don't you believe that?"

"I don't know what to believe," Marc said bewilderedly, wanting to believe her. "I know what I see though." He turned to face her.

"Baby, we were only kidding, honest! Do you think I could go for anyone else?"

"I don't know, baby. Women are kind of funny. I just see red when I see you fooling around with another guy."

"I wasn't fooling around, baby, honest. If I wanted to be with him, I wouldn't have run after you, would I?"

"I don't know, would you?" Marc slipped his arms around Rita's waist.

"No, baby, I only run after you."

Yet, even as she spoke, Marc's eyes were studying her, wondering.

Rita's insides ached with desperation. She wanted, needed him so much. But the scars on his soul, his bitter agony of loneliness and fear, clawed at him, destroying him and the bird of love and beauty he had created. Their love, being bigger and stronger had more strength to destroy itself. Rita realized Marc was weakening under the greater strain of accepting their love, trusting her. She kissed his mouth. It was warm. Even if she had to fool herself, she wanted Marc.

Marc lost his balance on the steps and grabbed the rail for support.

"Let's get on some level ground," Marc smiled.

"Okay," said Rita smiling softly.

Marc's smile broadened. He watched her from the side of his eyes as they descended the steps one arm around each other's waist.

23

POUNDING MUSIC DRIFTED THROUGH THE HUMID HEAT. The yellow overhead lights fused with the engulfing heat, forcing the walls of Johnson's down upon the people standing along the bar and seated at the tables. Their voices seemed to crack across the room with an unusual rapidity, resounding and reverberating like an echo inside an empty cavern. It was the heat, the slowness of moving, the forced languor of the people that gave sound a staccato which assailed the ears.

Rita walked into Johnson's with Jeannie, Laura, and Johnny. Sammy looked up.

"Hey, baby, long time no see."

"Hi, Sammy, how're you?" Rita replied.

"Not bad. What's been happening?"

"Nothing very exciting. I've been out of circulation for a while . . . ." She smiled weakly, not really feeling like smiling; it was more a snicker of resignation. "But I'm back swinging again."

"Yeah, I heard you and your boy split."

"That's right . . ." Rita swallowed hard. "You got a wire service, or what? You know everything, don't you?"

"You know, baby, we're all interested in our friends."

Someone from the far end of the bar called Sammy and he walked toward them to refill their orders.

"Everything's just about the same, isn't it?" Rita remarked, looking around.

"A few more pieces of junk here and there, but the same dive," replied Jeannie. "Let's sit at this table."

They sat at a table opposite the bar.

"Excuse me," said Johnny. He walked toward the men's room.

"You and Johnny really hit it off good, didn't you," Jeannie remarked to Laura as the three girls watched Johnny walk toward the back.

"Yeah, we get along fine. Now that you're back, Rita—I know it's one day—but why don't you and Jeannie come over to our place. Maybe tomorrow? Johnny's been asking me to have you over."

"Maybe. Want to go tomorrow?" Jeannie asked Rita.

"Hmmm . . . sure, sure." Rita was absorbed in thought.

"What are you thinking about, babe?" asked Laura. "Marc?"

"What do you think? I met him in here, didn't I?"

"Yeah. You'd never think so much could happen in so short a time. You and Marc getting together and splitting. Me and Johnny getting married. Jeannie's the same though, same as ever."

"You're not kidding. Me and God. We're always the same."

Laura snickered. Rita smiled uneasily, sadly.

"But what started the whole thing?" Laura asked. "I thought you two were going real smooth."

"We were—for a while. We were going great, but then Marc started to get real nervous every time I was within a hundred yards of another guy. You remember what happened at Jimmy's party two weeks ago, don't you Laura? You remember Tom?" Rita asked Jeannie. "Well, he comes to the party a little gassed and kisses me on the cheek. I think you were at the party, weren't you?"

"Yeah, but like I didn't see *anything* happen."

"Yeah, well, Marc flipped over that scene with Tom—how come I was balling with Tom, you know? And he just kept bugging me after that. Every night we'd start in on a new argument. Same story, different correspondents—every night. Who was I fooling around with? Was I trying to put him down? On and on and on and on. He didn't do it to be mean, you know? He loved me, I'm sure. I think that was the trouble. In the beginning, when it didn't affect either of us too much, he was wonderful, kind, considerate, opened up a new world of warmth and beauty, pared away the dead skin; but as we got to mean more and more to each other, Marc tightened; he froze in the clutch. If I could only have assured him; if I could only have reached him. But it wasn't me. It was inside him; it had to come from inside. But it didn't." She sat silently, sadly.

"See . . . that's why I'm the same," said Jeannie. "I want none of that crap."

"You can take so much of that . . . . " Rita's eyes filled with tears. ". . . and then it's the end. And here we are, you know, it's all over." She shrugged hopelessly and glanced around the bar. She batted her eyelids closed a couple of times to try to disperse tears . . . but a few escaped and rolled down her cheeks.

"You still love him, don't you?" Laura asked.

"I guess I'm still in love with the guy I fell in love with, not with the raving idiot at the end. He just wouldn't believe that I didn't want to make it with another guy."

"He was probably making it on the side himself and felt guilty," Jeannie suggested.

"Come off it! Rita feels bad enough without that kind of talk," snapped Laura.

"Hey, man, listen to this little one come on," Jeannie remarked surprisedly. "That guy must feed her vitamins."

They all laughed and it helped to ease Rita's tension.

Johnny came back and sat down. They ordered four beers.

Raoul Johnson entered the cafe. He was wearing a light green, short-sleeved shirt and skin-tight white pants. He saw Rita, smiled his sneer, and walked over.

"Hello, baby, back in action again, hunh?" He gazed at her through half-closed eyelids. "Crazy, I'd like to get in on some of that action," he said, slowly fluttering his eyebrows. He tried to arch one eyebrow higher than the other, but it just lifted slightly and fell back in line with the other.

Rita made a disapproving face and waved a weary hand at him, as if to chase an irksome fly.

How crazy this all seems, she thought. I've returned, and this place—the whole Village—is the same as ever. Yet something about it is strange, cold, shallow now. I've changed!

It's all the same. The same guys around, looking for women, but now they seem merely slimy voluptuaries trying to bed every girl they can get their eyes on; the same frustrated searching; the same forlorn people doing the same things, the same uninteresting, lonely, time-absorbing things every night.

The thought that she had been so much a part of this place was confusing to Rita now. She saw the people as sick, searching for a cure.

They are all looking for something and they don't know what it is, nor where to look. They are looking for themselves, but don't know it and can't find anything but nonsense and little games and bits and sex. The whole place is cold and rotten and dirty and sick and lonely. They don't know anything about life. They've never felt the warmth and tenderness of love, and that's what they are really after, but they don't know it, and they say they aren't because they can't find it anyway.

Now that Rita had loved, now that she was still in love, in love with love, now she realized. She knew that there was more warmth to love than the warmth of a bed.

But these people don't know, because they've never loved. They are so full of thoughts of themselves, of their own satisfaction, of their own security, they can love no one but themselves. How boring, how terribly empty their lives must be, she thought to herself, recalling the vacuousness of her prior existence in the Village. They only know an insatiable hunger and drive, a need to do something—but what? None of them are sure, and not being sure, nothing can satisfy them. They're just drifting and grabbing.

She pitied them.

They're animals, that's all they are, she thought. That's all I was. Man's nature is to be rational . . . but these don't think, they only feel— feel sorry for themselves.

Rita looked around at the tables of people. Books were piled on the tables, books from acting or painting or dancing or some other school.

Everybody is still going to school, preparing to enter life—but not yet—some day. People are sitting and talking and drinking, waiting for a late hour so they can escape to the soothing arms of Morpheus. Oh, heavily burdened, ethereal arms of Morpheus, the salvation of the world, thought Rita to herself. They just keep sleeping until they can't sleep longer, and then they arise to tire themselves with unimportant dabbling until it is time to rest again. They are missing the whole point of it all. They are grabbing for something and only grasping at its shell. Love isn't sex. Sex is merely a physical thing which can be delved into by anybody, anything, anytime. It isn't special, it didn't take brains.

And what about all those men making all kinds of advances to women walking in the street? And yet, what is it that is different from their wives who they deceive? Is what the young girls have to offer them any different than the little hunched-over woman with the hair sticking out of the moles on her face who sells newspapers in the bars around the Village? Is it so much different, really? Or is it merely the mind of the person who wishes to make the younger girl something more, who wishes to think that the young girl is wonderful and maddening; who wishes to think that promiscuity is great? Even their mothers and daughters are the same as the other women whom they crave, but thinking of their mother would only be in matters of respect. Any thoughts that she be capable of being desired by another man would be horrible, disgusting. Only the thoughts of wild sex excites these animals, not love, not even sex itself. They go to bed with an idea, and their partner in bed is just to fill the role, and anyone could fill that role.

Sex can't be taken so lightly, thought Rita. Not that it can't because it's wrong . . . but it can't be because it just doesn't work. Sex the over-advertised, love the undermined. And this is what Marc was afraid of, she thought sadly. Pity that so many people don't realize the importance of love and tenderness. Love is something warm and friendly and protecting and happy.

And what about the men who have been found doing erotic things with animals? Aren't these men in the Village, who constantly crave sex, the same as the sheep maulers? she thought. A woman is nothing but an animal to them, and they in turn are only animals. And what they do could as readily be done with an animal. What would be the difference? Nothing but animals! Rita shuddered with contempt.

Raoul Johnson was in the back of the cafe dancing. He was trying to catch the attention of a blonde girl who had just come in with her boyfriend.

Rita looked around the bar again. People were hanging from the bar, drinks in their hands. Others were sitting at the tables. They all looked sad, lonely, desolate. They repelled Rita and made her feel lousy and lonelier. They were trying to forget time, trying to forget life.

"I'm taking off," Rita said abruptly, standing up. "I'm going to see if I still fit into my old bed. See you later."

"So early?" asked Jeannie.

"What else is there to do . . . fuck?"

"Why not?" Jeannie said bluntly, half joking.

"'Cause I'm not an animal whore. I'm a woman . . . and that's just part of the deal, not the whole thing. I can walk and talk and think. Just because all these idiots can't—only understand sex—that's their problem, not mine." Rita turned and walked out.

"Man, she got the damnedest mood on tonight. I guess she figures I'm a whore 'cause now she's been in love. What're you supposed to do, buy it on the corners? Sure, I guess I'd like to be in love, if that means finding one guy that I dig the end, and always have a ball, and not fight or anything. Where is he? I can't find him."

"If you looked any place else but in bed you might find him," Laura suggested.

"You're a regular hot shit, aren't you?"

"Come on, let's knock it off," interposed Johnny. "How about another beer?"

"No, I don't want one," said Jeannie, glaring at Laura. "I'm going to the back for a minute." She walked toward the back. Raoul Johnson stopped her and they started talking.

"Rita is all mixed up, you know," Johnny said to Laura.

"Yeah, I know. I think we should go over to the apartment and see what's happening."

"Okay . . ."

They stood and started over toward Christopher Street.

24.

LAURA UNLOCKED AND SWUNG OPEN THE APARTMENT DOOR. Lamps were
aglow in the front room. In the middle room, only a dim night light above
the covered tub was lit. Rita was not in sight. Laura and Johnny walked
into the front room. On the couch was an open valise, half filled with
clothes Rita had not yet unpacked after returning to the Village. On the
floor in the center of the front room was the skirt which Rita had just been
wearing. It lay in a heap along with the sweater she had been wearing. Her
shoes were on the floor near the phonograph. There was a black mark
above them on the wall where they had left their imprint after having
been flung there. Long black stockings hung draped from the lampshade
above the phonograph where they had caught after flying through the air.

"It looks like Rita did a strip," remarked Johnny.

"You're not kidding."

They twirled around simultaneously when they heard a scrap-
ing and bumping in the other rooms. They walked to the doorway
between the front and middle room, looking toward the back room.
Suddenly, the curtains parted and Rita stomped out of the bedroom,
clad in panties and a bra, carrying a valise. She gaped, astonished by
the two people standing in the doorway.

"Ooopps," she exclaimed, pivoting around and rushing back into the bedroom, breaking into a loud laugh. "Why didn't you shout or something? I didn't even hear you come in."

Laura was laughing too.

Johnny, embarrassed, just smiled.

"What's coming off here, besides all your clothes? What're you doing?" Laura asked.

Rita came out of the bedroom again, this time wearing a white slip. She carried the other valise to the front room and hoisted it onto the bed next to the one already open.

"I'm checking out," she snapped determinedly, her face set hard. "I'm going to leave this God damn hell hole. I'm leaving tonight and just getting as far away as I can possibly get."

"Where're you going?"

"I don't know. I don't give a God damn. I'm just getting out of this place. It doesn't matter where I go, what I do. I just want to be alone—brood for a while—maybe start again."

"But Rita, what the hell happened? You just got back today. You didn't even finish unpacking."

"What happened? You see what's happening right in front of you—all the time. Are you blind?"

Johnny was puzzled. "See what? . . ."

"See this God damn rotten Village for what it is—a rotten hole filled with rotten, lousy, sick people. I gotta get out," she screamed tremulously. "I gotta . . . I gotta . . . gotta." She covered her face with her hands, crying violently, sinking down into a slump in the armchair.

Laura dashed to her and bent over her consolingly.

"You all right, honey?"

"I'm all right—I'm all right," Rita moaned in a cracked, spent voice, not raising her head.

"C'mon, . . . what's bugging you, baby?"

"What's bugging me is the fact that I woke up, that's what's bugging me. Before, I was dumb and happy-go-lucky; now I've had the misfortune to love somebody for a fleeting second—be loved—to taste the stream of life full strength, and now I'm unhappy—unhappy because it was good, because I liked it, because there's no love down here in this lousy Village. This is all a bunch of bullshit." She was now screaming impatient anger at Laura and Johnny. "All these finks, dressing the way they do, talking their hip trash, they're afraid of life. They try to make themselves believe they don't need ordinary emotions, . . . they're above ordinary feelings. They try to rise above it, . . . but they protest too much." Rita buried her head on her arms, sobbing uncontrollably.

"Take it easy, baby." Laura looked at Johnny and shook her head to indicate he shouldn't say anything.

"It's all a rotten bunch of shit," Rita moaned, looking up at Laura. "All of these bastards are sick, . . . you know that? That's why they're here . . . because they're sick . . . because they're all running away. And they're so damned scared they can't even look back to see how far they've run. They just keep getting further and further away. They're in their own little world, and, like they say, . . . it's way out. So far out that they've left all their sense behind them." Rita bit her lips to check her tears. She grew pensive, unconsciously rubbing the upholstery on the arm of the chair as she stared at the wall. "What happened? Nothing happened! Not tonight, anyway . . . It's been happening right along—to me. I've changed. I'm not the same anymore. But the Village is. It's the same now as it was ten years ago, and it'll be the same forty years from now. They've been sick here for years. It's nothing new; it's been here all the time—no new beat generation. They should'a come down here. They would'a found the beat ones twenty-five years ago. It's all phony and rotten, and none of it means anything. They're all only lonely and mixed up and sad, trying to lose themselves, trying just to cover themselves over with the streets down here, and hope that the lousy world that rejected them, that doesn't love them, doesn't uncover them to hurt them any more. But not me . . . not me." Her face shattered into tears again. "I'm through . . . through with this shit. You just can't run from it . . . ."

Rita stood suddenly and walked to the bedroom. Johnny and Laura watched her go out of the room, then looked at each other questioningly. Rita returned carrying a pile of clothing which she began to fling lustily into the open valises.

"Where you going?"

"I don't know. I'm just going. I'm giving this place back to the couks who had it before—and if they want their twenty-four pounds of pot back, they can have it." Her voice strained with the effort of heaving her clothes into the valises.

"But you gotta go somewhere. Do you have any money? I've got some extra from my job."

"Thanks baby, thanks," she tried to smile gratefully but her smile was more a grimace. "I won't need any money. I don't need anything— just breathing space. Thanks anyway." She stopped packing and looked deeply into Laura's eyes. Sadness and loneliness pervaded her features. She closed her eyes and began to weep silently, her body throbbing softly. She lowered herself into the chair, her head sinking to the arm rest, Laura lifted Rita's throbbing head, sat on the arm of the chair and rested Rita's head on her lap.

"Come on, baby . . . Take it easy."

Rita moaned. She began to cry uncontrollably, whining and muttering and cursing intermixed.

"I never loved anybody . . . never . . . never in my life . . ." Her words, hardly intelligible, were released in spasms of pain and lamentation. ". . . Except Marc . . ." She groaned painfully. "Marc . . . oh, Marc, baby, . . . I never loved . . . anyone but you . . . Never . . . never . . . never . . . no one but you . . ." She beat her hands into Laura's lap, screaming into her skirt.

Laura accepted the blows, whispering words of comfort to Rita, but Rita didn't hear.

"He went away . . . He went away because he . . . thought I didn't love him . . . He couldn't believe I loved . . . him. He was too . . . frightened to love me back, . . . afraid I'd turn out to be like the rest . . . of this selfish world . . ." She gasped convulsively. Her crying became deeper, more soulful, more painful. She gripped the cushion of the chair and crushed it against her face as if to press her rage and sorrow into that mute, absorbing cloth and cotton. She remained with the pillow on her face for many seconds as she tried to control herself. Her weeping was replaced by a throaty rattle. She looked up. Her eyes were two red ovals slit out of her face. They were deep and dark, surrounded by redness.

"Johnny, boil some water for tea," suggested Laura.

"Sure, sure thing."

Silent steps carried him into the kitchen. Tinny clatter accompanied the pots out of the closet, disturbing the hushed, breathless room.

"He didn't believe me . . . He didn't believe me . . ." she pleaded to Laura. She shrieked mournfully, piercing the apartment with the ominous dread of a funeral parlor just before the casket is sealed.

"Come on now, honey, try not to cry. Marc'll be back, you know that."

"He'll never be back . . . never . . . never, nev . . . er . . ." Rita's words disappeared into chilling moans. She was exhausted, out of breath now, just gasping out her words. She twisted and sat back in the chair, still sobbing, her eyes glassy and shiny, as she stared ahead unseeingly.

"The water's boiling," said Johnny.

"Come on, have a cup of tea."

Laura helped Rita to stand. They both walked into the middle room. Johnny poured tea into the Chinese teacups.

"Here, have some nice tea," Laura said, handing a filled cup to Rita.

"Thanks," Rita whispered wearily. She sat on a pillow at the low table.

"Try not to think about it."

"I can't help it. I just can't help it." Her head shook slowly from side to side as she stared at the floor. Tears rolled slowly down her cheeks, reflecting the lamplight. She sipped at her tea but it wouldn't go down.

Laura sat on another pillow watching Rita. Johnny stood propped against the covered tub. They both drank their tea, not speaking, smiling comfortingly when Rita occasionally raised her head.

Rita stood abruptly. She put down the tea and ran into the bedroom. Muffled, heart-rending weeping filtered from the bedroom.

Laura and Johnny remained still, quiet. The weeping continued for a long time. Later, it grew softer, then there was silence.

After a while, Rita walked slowly, dazedly, from the bedroom, looking about the middle room as she walked. In the front room, she found her nylon stockings. She sat on the side of the couch and began to slip them on. Laura and Johnny had followed her and stood watching. Rita was not crying now. Her face was calm, blank, determined.

"I'm going," she said finally. "I'm fed up with this place." She lifted her slip and fastened the garters to her stocking thoughtlessly.

"Where you going, honey?" asked Laura.

"I don't know, I don't care. I'm just leaving this place. I'm getting out . . . out . . . anywhere." She fastened the other stocking.

"But you don't have any money. How're you going to get along?"

"I'll go home, I guess. I'll go to that other rotten hole and stay there for a while until I can get some money to get out on my own. I think I know where to go from here. I have to get there by myself now. This Village isn't a crutch, it's a conglomeration of cripples." Rita stood shakily. "I'm glad I still have some of my old clothes left. I don't even want to see these Village things again." She picked up the clothes that she had taken off. Suddenly, anger flared in her face. "I don't want to see them again . . . Never . . . never . . ." She tossed the clothes about the room with all her violent anger. "Never . . . never . . . never," she wailed no louder than a whisper, her voice becoming a muffled rasping. She grabbed the long black stockings from the lamp and pulled at them with all her strength until their very strands began to come apart. "Never . . . never . . . never," she screamed hoarsely. "I never want to see any part of this place again." Her voice was coarse and cracking and hurt the ears.

Just as suddenly as it had come, her anger left her. She stood bewildered, feeling her emotions disappear into exhaustion and hopelessness. She picked a skirt from the bed and slipped it over her head.

"When I have some money, I'll leave that hell hole of a home and start some place else. Some place's got to be different. It can't all be like this." She slipped the jacket of her suit on. "It just can't." She looked to Laura and suddenly her determination faded. She put her hands to her face and sank on the edge of the chair, throbbing silently.

"Come on, kid . . . take it easy. You're doing fine." Laura assured her, lifting her to her feet. She started to run a comb through Rita's hair.

"I'll take it," said Rita, smiling weakly. She took the comb and started to pull it through her tresses. "Good thing I kept some of my old clothes. This way they won't start in right away when I get home," she said with a hint of a smile on her face. "Jesus Christ." She tossed the comb to the floor and started to sob again, sagging down toward the chair. "Does everything have to be fucked up . . . everything . . . everything . . . the whole world?"

Laura supported her and helped her into the chair. She picked up the comb and started to straighten Rita's hair again.

"It'll be different next time, Laura."

"Of course it will. It's different now."

"Next time, it'll be good, it'll be clean, and fine, and wonderful, and it won't stop, . . . because next time . . ." She sobbed and a rattling came out of her throat, and her mouth was suspended open. ". . . next time I'm going to be smart. Next time I'll know what I'm doing. I needed me first, then somebody else. But I've got me now, and it's not a place I need anymore. I'll always be with myself—everywhere, anywhere."

Laura finished combing Rita's hair. Rita, trying to control herself, stood up, pressing her lips together so that she wouldn't cry again.

"What a life," she said, shaking her head sadly. "I know now, . . . but it's too late. Next time . . . soon." She put some powder on her face to cover the signs of her crying. Her eyes were swollen.

"I'll take your bags down," Johnny suggested.

"Yeah, okay," Rita said wearily, almost inaudibly.

Rita walked to the door. Johnny followed her out. She turned and watched Laura snap the light off. She stared silently, pensively, into the darkened room as Laura emerged out of the darkness.

"All set?" Laura asked.

"Yeah, . . . all set." Rita watched the inside of the apartment until the door joined the frame. The metal tipped steps raised a cacophony of tinny sounds as they descended.

It was quiet on the street. The three shadows, their footsteps resounding, walked slowly toward the well-lit area at Sheridan Square.

"Well, take it easy, honey," said Rita.

"You too. Don't let it throw you."

"Maybe it wasn't so bad anyway. At least it taught me enough to leave."

"That's right," Laura said, trying to be light and happy. "Look at the bright side."

They smiled at each other pathetically. Laura felt tears welling up in her eyes. Johnny walked silently beside them. They reached the corner and crossed the street to where the subway entrance was. Johnny put down the valises. Rita bent down and grasped their handles. They pulled against her arms as she straightened up.

"Take it easy now. Maybe we'll get together soon," Rita suggested, looking tenderly, yet sadly, into Laura's eyes. Hot little balls of water escaped her eyes and rolled down her face. Laura bit her lips hard to stop her own tears.

Josh Minot had been sitting alone in Jim Atkins'. He saw the trio by the subway entrance and walked out of the eat shop and toward them.

"Hey, baby, what's happening?" he called.

Rita turned and looked at him silently, blankly. "Nothing! You know God damn well nothing is happening or is going to happen." She turned and descended the stairs.

Josh, openmouthed, Laura, and Johnny watched her disappear around the corner of the staircase. Soon the footsteps that shuffled under the weight of the valises stopped. Then they heard the heavy twang as the turnstile twisted around.

"Well what the hell is wrong with her?" asked Josh.

"Nothing really . . . not now . . . . " Laura took Johnny's arm and they turned and started walking downtown on Seventh Avenue.

GLOSSARY

Ball	—A good time.
Bit	—An act, a scheme, a bit of chicanery, a scene calculated to bring about a desired result.
Bread	—Money.
Bug	—Bother, vex, harass, annoy.
Bugged	—Someone who is bothered, vexed, harassed, or annoyed.
Butch	—A Lesbian who assumes a male role.
Cat	—An individual, a person, a being.
Chow	—Food.
Cool	—Something is admired, approved, if it is cool.
Cool it	—Desist, stop from a course of action.
Come on	—Appear, do in a certain way.
Couk	—Someone who is bugged; an emotionally disturbed person.
Crazy	—An expression of approval; also bizarre and therefore good.

Cut, cut out	—Leave, quit; also desist, stop.
Dig	—Understand, appreciate, enjoy exceedingly.
Drag	—Something boring and tedious.
End	—The ultimate perfection; something very good.
Far out	—Another word for closeness to perfection; close to the end.
Fern	—A Lesbian who assumes a female role.
Flick	—The cinema.
Flyers	—Homosexuals.
Flying	—Someone who has been relieved temporarily of his earthly bounds by alcohol or drugs; in high spirits.
Gay boys	—Homosexuals (male).
Hip	—To be "hip" is to understand, to be among the "knowing."
Like	—A ubiquitous, universal word used to punctuate the conversation of hip people. It can be used anywhere and means nothing.
Loot	—Money.
Mad	—Very bizarre; very pleasing.
Man	—A form of address to either sex; also used ubiquitously for punctuation.
Nails	—Cigarettes.
Pad	—An apartment.
Pot	—Marijuana. Used more broadly to refer vaguely to any narcotic.
Put down	—Disapprove of or avoid someone.
Sack	—A bed; to go to bed.
Scratch	—Money.
Sick	—Emotionally unbalanced—couk is sick.
Split	—Leave, quit, desist, cut out.
Square	—Not hip, as someone who must refer to the foregoing to understand hip talk.